on the
other
side

Also by Carrie Hope Fletcher

All I Know Now

Carrie Hope Fletcher

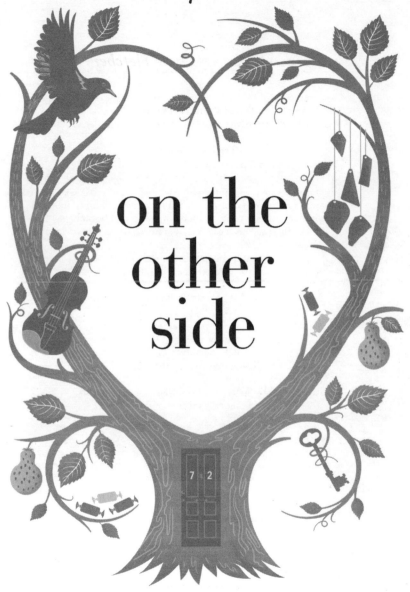

on the other side

sphere

SPHERE

First published in Great Britain in 2016 by Sphere

3 5 7 9 10 8 6 4

A CIP catalogue record for this book
is available from the British Library.

Hardback ISBN 978-0-7515-6314-6
Trade Paperback ISBN 978-0-7515-6313-9

Typeset in Sabon by M Rules
Printed and bound by CPI Group
(UK) Ltd, Croydon, CR0 4YY

Papers used by Sphere are from well-managed forests
and other responsible sources.

MIX
Paper from
responsible sources
FSC® C104740

Tameside MBC	
3801601915430 3	
Askews & Holts	08-Aug-2016
AF	£12.99
CEN	

This book is dedicated to those
who constantly push forward, no
matter what is in their way.

And to my mum and dad,
who taught me to push.

1

new arrival

Steady lights flickered across her closed eyelids, and in her ears she could hear the rhythmic hum and rattle of a train on its tracks. Evie Snow opened her eyes, expecting to find herself on the 20.32, pulling into an unfamiliar station in an unexplored part of the city, having drifted off to sleep as she so often did when she was younger. Instead, when her eyelids fluttered open, like two twitterpated butterflies, she found herself in the lift of the building she'd lived in when she was twenty-seven years old. She glanced at the button board and saw that the number 7 was lit up, beaming at her. The doors slid open and the rickety lift gave a tiny shudder, wobbling Evie's already unsteady stance, urging her to get out and keep going. She was sure she hadn't been in this lift before she'd fallen asleep. She was sure she hadn't been in this building for over fifty years.

Evie's gaze flickered up to the polished gold surface of the lift's walls. She noticed someone else in the reflection, someone standing exceedingly close to her. She spun around to catch the woman she'd seen, but the lift was empty. She was alone. Looking back into the gold, she examined the only reflection it showed her. That of a woman in her twenties, blonde curls tumbling over her shoulders in an unruly fashion, curls that Evie had only seen as thin and grey for a long time. Chocolate eyes stared back in disbelief, full of life and vibrancy. Eyes that hadn't yet forgotten how to shine. The skin on this woman's face was smoother than her own; it hadn't yet been weathered and worn from years of crying, laughing, frowning and smiling. Evie reached a hand up to her own face and felt the silky skin under her fingers. A quick, breathy laugh escaped her lips, like she'd been punched in the gut, forcing the memories of this face to the forefront of her mind. When she tilted her head, so did her mirror image, and when she smiled at the sudden realisation that this reflection was indeed her own, the beautiful twenty-seven-year-old Evie in the polished gold smiled back too.

Evie finally stepped out of the lift and the heels of her favourite shoes clicked against the marble floor. She called them her 'carpet bag shoes' because of their resemblance to the carpet bag that held Mary Poppins' impossible treasures. The hem of her floral dress swished around her

2

knees, and suddenly the warmth of her cherished emerald-green coat sank into her bones and she was enveloped in a snugness she'd not felt for a very long time. She wiggled her fingers, realising that her left hand did not yet bear an engagement ring. A ring that had not only weighed down her hand with its extravagant, too-big emerald, but had weighed down her heart too with its significance. She held her hands in front of her, smiled at their emptiness, then swung them by her sides all the way down the corridor.

As she turned a sharp corner that led to her apartment, she stopped dead in her tracks at the sight of her neighbour, Colin Autumn, a man who'd always been kind to her, if somewhat introverted and quiet. She remembered him as a tall, well-built man. The Oxford professor type. He favoured tweed jackets with suede elbow patches and sweater vests, often orange or green in colour. The smell of his pipe had never been a pleasant aroma, but he had a sweet, rarely revealed smile, one that Evie had managed to coax out of him only a handful of times. He'd died suddenly of a heart attack while Evie had lived next door. It was a shock to see him here at all, let alone in such a state. Mr Autumn was now a shell of his former self, huddled on the floor by the door to his apartment, clutching his knees to his chest and rocking himself back and forth. His tweed jacket and sweater vest were gone, and instead he wore faded white-and-blue-striped pyjamas that seemed to swamp his frail, sunken frame. His skin was white and almost transparent. He was quivering, muttering something under his breath, and as Evie cautiously approached him, keeping her back to the opposite wall, she thought she heard him say, 'Heavy. I'm too heavy!'

Evie reached tentatively into her right-hand pocket, hoping she'd feel the familiar shape of her keys. Yes, there they were. Cold in her slightly clammy hand. She brought them out and jangled them happily, momentarily forgetting the sight of Mr Autumn in his hysterical state. She quickly slotted the key into the lock, but her heart sank into her carpet bag shoes when it did not turn.

She tried again.

No luck.

And again, a little harder.

Nothing.

Now she desperately twisted her fingers against the key, but it just wouldn't budge. Tears pricked her eyes. She stepped back and looked at the door. It was definitely hers. Apartment 72. The gold numbers shone brightly on the polished wooden door, taunting her now that she couldn't get in. She looked at Colin, who had stopped rocking and was watching her.

'Mr Autumn?'

'Miss Snow? It's been years.' His voice crackled like an old record player.

'Where are we?' She crouched by his side. She wanted to embrace him, but he looked so weak and fragile she was afraid her arms may break him.

'Where are we, you ask. We lived here for years. You know this place.'

'Of course but . . . I can't get in.'

'Too heavy . . . you're too heavy. Oh goodness, Evie, not you too. Too heavy. Too heavy.' And with that, he returned to his rocking and muttering.

Evie stood and stumbled back to her door. As she beat her fists against it, a few tears spilled over and ran down her rosy cheeks. She clenched her eyes shut, wishing with all her heart she knew what was going on.

'Why can't I get in?' she whimpered.

Through her closed eyelids she saw yellow dots twinkling. She quickly opened her eyes to see her door sparkling with thousands of delicate little lights, dancing about the wood. They moved smoothly into formation, creating words for her to read.

Your soul is too heavy to pass through this door.
Leave the weight of the world in the world from
    before.
Once it is lighter your key shall then turn,
And you will be able to have what you yearn.

'My soul is too heavy? What does that mean?' She took off her coat, now feeling hot and flushed.

'Taking off your coat won't help you get any lighter, little Evie.'

A short man stood at the end of the corridor. Mr

Autumn had gone quiet, and Evie could see that he was now sucking his thumb, his eyes squeezed shut so tightly that they'd turned into mere lines. The man who had spoken was in his mid-forties but looked far older. A cigarette was hanging out of the side of his mouth, but he talked like it wasn't there at all.

'Dr Lieffe.' Evie let out a sigh of relief when she saw him. He was a plump, slightly balding Dutchman, with the sweetest button nose, who had been the apartment building's doorman. Warmth radiated off him in inexhaustible waves, as it always had done when Evie had lived here. Dr Lieffe knew the name of everyone in the building, and all their business too. Not because he pried, but because you couldn't help but trust him. He made sure everyone got their letters and packages, and at Christmas time he snuck bags of chocolate coins in with their post. He also thought of himself as a bit of a matchmaker, and was always trying to pair off the single apartment dwellers. On one occasion, long before Evie moved to the building, he'd succeeded, and had been honoured to be an usher at the wedding of Danny Thorn and Rose Green. From then on he referred to himself as Dr Lieffe, derived from *liefde*, the Dutch word for love, but being a unique and individual man he wanted a unique and individual name and so he became Lieffe. Eventually it caught on, until no one in the building remembered his real name.

Evie was one of his favourite tenants because she took him cups of hot chocolate when it got cold, and chilled pink lemonade in the summer when his little desk fan just wouldn't do. He'd passed away soon after she had moved out of Apartment 72, and she'd attended his funeral, along with most of the people who'd lived there past and present. The apartment building had been his favourite place in the world.

'I can't begin to tell you how pleased I am to see you!' Evie ran to Dr Lieffe and he gave a throaty laugh as he embraced her, a little awkwardly, as she was a good foot taller than he was.

'I wish I could say the same. I do hope it wasn't painful. Did you go in your sleep?' His English was impeccable. If not for the very slight accent and the pride he had in his country, Evie wouldn't have known he was Dutch. He took the cigarette from his lips and stubbed it out in a wall-mounted ashtray in the corridor. He never usually smoked inside the building, but strangely, Evie couldn't smell the smoke at all.

She frowned. 'I'm not sure I follow.'

'Oh Evie.' He gave her an affectionate smile, tinged with sadness. 'This is the afterlife. Well, it's the afterlife's waiting room, at least.' He reached out to her and they linked arms as he started to lead her back to the lift.

'The afterlife's waiting room,' she repeated, trying to make sense of it all. She felt like she'd fallen down the rabbit hole, except it hadn't led her to a fantastical world where animals could talk and tell the time. Instead she was in a world that belonged in the past, where people long dead were alive once more.

'You see, when you die, provided you've lived a good life on earth, always trying to be the best version of yourself

7

that you can be, you go to your favourite place,' Dr Lieffe explained.

'Heaven?' Evie asked, her brow furrowed in confusion.

'Ah, yes, but your own personal heaven. You've passed on, Evie. I'm afraid you're dead.' He squeezed her hand.

Of course, she thought.

'Yes, I ... I think I remember. Now that you mention it.' She concentrated hard, squeezing the memories out of her head. 'I lived a good long life. I married. Had two children. I was ...' she paused, 'happy. And I died with my children and grandchildren at my bedside. Yes, I remember now.' Her lips turned up at the corners and she lost herself in her mind's eye, recalling images of her children all grown up. Then she shook her head slightly and brought herself back to Dr Lieffe, who was standing before her, ushering her into the lift.

Evie looked at herself in the polished gold, and saw that she still looked twenty-seven. It's not that Evie was vain, but when she'd been so fond of her own assets, like her caramel curls and her chocolate eyes, it had been hard to watch them fade into shades of grey, along with all the life and excitement she had once felt.

'Clearly you were at your happiest here, in this very building. As was I. So when we passed on, we came back here.' Dr Lieffe pressed button number 2, but it didn't light up. 'Damned thing.' He pressed it again with a little more force, and the yellow light shone dimly through the small frosted number. 'However ...' He paused, still looking at the button, a troubled expression on his face.

'Ah, there's always a catch. You may have three wishes, but you can never wish for more wishes.' Evie chuckled lightly, but the look on Lieffe's face gave her the feeling that it might not be as easy as she'd like.

'It's only a small catch, Miss Snow. You couldn't open your door, could you?' Evie shook her head. 'That's because you're holding on to possessions that aren't allowed to pass through with you.'

'Possessions? But I didn't bring anything with me. I found myself in these clothes when I arrived here, wearing these shoes, with my keys in my coat pocket.' She felt again for the keys, and when her fingers wrapped around them, she pressed them into her palm as hard as she could, forcing herself to believe that they were there and she was here and everything was all right.

'Not all possessions are material, my dear girl.' The lift gave a sudden jolt and started to shudder its way down the shaft. Dr Lieffe hit the wall with a clenched, white-knuckled fist – suddenly disproportionately angry with the situation. Evie gave his arm a gentle pat. At last the doors opened, slowly, as though they didn't want to reveal what lay beyond them.

'Evie,' Dr Lieffe took a deep, unsteady breath, 'this is the second floor.'

'Yes . . .' She waited for him to continue but he said nothing, nor did he move to exit the lift. 'Is there something wrong?'

'I'm sorry, but I've not been down here in a long while. I

try to avoid it as much as possible, but you must see what's down here.' He took a step towards the door, holding tightly to her arm. 'Our souls are very delicate, and there are certain things that can weigh them down. When we feel guilty, hold in feelings, bite our tongues, keep secrets – that puts a great burden on our fragile souls. These man-made weights attach themselves to our spirits and start to drag us under.' Dr Lieffe hadn't looked at Evie once since they'd arrived on the second floor. His gaze was concentrated firmly up ahead, at the approaching turn in the hallway, his steps slowing. Blue-tinged lights flickered over their heads, and electricity buzzed.

'To be able to pass on, to step through your door, you must rid yourself of those weights. Let your feelings be known, open your heart, forgive people. Whatever those burdens are, you need to let them go. Otherwise, there's no way through the door and you'll become stuck.'

As they moved further down the corridor, the sound of groaning became audible. Not just one voice, but several, in a strange and aching chorus.

'Dr Lieffe ... why are we on the second floor?' Evie was now clutching his sweaty hand, their fingers interlinked as they edged towards the haunting voices.

He sucked in a breath. 'This is the floor on which the more ... reluctant residents of this building reside.'

They turned the corner, and Evie gasped.

2

the second floor

'What are they doing?' Evie stopped, and pulled at Dr Lieffe as he tried to continue forward. 'Why aren't they inside their apartments?'

If she'd known these people once, she didn't recognise them now. Their faces were grey and gaunt, their skin transparent. They were all dressed in the casual clothes they'd usually wear for lounging around their apartments. Pyjamas, dressing gowns and gym gear that had probably never seen a day of exercise. Everything in shades of black, white and grey. Around them were puddles of colour – blues, reds, pinks, oranges, greens – that had melted from their bodies and garments and were now soaking into the carpet and smudged on the wallpaper.

'What's wrong with them? They've lost all their ... colour,' Evie whispered.

'They're stuck, my dear girl,' Dr Lieffe explained. 'They refuse to let go of what it is that's keeping them here. They've been here so long, they've become shells of who they were. They've got no life, no colour left in them. It's all just ... melted away.'

One man was leaning up against his door, scratching pathetically at the wood. The door remained glossy and unscathed, but his fingers were bruised and bleeding stumps, his blood jet black. A woman was muttering, speaking rapidly, some words louder than others. She was cradled against her door, banging her head on the frame. Another woman was trying to catch imaginary phantoms in the air around her. As Evie watched her flailing about, the woman hit herself on the nose, which made her yelp. Judging by the stream of black running down her face, it wasn't the first time she'd done it. There was a large patch of dried blood on her white tank top, and her hands were covered in black stains. Evie could see the liquid caked under her fingernails as she swiped her hands through the air.

The constant cacophony was too much. The sounds came in waves and started to make Evie feel queasy.

'I've seen enough,' she whispered. 'I want to go back to my apartment.' She tried to turn, but Dr Lieffe pulled at her arm, not letting her go.

'Look at them, Evie. Take it all in, and make sure you don't turn out the same.' He spoke sternly, looking more serious than she'd ever seen him – a completely different person for a moment – but then his face softened, he loosened his grip and together they walked swiftly back to the lift. Evie pressed number 7 continuously and fast until the doors closed and the lift began to rise. Then she leaned against the wall and let out a breath she didn't know she'd been holding.

'I can't be one of them.' She shook her head fiercely, hammering home the point to herself as much as to the little Dutchman.

'We call them The Hopeless. And I'm glad to hear you say that.' The relief was clear on Dr Lieffe's face.

'No, I won't be hopeless. I am full of hope. I'm a Hope-*ful*.' Evie spoke fast, convincing herself that the words were true. 'But I don't know what it is that's weighing down my soul. I don't know how to fix this.' A lump had formed in her throat.

The lift doors opened and they both stepped out immediately, wanting to be rid of the memory of the second floor, though they didn't yet move towards Apartment 72.

'Evie, I've heard every single person who's come back to this building say exactly that, and not once has it been true.' Evie looked down at her carpet bag shoes sheepishly. 'Remember, I was the gatekeeper to this building, and everyone within it told me their business. You and I both know what it is that's keeping you here. You just need to admit it to yourself first.' He started walking towards her door.

Evie understood what he was saying, but something

else now puzzled her. 'Dr Lieffe, if this is the afterlife's waiting room, and people get stuck here because they can't move on to the *actual* afterlife, and if you know exactly what it is that lets people pass on, why are *you* still here?'

Dr Lieffe stopped halfway down the corridor. He looked her right in the eyes as his own filled with tears. She felt embarrassed and gazed down at her shoes, letting him have a moment to himself.

'Well,' he said, after what seemed like an everlasting moment, 'I've never had anyone ask me that before.' She glanced up as he wiped a tear from his cheek with his thumb. 'Evie, this building, these corridors, they are *your* waiting room. Just like everyone's heaven is different, everyone's purgatory is too. My own life was so miserable that I found my happiness through other people, through getting to know their stories and occasionally being part of them. When I arrived here after I died, the entrance doors to the building wouldn't open. Not until I forgave my ex-wife for divorcing me. I knew deep down that it wasn't her fault; she just wasn't in love with me any more. But I'd blamed her for years. My waiting room was in front of this building, and once I'd let that grudge go, the doors opened for me and I got to be in my own personal heaven.' He gestured around him at his happy place, his little piece of paradise. 'Talking to the people in this building and offering my services where I could was my entire life. So it makes sense that my heaven is back here, helping people like you find their way into their apartments.'

In that moment, Evie couldn't think of anyone she'd met who had a bigger, more selfless heart than Dr Lieffe. Then she remembered another man she'd known, once upon a time, and a weight in her own heart tugged her downwards. Dr Lieffe saw the pain flicker across her face.

'Evie. You know what it is that's keeping you here. Don't you?'

'Yes,' she sniffed. 'I do.' She didn't realise she was crying until Dr Lieffe moved to her and tentatively rubbed a tear from her jawline with the same thumb he'd used to wipe away his own. 'It's . . . it's my secrets.'

'Secrets, Evie? You're sure?'

'Yes. Positive. There are certain things I kept from my family. Partly because nobody needed to know, and partly because I couldn't bear to relive them. There wasn't a day that went by when they didn't catch me off guard. I'd be walking up the stairs in my own home and think there was an extra step, only to find there wasn't. I'd be in the garden, tending to flowers, and my breath would catch. If you threw my heart into the air, it would fall to the ground twice as fast with the weight of those secrets, I'm certain.'

The idea of sharing the things she'd forced herself to keep hidden for so many years felt all wrong, but at the same time oddly right. There was a chance she could feel light again. A chance to dance without her feet being

15

nailed to the floor. A chance to put her unlived past to rest.

Sometimes, she thought, we reach a fork in the road and choose to go one way, then wonder what would have happened had we chosen the other path. Even more so when the path we end up on was chosen for us and the other path is so far away, there's no chance of ever turning back. Evie had once reached a fork in the road and had had no choice but to take the wrong path.

Dr Lieffe sighed heavily and gave a small smile of relief. 'Well then. That's the hard part over. The next bit is comparatively easy, you'll be glad to hear.' He started leading her back down the corridor to the lift, past Mr Autumn, who was now curled up fast asleep outside his door, still sucking his thumb.

'But how do I even begin to fix this? I'm dead. I can't go back to the . . . ' she paused, trying to think of what to call the world she'd left behind, 'the land of the living and seek out all the people I'd need to talk to in order to open my door.'

Lieffe took her hand in his and squeezed it, whether to calm himself down or to comfort her, she couldn't tell. Then he led her back into the lift, which Evie was already sick of seeing. This time, he pressed the button marked 0.

'There's always a way, Evie.'

The doors closed.

16

3

the wall

The lift sank down to the ground floor. Lieffe then led her through the foyer, behind his desk – where he stopped to pick up a cigarette and light it – through a kitchenette and down a flight of stairs that seemed only to lead to darkness. Lieffe flicked a switch and a dim, yellow light revealed a disappointing basement. A floor that Evie had never had cause to visit all those years ago. She'd guessed it was just storage space for the things previous residents had left behind, or where lost property lived. She herself had lost a few things while living here: a red and white polka-dot umbrella, three pairs of sunglasses that she'd bought in progressively bigger sizes in the hope they'd be too big to lose, and a pair of flip-flops that she'd kicked off in the lobby while chatting to Lieffe one warm summer's evening after having been out at a party in a park where she'd got a little tipsy. Each time she'd noticed something missing, Lieffe would disappear down to the basement and reappear a few minutes later holding the ever-overflowing Lost and Found box.

'It should just be the Lost Box,' Evie had once said. 'Even if someone finds something and places it in the box, it's still lost until it's found by its owner. And once it's found, it no longer has a place in the box!' With that, Dr Lieffe had taken his marker pen and scribbled out the words 'and Found' on the side of the box.

Evie's eyes adjusted to the light. The Lost Box sat in the corner on the concrete floor; no green carpets like upstairs. Lieffe flipped a switch that provided a weak yellowy light, just enough so he could make his way across the room to the very back wall. It was a pale cream colour, but Evie could see that it had once been covered in blue-and-pink-striped wallpaper, which had since been torn away in uneven strips, leaving scraps around the edges, giving the wall a jagged border. The large cream patch in the middle shimmered gently in the faint light, and Evie could swear there was a hum in the air, like the sound of an electrical storm on its way.

Dr Lieffe stood facing her in front of the wall and gestured to it with a hint of a smile, as if presenting it to her. She stared back blankly.

'The wall, Evie!' he growled, excited now, and slightly annoyed at her lack of understanding. 'The wall is the way back that you're looking for.'

She stepped closer. The hum was now a little louder, and she could hear that, much in the way that the second floor's cacophony was made up of voices, this sound was made up of chatter too, although much less aggressive, far calmer. Like soft whispers to a secret love, hearts spilling over with champagne, or that gentle, hushed tone mothers use when tucking in their children.

'What is it? Why can I hear the whole world at once? Everyone's so . . . ' Evie's eyelids felt heavy, and she let her forehead rest gently against the wall's oddly warm surface, 'content.'

'Is that what you hear? Contentedness?' Lieffe had pulled a desk chair to the centre of the room and was sitting now, watching Evie.

'Isn't that what *you* hear?' Evie let herself sink to the floor and settled on the concrete, her back pressed firmly against the wall, unwilling to be parted from it. She turned her head to the side so she could keep one ear to the hum.

'Everyone hears something different, depending on what sort of life they lived and who they've left behind. I hear laughing. Lots of it.' Through her half-closed eyelids, Evie could see Lieffe smiling.

'To me the world sounds warm and hushed,' she said. 'It makes me feel the same way I felt once when I was a teenager, and I came home from a wonderful evening out with a friend and tiptoed upstairs, trying not to giggle and wake my parents.' Images danced in her mind, and she smiled, drunk from the wall's warmth.

'The sound of a happy life, no doubt.'

Lieffe seemed far away to Evie now. She let herself sink further into the wall, feeling it wrap around her, hugging her and rocking her to sleep.

'Alley-oop!' Lieffe had taken her hands and was tugging her upwards to a standing position. Taken by surprise, she toppled on to him slightly but managed to regain her balance after a few deep breaths. 'Seems like you and the wall will get along just fine.'

'Get along? You make it sound like a person.' Evie brushed down her skirt and undid her coat, a little warm and flustered now.

'I'm not entirely sure what it is, Evie, but it's definitely more like a person than a wall.' Lieffe ran a hand across it and his brow creased. 'It's sort of ... sentimental. It has an understanding of who we are, but it's like a child. If you're nice, it'll play with you. If you're not, it won't. I had no doubt it would like you, Evie, but it's nice to see the effect you have on each other.'

'On each other? It made *me* feel wonderful, but I'm not sure I had any sort of effect on ... ' She turned to where she had been pressed against the wall, and saw that that feeling of being hugged had, in fact, been literal. The wall had sunk in on itself, moulded itself around her, and the imprint of her body was embedded in its surface. Now it was shifting and shimmering, remoulding itself back to its former flatness.

'Come, let me explain.' Lieffe wheeled the chair around

20

behind Evie, scooped her up in its seat then guided her over to a desk in the corner. He picked up a pen and drew a notebook towards him, then started to draw on the faded blue lines. He marked five parallel horizontal lines. Between the top two he wrote HEAVEN. In the next space, between the second and third lines, he wrote AFTERLIFE'S WAITING ROOM, in the next gap LIFE and in the space below that HELL. He took his pen to the line between HEAVEN and AFTERLIFE'S WAIT-ING ROOM and darkened it considerably, then did the same to the line between LIFE and HELL. The middle line, between AFTERLIFE'S WAITING ROOM and LIFE, he scribbled over, making it jagged and messy.

'The gateways to heaven and hell are very well protected. You've seen for yourself that the doors to heaven are securely locked.' Dr Lieffe used the tip of the pen as a pointer, guiding Evie through his diagram.

'And what about the doorway to hell?' She swivelled the notebook towards her so she could get a better look.

'If you knew you were going to hell, would you be keen to knock on the devil's door? No. If you're going there, you get collected. I pray you never have to witness that.' Dr Lieffe's eyes glazed over and he shook a little as he looked down at his drawing. His pen drifted to the thick black line between LIFE and HELL and he added to its darkness a bit more. Evie wondered what had made him shudder. Lieffe had always proved to be a brave, bold man; if something made him quiet, you knew it was bad.

heaven

afterlife's
waiting room

life

hell

'What about this line here?' She pointed to the jagged line in the centre; the gateway between where she was now and where she needed to go. 'It's not the same as the others.'

Lieffe leaned against the edge of the desk and looked towards the wall. He took the cigarette from between his lips and flicked it to the floor, squashing the dying embers under one of his brogues.

'No, it's not the same, Evie. This place,' he held up his hands, gesturing to the room around them, 'is not like heaven or hell. It's not as solid or as sure.' Evie raised an eyebrow, trying desperately to follow. Lieffe changed tack, hoping to make it easier for her to understand. 'If life is a full-colour drawing, a beautiful animation, then this place, the afterlife's waiting room, is the tracing paper over the top of that animation. It's close to the original, but not quite the same. It's faded and translucent, like looking at the world through a frosted window. Everyone in this world is neither here nor there. We're certainly not alive, but we're also not entirely dead yet either.'

Evie looked at the wall, shimmering under the weak light. The flat surface appeared to wobble, almost like it was waving at them, trying to get their attention. *It really is like a child*, she thought.

'The wall between this world and the land of the living has always been more permeable than the walls to heaven and hell. Over the years, hundreds of tortured souls have tried to force their way through, trying to get back home, unable to accept their death. It has made the wall even weaker in certain places. It's sad for those still alive but quite helpful for you, Evie.'

'Sad for those still alive?' she asked. 'What do you mean?'

Lieffe sighed, worry creasing his already wrinkly brow. 'There aren't supposed to be ghosts on earth. Not the kind people can see and be tormented by, anyway. When *you* cross over, you will do so with good intent. For the sole purpose of completing your ... your unfinished business, as it were, which means you'll be completely invisible to those still alive. You won't even cast a shadow. Those who *force* their way back with the intention of staying are not peaceful, and aggressive souls upset the nature of things. Living people catch glimpses of them when those souls are in their most aggressive, frustrated state. Their energy can also knock things off shelves, slam doors, shatter glass ... No, that's not supposed to happen. Ghosts are not supposed to exist. But they've made it easier to get you back home.'

Evie walked back to the wall, partly because she liked the feeling it gave her but also because she needed to inspect it. If she was going to ... befriend it, so that it let her cross through it, she needed to get up close and personal.

'And you've done this before?' She eyed Lieffe, hoping she wasn't his first experiment.

'Myself.' He nodded with a faint smile. 'When I went back home to forgive my wife.'

24

'Is it easy?' Evie was stroking the wall with the back of her index finger, and she swore she heard it purr like a satisfied kitten.

'It's ... simple enough. It just requires a few things.' Lieffe walked across to where the Lost Box sat. He picked it up and brought it over, placing it in front of Evie's feet.

Inside the box was a pink sock and a child's yellow rain hat. Evie balanced the hat lightly on her own head, although it was far too small for her. Lieffe laughed at her serious expression underneath such a daft hat.

'You never changed, Evie, did you?' he asked, still chortling. She took the hat from her head and looked down at it, rubbing her thumbs over its plastic edges.

'Oh, I did, Lieffe. Quite a bit, actually. But it's so nice to be back.' She looked up and noticed the little man's soft expression. 'Why have you brought me this box?'

4

the lost box

'Evie, do you remember how things used to turn up in this box that seemingly belonged to no one?' Lieffe asked. 'Items used to sit in there for weeks, months even, with no apparent owner, then all of a sudden, one day, some-one would come to claim something. It was a victory worth buying a cake and streamers for.'

Evie laughed. She remembered how they'd sit and make up stories about the people who owned each item, and how they came to lose it. When someone turned up to claim something, they'd interrogate them to see how right (or, more often than not, wrong) they were.

'Yes,' she said, settling back into the chair, 'I remember.'

'Well, this box has a sort of magic to it here.' He picked it up and placed it in Evie's lap. She stared at its very plain and ordinary – parcel-paper brown – cardboard interior.

'Magic?' She raised an eyebrow.

'Evie, you died at eighty-two, but now you look twenty-seven, you're back in a building you haven't visited in over fifty years with a man who died long before you did, and you just had a hug from a wall. Surely we're well past questioning the supernatural?'

He had a point. Evie shrugged and put her palms flat against the sides of the box. She lifted it above her head so she could look at its underside.

'Is it like pulling a rabbit from a hat?'

Lieffe's face scrunched as though he was ready to scold her again, but then the wrinkles softened. 'Actually, I suppose it is.' He took the box out of her hands and placed it back in her lap, gesturing with his index finger for it to stay there, as if it was an obedient dog. Evie tucked her eager, fidgety hands underneath her thighs. 'In order to get to where you need to go, you have to give the wall something to go on. Something to tell it exactly where it should take you.'

Evie's head cocked to the right.

Lieffe smiled inwardly. He was reminded of his daughter when she was young, trying to understand her maths homework while he attempted to explain it to her with his own very limited knowledge.

'Sort of like a magic trick. Well, no. Not really. It's quite a bit *sweeter* than that. You see, the wall is sentimental. It feeds off feelings and memories. So you need to give it something that has a strong connection between you and the person you're trying to find. A word. An object. A song. A secret handshake. Anything. It'll feed off that connection and line itself up with whoever it is you're looking for.'

Evie eyed the wall. It was just a wall. How could it take her back to a place in which she was dead and gone, buried six feet underground?

'Are you sure a *wall* can do all of that? This isn't a hoax, is it, Lieffe, some strange dream?' As soon as she cast that shadow of doubt into the room, the wall's hum jumped in volume. Eventually it resumed its gentler song, but it sounded slightly disgruntled, projecting the sounds of people whose flatmates had left their shoes on the stairs for the tenth time that week, or the people who had worn flip-flops that day only for it to rain unexpectedly on their way home.

'Sorry,' she whispered from the corner of her mouth. With a sigh, she said, 'All right, Lieffe, what do I need to do?' The urge to remove her hands from underneath her legs and start playing with the box was unbearable.

'That box can conjure objects. You came here with no personal possessions, so it will allow you to retrieve the things you need to get you through the wall. If words or actions are your key, then you have no need for the box, but most people need *something* they left behind, and the Lost Box has volunteered its services.' Lieffe looked proud of the box and what he'd discovered it could do.

Evie eyed him from under her curls. 'How do you know all of this?' Her hands slipped out from under her thighs, but she placed them on her lap, still resisting the urge to touch the box. Lieffe shrugged, a little smile on his face that looked like it could turn into a childish giggle at any moment.

'Trial and error!' he said. Evie got the feeling there was a little more to it than that, but she didn't want to pry, and there were far more pressing matters at hand.

'So how do I work it? Is there an on switch? A magic word? One side makes me larger and the other makes me teeny-tiny?' She held up her thumb and index finger to indicate how small she might become, and looked at him through the gap with one eye.

'No.' He walked to her and swatted her hand away playfully, then looked down into the box. 'It's a Peter Pan kind of deal.'

'You mean, think happy thoughts?'

'Bingo. You need to think of the connection you have to the person you're trying to find, and what the significance of the object is to you both. What makes it so important that it will tether you between worlds?'

A little knot had formed in Evie's stomach, and now it grew tighter. She thought about her secrets and how much they'd weighed her down almost all her life and she knew that there were exactly three of them. Three rather large secrets. It wasn't hard to figure that out when she'd spent years trying to hide them from the people she loved

30

simply for that reason – because she loved them. Evie wanted to avoid any risk of hurting them. Three secrets, and three people she'd need to cross the wall to visit. Finding their keys was easy. The first required a song. The second required an action. And the third ... well, the third required the box.

'Is that it? I just think about it and it'll appear?'

'Yes, though the box is a little ... excitable. Unlike the wall, it only needs the smallest amount of encouragement, so don't think too hard or too loud. Just place your palms flat on either side of it and think about what you need and why you need it.'

Evie closed her eyes and did as she was told.

She thought of raven-black hair that curled at the ends and jade-green eyes that twinkled. She heard the sounds of soft violins and rickety rattling trains. She smelt burgers and salty fries. And her mouth watered at the taste of hard boiled sweets.

'Evie,' Lieffe said tentatively as his skin started to prickle, 'you're thinking too loudly.'

The sides of the box pushed against Evie's hands and then shrank in towards each other. To Lieffe it looked like the box was breathing, quickly at first and then the breaths started to get bigger. With each breath in, the sides of the box expanded a little further, and with each breath out the top edges of each side almost met in the middle. Evie was lost in an oblivion of thoughts. She'd not dared to let herself wallow in them for the longest time, but now she'd opened the floodgates and she wasn't about to get out of her own head without a fight.

With one final mighty inhalation, the box burst with a bang, knocking the chair over backwards with Evie still in it. Hundreds of individually wrapped hard boiled sweets of all different colours and flavours rained down over them. Evie sat up and plucked one out of her hair, ignoring the last few still tumbling down around her. She quickly unwrapped it and popped it into her mouth, sucking on it with relish. *It tastes of hope*, she thought.

She looked around the room. There was no sign of Lieffe, and she thought he must have left in all the commotion, but then she caught a glimpse of his watch face in the corner of the room, reflecting the dim light, and realised he was huddling a little pathetically underneath the desk.

'Oh stop it,' she said teasingly. 'A few sweets never hurt anyone!'

'I did tell you not to think too hard. What if it was a family pet you were remembering? The poor creature would have been catapulted out of the box at high speed and might not have survived the journey!'

'I'll bear that in mind when I need to summon Horace, the family cat. For now, all I need are the sweets, though they're for my third and final journey.'

'You won't be needing them now?' asked Lieffe.

'No,' she said more sternly than she'd intended. 'That's something I'll have to ... erm ... build up to.'

'Saving the best till last?' Lieffe asked hesitantly.

'Something like that.' The sadness reached Evie's eyes before the half-hearted smile did. She started to collect the sweets, putting them into the box, with a few making their way into her pockets. Lieffe helped, the two of them moving round the room on their haunches in a heavy silence, wading through the inch-high carpet of crackling wrappers.

'Evie?' Lieffe held her name in his mouth as though it was made of thin glass that might break should he be too fierce or too loud. He sensed he needed to tread carefully here. There was something about a quiet, pensive Evie that made him uneasy.

'Yes, Lieffe?' But Evie knew exactly what was coming.

'Why the sweets?'

November

The Violinist and the Artist

Her back aching from her awful desk chair and her head reeling from the constant hustle and bustle of office life, Evie sat on the train home, a book on her lap, staring contentedly out of the window, the hint of a smile playing at the edges of her lips. First days weren't meant to be easy. They were filled with anticipation, nerves and stress. She had expected the worst, which meant she wasn't the slightest bit disappointed when the worst had indeed shown up. In fact she'd welcomed it with open arms and an open heart.

Evie's big ambition was to be an animator for motion pictures. For now, at least, she had had to settle for drawing cartoons for a local newspaper that would end up wrapped round fish and chips. But that was OK, because she knew that all great artists started small, and it was certainly a step in the right direction. It also shut up her insufferable mother, who thought that her doodling daughter was nothing short of scandalous. No, it wasn't right for a lady of her class to want to make silly little drawings dance and wobble about on a screen. Evie had to constantly fight off her mother's nagging that she find a man to marry.

Eleanor Snow's lips had been pursed for so much of her life that her mouth now closely resembled a cat's behind. She was tall and bony, her clothing always drab and horribly appropriate, and her stony eyes were absent of any colour or life. She didn't walk; she scuttled like a centipede, sucking the fun and happiness out of the world as she went. She was a severely old-fashioned lady who felt a woman hadn't done her proper job as a female if she was unmarried and childless, so to have a daughter of twenty-seven who was both was life-threateningly embarrassing.

Up till now, Evie hadn't had a job, and had been kept hidden away inside the family's rather large mansion, complete with tennis court, indoor swimming pool and six luxurious bathrooms. Being unemployed meant that Evie had been Eleanor's *secret* embarrassment and the fewer people that interacted with her and knew her sad situation, the better. Although she wanted for nothing, Evie had become horribly bored with her life. She had a butler and a maid and a cook to bring her everything she could possibly desire, but she never used them. She wanted to do things for herself so that she could feel she was actually living, not just existing. And even though Jeremy the butler, Jane the maid and Isla the cook were wonderful friends, Evie was still awfully lonely and excruciatingly fed up.

Finding a husband had never been at the top of her list of priorities. Her mother and father set a poor example, as they hadn't married for love – they had married for the sake of money and convenience. They were a terribly smart match according to *their* parents. Evie's father, Edward Snow, was the son of Edward Snow Senior, of Snow and Summer Ltd, a terribly successful law firm built on the fortune of Evie's great-grandfather, yet another Edward Snow. Great-Grandfather Snow had been ostracised from the family for reasons Evie had never been told and knew better than to ask about. Yet the family that had exiled him felt no qualms about using his money to set up a business of their own, and it made Evie sick to her stomach.

Eleanor was the daughter of Elaine and Ewan White, another rich yet loveless couple, who'd known the Snows for generations. They made an undeniably airtight case to the young Edward Snow's parents that their respective children would benefit from marrying when they were old enough, as Edward was set to take on the law firm after Edward Senior retired, and Eleanor was well prepared to bear children and had been trained to keep a household in shape. And so it was done.

All that any of this taught Evie and her little brother Eddie (another Edward, of course) was how *not* to marry.

37

Evie witnessed her parents' cold stares and clipped conversations and their palpable lack of love and vowed never to end up in a relationship of that kind. It also turned her off the idea of looking for love at all.

Although her mother was well aware of Evie's aversion to marriage and men, she had made several attempts at pushing her daughter in the direction of young James Summer, of Snow and Summer. James was a few months older than Evie, and was apparently everything women looked for in a mate: wealthy, witty and gorgeous. Because their fathers were business partners and their families lived on the same street, Evie and James had been friends since infancy, and Evie knew a side of James he never dared to show his family and it was the side of him that liked to 'make believe'. He would think up stories that Evie would in turn try to draw and together they created imaginary worlds that they'd live in, only to be snatched away by their disapproving mothers. But what had really sealed their friendship was the fact that Evie refused to address him as James. Even at eight years old, she had no time for absurd traditions, especially the one that meant that all the men in a family had the same name. It caused great confusion when she called for just one person, and several answered back. So to Evie he was Jim, which caused his cheeks to flush every single time she spoke to him.

Eleanor Snow couldn't have hoped for a better friendship to bloom between Evie and Jim. But even though Evie knew her mother wanted that friendship to grow into something more, and even though she knew what a wonderful husband Jim would make, she just couldn't force herself to love him.

Finally, after enduring years of Evie's brilliantly planned, well-executed arguments, Eleanor compromised and told her that if she could get herself a job as an artist within the week, she would pay for an apartment close to work, but only for a year. If she hadn't climbed any further in the field by the following November, then Evie was to leave the job to be married off to whomever her mother saw fit and do what women were supposed to do: bear children and run the house.

Eleanor had not expected her to succeed in finding a job within the week, but Evie had never been more determined to achieve anything in her life. She'd snuck into her father's study, flipped through his Rolodex and was thrilled when she found someone who worked for the local newspaper. She had an interview lined up by day two, and because of her portfolio full of years' worth of drawings, which she'd hidden from her mother, by day five she had the job. She had been over the moon. A real job for a whole year. A proper adventure. Now, with her foot on the bottom rung, she needed to climb the ladder, maybe illustrate a book during the year, and then she wouldn't be forced to marry her best friend, Jim.

The train came to a stop at the end of the line and the driver announced, 'All change, please!' through the crackly tannoy. Evie hurriedly stuffed her book into her bag. As she stepped out of the train, she caught the right heel of her new shoes on the edge of the train and stumbled, her bag slipping from her shoulder and her book falling to the ground. It skittered down a passageway, disappearing amongst the hurrying feet of the evening commuters. Evie gathered herself and straightened up just in time to see a bustling businesswoman accidentally kick it out of sight.

'Damn,' she said.

Pushing her way through the crowds, despite her sore foot, Evie saw that the book had landed at the bottom of a downwards-moving escalator and was being pushed against the raised lip where the escalator disappeared under the floor, its pages creasing and crunching with every step that passed beneath it. Her heart gave a slight jolt at seeing it in that state, and she rushed to its rescue, being careful not to step on to the escalator herself. It was then, at the moment when she bent down to snatch her book from the clutches of the sliding metal stairs, that she heard it.

It was very soft but definitely there, and her heart swelled at the sound: a violin being played by what sounded like an extremely talented violinist. Evie still hadn't figured out the best route from work to her new flat, and she wanted nothing more than to soak her tired muscles in a hot bath and then curl up in her warm bed, but ignoring the ache in her back and her still reeling head and her sore heel, she abandoned thoughts of heading for her next train and stepped on to the up escalator.

As she was carried higher and higher, the sound grew louder and more beautiful, and slowly the violinist came into view. She saw his scruffy raven-black hair and matching black coat with dark purple piping that was so dark you wouldn't know it was purple unless you were really looking – and Evie was really looking. Very few people passed, and not one seemed to notice the talent standing before them. His wildly untamed eyebrows were knitted together so tightly that Evie wondered if they would ever come apart. Then, as the music softened, so did his face. His expression changed to one of contentment, and his eyebrows separated with ease and settled over his closed eyes.

He was handsome in a funny sort of way. His nose had a notch in its bridge, presumably from where it had been broken, and the tip was large and rounded, the kind of nose Evie would give to her more adorable cartoon characters. His mildly curly hair hadn't seen a brush in at least a week, and hunched as he was over his violin, she guessed that if he stood up straight, he'd be nearly a whole foot taller than her. But what she found most mesmerising was that he *lived* his music. If he played in a minor key on his black wooden violin, his face would be melancholy, scrunched or twisted. If the music was in a major key, his lips would twist into a smile and his whole expression lifted. If the notes moved, so did he. He didn't exist in this world, only in the world he created with his fingers and his bow.

Evie didn't know or care how long she'd been watching him. She'd settled her back against the wall opposite where this man was busking and become transfixed. She noticed the violin case at his feet. Despite the passing people not taking much notice, he had still made quite a bit of money today. She wished she had something to contribute, but she'd spent the last of her change on a bag of her favourite hard boiled sweets from the shop near where she worked. She took a handful of the coloured sweets from her pocket. They were individually wrapped in coloured plastic and each sweet was glassy with a few little bubbles inside. Evie picked out a green one, to match her coat. Then, hitching her bag firmly on to her shoulder, she walked over to his case and placed the sweet on top of the pile of coins.

With his eyes still closed and his mind firmly in his music, he didn't notice anyone was there. Evie looked at him one last time, swaying to the melody he twirled in his fingers, then left to find her platform. Coincidentally, the entrance happened to be right next to the violinist. It was almost as if he'd guided her there with his music.

After a month, Evie's job had settled into a routine. She adjusted her desk chair to the perfect height so that she never hunched over when she drew. If she got to the office at quarter to nine, rather than nine exactly, she could miss having an awkward elevator chat with her seedy boss. She learned that in her ten-minute mid-morning break she could make it to the nearest coffee shop and back if the queue wasn't too long. And most importantly, in the evenings on the way home, the sound of that single violin would mellow her out. It flicked an off switch in her brain and sent her on her way completely unwound. A bad day at work was forgotten in a single note, and in return for the violinist's unwitting musical help, she would drop a sweet into his violin case every time she passed him.

One particular evening, Evie was walking past the violinist, a dark purple blackcurrant-flavoured sweet in her hand. She was about to drop it into his case as usual when a small piece of cardboard caught her eye. She looked up at the man, his eyes closed as always, and she bent down to read the note written there in a round and swirly hand.

I like the orange ones best.
Thank you, Sweetie
xxx

She looked up again at the man with his black violin tucked under his chin. He didn't know who she was, or even that she was there, and yet she felt closer to him than she did to anyone else in the world. The people she worked with treated her as though she thought herself a princess because of the family she couldn't help having been born into. All she wanted was to draw until her fingers had splinters from her pencils so she could be promoted by a boss who thought her eyes were on her chest, just so she could have a career and live the life of an independent woman, rather than giving in to her mother and marrying a man she didn't love.

Now, she sat on her haunches looking up at a man she passed every day and who provided the soundtrack to her journey home, a man who'd never spoken a word to her or even looked at her face and yet he knew she was there by the sweets that she left and now he was reaching out for the first time, and Evie felt more connected to him than the people she was supposed to feel connected to. Her father might as well be a stranger, given how little involvement he'd had in her upbringing. On the rare occasions he saw her now, it took him just a split second too long to remember that the grown woman in front of him was in fact his daughter. Her brother had gone unusually quiet in the last couple of years. They'd been close during their childhood, and Eddie had always looked up to Evie, but recently he'd started to shy away from long conversations and hidden himself away. Before she'd moved out, Evie had seen him talking to their cook, Isla, an unusual amount, so she had a strong hunch that she knew why he'd retreated into himself. And her mother . . . well, her mother was the source of the majority of her problems.

There was a little flicker in Evie's heart, a crackling spark inside her that triggered a thought in her brain: *Is this the start of a new adventure?* For a woman who'd only ever used her heart sparingly in her illustrations and animations, and never in matters that involved men, it felt odd to look at someone she barely knew and feel a gentle squeeze in her chest. The laws of gravity had changed and she was no longer being pulled towards the earth, but towards him.

She pushed her hand into her bag, past the sketchbooks and loose pencils, right to the bottom, where her finger-tips encountered empty wrappers and her last few sweets. Excitedly, she pulled out as many as she could and picked out her last three orange ones. Then she took out a pen, flipped the cardboard to its blank side and quickly scribbled out a little cartoon self-portrait that accentuated her curly hair, chubby cheeks and big grin. She signed it, *Love, Evie*, then placed it back in the case and arranged the three orange sweets in a line on top of it.

He was still playing, eyes tightly shut, as she stood upright in front of him. She realised this was the closest she'd ever dared to get, and never before had she wanted him to open his eyes as much as she did now. She wanted to know what colour they were, whether they were full of life or cold and hard, whether when he looked at her, he'd actually *see* her. But for now, he played on, and she was reluctant to disturb him. She thought that maybe disturbing a musician mid-song was like waking a sleepwalker mid-dream, and she'd hate for his first impression of her, if there was ever to be one, to be bad.

Evie took the lift to the seventh floor and trudged to Apartment 72 in her flat brown ankle boots. Much as she loved her new shoes that looked like Mary Poppins' carpet bag, the three-inch heels made getting off trains more difficult than she would have liked, so they now sat unnoticed under her office desk. She slid the key into the lock, pushed open the door and walked into her living room. She was greeted by the smell of paint. She'd been spending her evenings painting the walls a deep shade of green, and had just the fiddly edges left to finish, but tonight she had something else to do. She shrugged off her coat, slinging it on an armchair by the door, pulled off her boots and ran on tiptoe to the kitchen.

To say that Evie had a sweet tooth was rather an understatement, and although her kitchen was empty of most of the essentials (bread, milk, coffee – she had tea, of course), she did have a tin of hard boiled sweets, which she now grabbed and took into the living room. Her mattress was on the floor, as she hadn't yet found the time to set up the bed frame, which stood against the wall in pieces. She'd lain the mattress so it was facing two tall windows that opened out on to a balcony. There wasn't much of a view, just another apartment building across the street, but the inhabitants of said building were highly interesting to watch and the majority of them kept their curtains open and their lights on. Evie plonked herself down on the mattress, opened the tin and started pulling out the orange sweets.

Every day at work had been somewhat difficult for the new girl and had presented challenges Evie hadn't even known existed. She worked in a department of two, together with a smarmy man named Grayson Pear. Grayson hated everything he drew, yet he still submitted his drawings to the editor and they were always picked above Evie's for every edition of the newspaper, even though they lacked heart and humour and were often derogatory towards whichever race, gender or sexuality he'd decided he didn't like that day. To make things worse, her boss seemed to think that the appropriate response to Evie's hard work was a slap on the behind. But despite all of this, Evie knew that the office would feel very small and unimportant to her when she heard that violin. When her first train pulled in at his station, she'd savour that distant sound as she walked through the passageway and then she'd revel in the swell of music as she moved up the escalator and his increasingly shaggy hair, his purple piped coat and black violin came into sight.

After a rather eventful evening, the day that followed had been dreary to say the least. Grayson had hidden her portfolio just before she needed to show the editor her work, which had still somehow earned her a slap on the arse, and by the time she left the office for the day, she felt that the sound of that violin was the one thing in her life she had to look forward to. The thing she held on to with all her might. The thing . . . she couldn't hear. As she got off the train, she strained her ears, but there was nothing. She thought maybe the hustle and bustle of evening

47

commuters was masking his music, so she ran through the passageway to the bottom of the escalators and stopped, causing someone to bump into her and mumble something rude under their breath. Listening even more closely she was now sure there was nothing, no sound at all, and her heart dropped through her chest and into her shoes. What if he'd moved to another station? What if she never saw him again? What if she never got to give him the parcel of orange sweets that was sitting in her pocket wrapped in brown paper?

She stepped on to the escalator and braced herself to see his busking spot empty, or worse, filled by someone who was far less talented and far less interesting to watch. But as the escalator carried her higher, there he was, in his usual place, his violin on his lap under his protective hands. Her heart lifted, then immediately thudded back into her heels as it dawned on her that this was the day she'd speak to him. She was caught completely off guard and totally unprepared, and when she received a jolt in the back from another commuter, she realised that she'd stopped dead as she stepped off the escalator and was blocking everyone's way. She moved to her right and took a moment to try to gather her thoughts, but her brain might as well not have been in her head for all the use it was being.

His eyes caught hers for a second before darting away again. He looked anxious. Like he was waiting for some-one. Evie tugged at the collar of her coat, wondering why the train tunnels suddenly felt so hot. But she had ink stains down her burgundy shirt, and if she were to speak to him (and she definitely *had* to speak to him), she didn't want to look a mess, so she kept the coat on and felt her neck and cheeks flush. His eyes caught hers again, and this time he held her gaze for a little longer, unsure.

She couldn't stand it any longer. With a deep breath in and a long shaky breath out, she started to walk over to him. As she got closer, a thought struck her: *I'm finally going to know the colour of his eyes.* Her stomach flipped. Then another thought: *What am I going to say?* It was too late. Her toes were now touching his violin case and he was looking up at her from his pop-up stool.

He smiled and she almost vomited her heart into his lap.

'Hello, Sweetie.' He was smiling, but the little crack in his voice gave away his nerves. This scruffy man dressed all in black, with hints of that very dark, almost not at all, purple, had the kind of smile that made you trust him with everything you held dear. You knew he'd keep it safe. Evie raised an eyebrow but couldn't help a smile.

'How did you know it was me?' *Evie, are you blushing?* she berated herself. *Stop that this instant.* But the voice in her head was her mother's, so Evie chose to ignore it. He held up the cartoon self-portrait she'd drawn him.

'You're very good. Although I don't think your cheeks are nearly as big as you've made them out to be here.' He put the drawing back in his pocket, and Evie realised he was intent on keeping it.

'Thank you. I'm Evie, by the way.'

'Yes, I know,' he said. 'And I'd like to thank you for all the sweets. The orange ones especially. They're—'

'Your favourite, yes, I know. Which is why I thought you might like this.' She pulled out the neatly wrapped brown paper parcel filled with every orange hard boiled sweet she could find in her flat. In an instant, this man transformed into a little boy, his eyes lighting up as if it was Christmas morning.

'For me?' A flicker of uncertainty passed over his face, his hand hovering but not quite taking the parcel.

'I don't know anyone else who likes the orange ones as much as you. Personally, they're the ones I avoid.' As she pushed the parcel into his hand, her little finger brushed against his thumb, and she snatched her hand away like she'd been burnt. Inwardly she rolled her eyes at herself. *Calm down, idiot.*

'Thank you.' He took the parcel without looking at it. His gaze was fixed on her and he noticed she had a twinkle.

It was right there in her eyes. It wasn't a trick of the light. It was actually, physically there. Maybe it was the slight scrunch of her nose when she smiled at him, which made the corners of her eyes crease that caused it, or maybe it was the way her eyebrows framed her eyes, but no matter what it was, when he saw that twinkle all he heard in his head was his heart laughing. He was very aware that he was sweating in this hot underground tunnel, with his coat done up all the way and with this very pretty, unusual girl stood in front of him, and he knew his hair was sticking to his forehead. He did his best to push it back so that Evie couldn't tell. But she could and it made her feel better for the beads of sweat currently rolling down her own back.

'And I'd like to thank *you* for the music . . . ' She trailed off. *That sounded* really *stupid*, she thought. 'I mean your playing. You really are quite something.'

He looked down at his calloused hands holding the neatly wrapped packet of sweets. 'Try telling that to every music school within fifty miles.'

'They don't already know?' Evie felt awkward standing above him now, looking down on him, and she wondered if he had an extra pop-up stool.

'As much as I enjoy playing, I don't busk for fun.' He gave his closed violin case a kick, making the change inside rattle.

'Looks like you do pretty well, though. Every time I've walked past, your case is spilling over.'

'It's enough to pay the rent on a very tiny flat in a dodgy part of town. How often do you walk past anyway? There have been sweets in my case for a while now.' He leaned his elbows on his knees, and she noticed how gangly he was, and how he didn't really know how to hold himself.

'I started working for *The Teller* a month ago. I got lost on my way home on my first day. I heard you playing, decided to investigate, and as it turns out, my platform is right there.' Evie gestured to the sign on the wall behind him. 'So thank you for leading me here. Without you it would have taken me a lot longer to find it.' She smiled, feeling warm on the inside, and he chuckled, but she could sense a dreaded silence approaching, and she didn't want there to be a pause because it meant . . .

'I should probably get home,' she said reluctantly. It was unlikely that he'd planned on speaking to her for long anyway. It was just a conversation out of common courtesy, after all the sweets she'd given him.

'Oh, really?'

A butterfly in her stomach fluttered its wings. Was that disappointment on his face? Was she horrible for hoping it was?

'Probably,' she repeated, with a tilt of her head. *So* this *is flirting,* she thought, feeling herself smirk and glance at him from underneath her eyelashes. It felt oddly natural. She wasn't sure if she liked that.

'Before you go, there was something I wanted to ask.' He leaned down and opened his violin case. Stuck to the inside of the lid, every orange coloured sweet wrapper she'd given him had been arranged to form the question *DINNER?* They caught the light and rustled in the breeze created by passing trains in nearby tunnels.

Any natural sense of flirting she'd felt before entirely deserted Evie. She looked up from the makeshift sign. Although he was clearly a little nervous (she could tell from his quivering eyebrows), his smile meant he was obviously enjoying her stunned silence.

'I'm not sure how I'm supposed to answer.'

His face immediately plummeted into embarrassment. His cheeks were already slightly pink from the heat of the tunnel, but now they were flaming, and the ruddiness spread right to the tips of his ears.

'Oh God, I'm so sorry. It's all a bit forward, isn't it? After all, I don't know you at all. We're not bloody Romeo and Juliet,' he scolded himself and closed the lid, keeping his head down. 'I just thought that you seemed really sweet. The sort of person I'd like to get to know, and—'

'No, no! That's not what I meant . . . '

'It's OK, you don't have to make excuses.' He spoke to the floor.

Evie bent awkwardly to try to catch his gaze. 'No, really, what I meant was—'

'Honestly, I totally accept it's a no.'

'NO! It's not a no!'

He peered through his hair, which he'd strategically flopped over his face, and his green eyes glinted.

'I just meant that with such a grand gesture, I don't know how to say yes in a way that matches it,' she said all at once before he could speak again. 'But it's definitely that. A yes, I mean.'

'Wow. Erm. OK.' He swiped his hair back off his face, which was still a light shade of red. 'OK. Yes. OK. Dinner. Me and you. Evie . . . '

'Snow.'

'Evie Snow?' He raised an eyebrow.

'Evie Snow,' she confirmed and held out her hand.

'I'm Vincent.'

'Vincent . . .' she nudged, wanting to know his full name. (Wanting to know *everything* about him, actually.)

'Vincent Winters.' And when she saw his eyes smile without having to see his lips, she got the feeling that this might be the start of her greatest adventure yet.

5

crossing the wall

Evie and Lieffe were sitting on the floor in front of the sweet wrappers that Evie had arranged to form the question *DINNER?* She beamed at him with a sweet tucked into her cheek.

'But all the wrappers were orange,' she explained, 'and he looked so dorky and nervous!' she giggled, as she finished the story behind the confectionery she'd asked the Lost Box to conjure.

'But you still said yes.' Lieffe smiled.

'I still said yes.' She smiled too. 'It wasn't just because he was handsome and I fancied him. It was because he was the first person in years, maybe even for ever, to actually *see* me rather than just look.'

'What's the difference?' Lieffe asked, adding one last wrapper to make the dot of the question mark.

'When someone looks at you, they only see what's on the surface and often miss a lot of the details. When someone *sees* you, they see who you are, what you're actually about. They see more than what's there in front of them. They're willing to find out more, at the very least.' Evie took one final look at the arrangement they'd made and then, with a swipe of her hand, she pushed the wrappers to one side.

'Are you visiting Vincent first?' Lieffe bunched the wrappers in his palm and put them into a waste-paper basket underneath the desk in the corner.

'No,' she said, very sure of her decision. 'That would be jumping in at the deep end.' She glanced at the Lost Box. 'I'll save that trip for last.'

'Well then. Where to first?' As Lieffe leaned against the desk and folded his arms, the air seemed to prickle with excitement. It was the same feeling Evie used to get when her family flew somewhere exotic for a holiday. That sense of impending adventure. Although the most adventure she'd had on any family holiday had been in Morocco, when she'd wandered off and almost been sold to a local man by a very persistent stallholder. Her father had been less than pleased when he'd had to buy back his own daughter. If it had been up to Edward Snow, he would have left her behind, but Eleanor persuaded him by squealing, 'What on earth would the Summers think if we came home without a future wife for their son?' From then on, Evie wasn't allowed out of their sight and adventures became non-existent.

The wall hummed more loudly, gearing up for what lay ahead. Evie took a deep breath. She slipped off her coat and placed it over the Lost Box, covering the mountain of sweets, then placed her palm against the wall. It was still warm and pulsing, a heart beating in a chest.

'I suppose I need to see my son.'

The wall stopped humming and pulsing and paused for a brief moment. It was holding its breath.

'Are you sure?' Lieffe asked. 'You can't suppose or think or wonder. You need to *know.*'

Evie knew she could make excuses to get out of making this trip through the wall, but there was no doubt in her mind, heart or soul that, some way, somehow, she needed to speak to her son.

'Yes.' She nodded. 'I am absolutely sure.'

'In that case, you need to figure out what to give the wall so it can find your son and take you to him.'

Evie stood back from the wall, looking at it through narrowed eyes. 'First of all, I need to know what to expect when I get to the other side. How do I speak to my son? Will he be able to hear me? See me? Will I have to explain why his dead mother is visiting him from beyond the grave?'

Lieffe smiled. 'I'm sorry, dear girl. I've not given you much of a briefing, have I? You've handled everything so remarkably well up until now that I forgot all of this is new to you.' He took the desk chair and wheeled it over to Evie again, gesturing for her to sit down. Then he stood between her and the wall, like a professor standing between his pupils and the blackboard.

'When you cross the wall, no living person will be able to see you, and you won't be able to make any kind of impact on the world around you. Your soul may be too heavy to pass on, but it's very calm and collected, is it not?' She nodded. 'Good. Now, as I've said, you won't be seen by your loved ones, and for the most part they won't be able to hear you either.'

'For the most part?' Evie asked.

Lieffe started to pace the length of the wall, back and forth. Evie imagined a pipe in his hand and a tweed jacket on his shoulders, much like Mr Autumn. *I should probably be taking notes*, she thought.

'There is a certain time when the living are more susceptible to our world. When their minds are most open to believing the impossible. Tell me, have you ever dreamed of people who have passed on? Have they ever said things to you in dreams that you never heard them say when they were alive?'

'Maybe . . .' Evie thought back through her life and vaguely remembered dreaming of a friend who had died suddenly of a heart attack in her forties. In the dream, her friend had told her that she'd once stolen money from her purse, and it had plagued her with guilt throughout her life. Evie had no way of knowing if this was true, so had written it off as an odd dream brought on by eating cheese on toast before bed, but she had been left with a strange, lingering feeling.

'When the living are sleeping, we're able to seep into their dreams and whisper our secrets to them. When they wake up, they remember those dreams because it was more than just their subconscious having fun while they slept. It wasn't even a dream at all, really. It was us.' Lieffe gestured around him, puffing out his chest, proud to be part of this weird world full of lost souls. His face was so full of affection and warmth for this place that he'd loved so much in life. 'The more open-minded the person, the easier it is to get into their dreams. Some poor souls here have had real trouble getting people to hear them, but eventually, in times of need, everyone is able to open their mind enough to let the impossible in.'

'So I just need to whisper my secret to my son while he's asleep?'

Lieffe nodded. 'Do you think he's open-minded enough to listen to you?' he asked.

Evie couldn't help but smile. 'Oh, I think my husband and I raised him well enough for that, yes.' She thought about her husband, left in the land of the living. She doubted he'd be far behind her. He'd never been able to cope without her, even when she was only in the next room, and he'd always made excuses to be close to her. She doubted it would be any different this time.

She used her feet to wheel herself closer to the silent wall, and Lieffe moved aside. 'Why's it so quiet now?' She tapped the knuckle of her index finger against the cream-coloured surface.

'It's trying to listen. It's waiting for you to tell it where you need to go.'

'Just one strong memory is all it needs? To make a connection?'

'Just one.'

Evie, eyes closed, the tip of her nose against the wall, breathed out slowly, the warmth of her own breath flushing her cheeks. She opened one eye and spied Lieffe on her left, watching her closely.

'Sorry. Shall I give you a moment?'

'No, no. I'm just being silly. No point in being shy when I'm dead, is there? But you are going to have to put up with my singing. That OK?'

'Nothing would please me more. If I remember correctly, you had quite a nice voice.'

'It wasn't anything to write home about, but for its ultimate purpose, it was perfect.'

Evie closed her eyes once more, and images of her first-born, her son, flooded her mind. Memories of rocking him in her arms only moments after he'd been born, and singing him to sleep with words she'd made up herself to a tune her childhood music box had played. When he was older, and fell off the tyre swing in the back garden, she'd sung to him to take his mind off his stinging knees and to stop him from crying. And as she lay in hospital, weeks before she ended up here, he'd held her hand and sung with her, just in case he never again heard her sing the song he loved so much. It was that song that she sang now, because she knew it would find him, no matter where he was.

> *If I were to follow you,*
> *Would you lead me astray?*
> *I'm trusting you with all my heart*
> *To lead me the right way.*
> *So hold my hand and take me through*
> *The darkest of my days.*
> *Because if you were to follow me,*
> *You know you'd be OK.*

The wall started to hum and pulse and shimmer, and the energy it created rolled Evie's chair halfway across the room. She watched its cracked paint smooth itself out and turn a charcoal blue. Small ripples started to appear, at first just a few, but then they came in their hundreds, dimpling the surface over and over, giving the illusion of a puddle in the rain. The hum turned into a low rumble that reminded Evie of her father clearing his throat, which he did whenever he felt uncomfortable.

'I think wherever your son is, Evie, the weather's bad,' Lieffe chortled.

A shock of light passed over the wall like lightning.

Instinctively Evie started to count – *one, two, three, four* – and then thunder shook the room. The wall wobbled and the chair rolled a little closer to it.

'The weather must be *really* bad,' Lieffe said, the laughter replaced by a nervous tremor as he held on to the desk to steady himself.

Lightning struck the wall again. *One. Two. Three ...* This time the thunder was louder, and as Evie's chair rolled even closer to the wall of water, she realised that it was more than just the thunder shaking the room and making the chair move randomly; she was actually being pulled towards it. Lightning filled the room again but it was brighter and Evie was sure she heard the zap of electricity. *One. Two ...* At the next lightning strike, the chair jolted so hard that she was tipped out of it and landed only inches from the wall. She looked behind her at Lieffe, who was righting the chair, its wheels spinning.

'I think the thunder's counting!' she shouted over the noise of the rain and the wind that was whipping at her hair and her dress.

'I'm sorry, Evie,' he shouted. 'Some souls are lucky enough to find their loved ones on holiday in the Bahamas, or at home, snug in their beds. This isn't the best introduction you could have had to the journey back.' He tried to smile, but flinched a little as the lightning hit once more.

One ... Thunder. Evie ran to retrieve her coat from

the Lost Box. It looked like she was going to need it. She had a feeling that she wouldn't have time to put it on, so she swung it by the shoulders around her body and held it over her head. The moment the fabric touched her hair, a fork of electricity pierced the wall, picked her up by the waist and dragged her through the water.

the
first secret

the black
bird

December

Dinner

Evie had been restless all day. She crossed and uncrossed her legs under her desk and tapped her pencil against her sketchbook, which didn't speed up time at all but did earn her some quizzical looks from Grayson.

'Something the matter, Princess?' he asked, putting his hand gently on her pencil to stop the incessant noise. 'Am I making you . . . nervous?' He smiled a wide smile.

Don't be taken in by his welcome grin, he's imagining how well you'd fit within his skin, she sang in her head. Evie hated the fact that Grayson was good-looking. Someone so arrogant didn't deserve to be attractive. She'd watched various women meet him after work for dinner dates, only to hear him brag the following morning about bedding them, tearing apart their performances in a minute-by-minute relay to *The Teller*'s photographers. His phone would buzz on his desk, flashing whatever horrendous nickname he'd saved them as in his contact list, but he'd press decline. Evie's blood would boil at the sight of the malicious delight on his face when he knew he'd conquered another woman's affections – affections he would never return.

'No, Mr Pear,' she replied, without so much as a glance in his direction. 'You're making me sick.'

It was Friday evening, and tonight was the night she was having dinner with Vincent. She hadn't thought through her wardrobe decisions hard enough this morning. She'd opted for comfort at work over dazzling for dinner and now wished she had chosen the latter. She was feeling a little sweaty and grubby in the stuffy office, and having Grayson leer at you was enough to make anyone feel as though they needed a shower . . . or two. She had perfume in her bag, so she hoped that would do. She'd watched the clock with nerves in the pit of her stomach all day, and her sketches were misbehaving, coming out scribbled and scratchy.

'Get a grip, Evie,' she muttered to herself.

The clock ticked over to five o'clock and Evie swiped her stuff off her desk, catching it in her open bag. She threw on her coat as she ran out of the door, without so much as a wave goodbye to Grayson.

She hadn't thought about where they might be going or what they might eat. She wondered if she was too nervous to eat at all. All she knew was that she wanted to learn about Vincent. Evie had led a sheltered life, but despite her parents' best efforts, she'd made sure she had plenty of adventures. One evening, when she was sixteen, she had snuck out of the house with Isla, the Snows' cook, to a bar in the centre of town. Eleanor was so sure of her daughter's obedience back then that she hadn't considered that the Evie-shaped lump under the blankets wasn't actually Evie at all, but cushions from the sofa arranged meticulously. They'd got back just as the sun was coming up, holding their shoes in their hands, giggling, hushing each other and then giggling more at their hushing. How they'd pulled it off was beyond Evie, when she awoke in her bed two hours later, fully clothed, smelling of champagne and cigarettes and with mascara smudged down her cheeks. Now that she was on her way to see this man whom she knew nothing about, she had that same mischievous feeling bubbling under her skin. She knew that this was a sure sign of an adventure about to begin.

They were meeting at Vincent's busking spot, and Evie had kept quite calm during the majority of her journey. It was only when the train pulled into the station that her skin started to tingle. As she stepped on to the escalator, she heard Vincent playing. She thought he must be getting in a last-minute song to round off the evening, but as he came into sight, so did a small round table covered in a red gingham cloth with a pop-up stool on either side, all squished into his designated busking spot. The table was set with two paper plates, one with a single yellow rose laid across it, and a lit candle stood in the centre. Yet again, Evie stopped moving as soon as she stepped off the escalator, and was shoved aside by a kid in school uniform. She shouted a sorry in his wake but her gaze was fixed on Vincent. As usual, his eyes were closed as he played. She slipped off her coat and sat down on one of the stools, trying to be as quiet as possible. She waited and watched him until he played one final, beautiful note, and when she was sure the song had come to an end, she applauded politely. Vincent opened his eyes.

'Miss Snow.' He nodded.

'Hello, Vincent,' she laughed.

'You've got a twinkle in your eyes,' he said.

'I do?' A finger instinctively went to the corner of her left eye.

'Yes, you do.' He smiled and balanced his violin in its case on top of the coins he'd collected that day, then sat down on the dark green canvas camping stool opposite her.

A girl with blobs of ink on her hands and permanently dishevelled hair, who looked like she could do with a proper night's sleep, but that twinkle, in Vincent's opinion, made her more interesting and more beautiful than anyone he'd met before.

'A yellow rose.' Evie lifted it to her nose and inhaled its subtle scent.

'Mm-hmm.' Vincent leaned his chin on his hand and

rubbed at his stubble. He hadn't shaved as he was trying to grow a beard. Meanwhile Evie was wishing he had shaved because she couldn't help remembering her mother's warning that men with beards weren't to be trusted. Maybe she was thinking too far ahead, but she was wondering what her mother would say should she ever meet Vincent. Yet despite Eleanor Snow's disapproving face flashing through her mind, Evie's main thought was what Vincent's rough cheek would feel like under her fingers, and suddenly the station felt very warm again.

'For friendship?' She set the rose between the paper plates and felt a little silly.

'Mm-hmm.' He hummed again in agreement, but this time Evie caught the hint of a smile between his fingers.

'I see.' She straightened her back and her expression, placed her hands in her lap and tried to pretend she was her mother: cold, hard and unwilling to play games. Vincent swiped his hair out of his eyes and gazed at her with sincerity in his expression.

'I want to be friends with you. I want to get to know you better. We've only properly met once before this, and like I said, we're not Romeo and Juliet.' He laughed, a rich and rounded sound. 'We can take as much time as we want to find out exactly who it is we're talking to. You might get halfway through this conversation and decide I'm a ruffian who you'd rather not associate yourself with, and I wouldn't blame you! But that's what all this' – he gestured to the table – 'is for. You and me, just talking for a while.

71

Then maybe, if it's OK with you, we could be friends, Miss Snow?' He picked up the rose and offered it to her, hoping she'd take to it more kindly this time.

Evie Snow studied him for a moment. She'd certainly not let her heart run away with her. It didn't know how. But maybe she had let herself think that his intentions were different. Romantic. And she didn't necessarily know how she'd felt about that, though she knew it had excited her, the idea that this unbelievably talented man was interested in her. But now that she knew it wasn't like that at all, she felt a little . . . No. She didn't feel anything, she decided. Like a tap turning off, she didn't feel disappointed, or disheartened, or foolish. Instead, she channelled her excitement into a new-found friendship and she took the rose with a smile.

Dinner had turned out to be burgers and chips that Vincent had bought from what he'd called 'the best burger place in town'. They'd looked atrocious when he'd tipped them out of brown paper bags on to the plates. Evie had struggled to pick her burger up without it falling apart, but once she'd taken a bite, she had to stop Vincent mid-sentence just to savour the sensation. They were indeed the best burgers in town.

'So, you're an artist?' Vincent asked, putting a chip into his mouth.

'Well, I'd like to be an animator for motion pictures. That's the dream.' In her mind, Evie could see her drawings moving around on the silver screen. 'But for now, I'm just a cartoonist for the local paper, my drawings destined for my boss's bin, while he fawns over my disgusting colleague's work just because he doesn't have boobs.' She sighed. 'And you're a violinist.'

'Yes. Doomed to play to an audience of uninterested commuters for ever.' He sighed too, but with an amused smile. He'd made his peace with his lot in life. He'd not given up per se, but he'd found contentedness in what he did have.

'Hey now,' Evie teased. 'Not all of them are uninterested.'

'Forgive me. All the unimportant ones are uninterested, but they're also the ones who pay my rent, so in a different and annoying way they're important too.'

'Yes, I suppose they are.'

'Any brothers or sisters?' Vincent asked, putting four chips in his mouth at the same time. For a first dinner together he was awfully comfortable around her, but that relaxed Evie too. In her family, every meal was a formal occasion and making conversation was frowned upon, so it was nice to have such a drastic change. She opened up her burger, peeled out the gherkins but instead of discarding them like Vincent had thought she would, she popped one in her mouth.

'One brother. Eddie. You?'

'I have a sister called Vanessa. She's a heart surgeon,' he said with a slight roll of his eyes. 'Any pets?' He changed the subject swiftly.

'None,' she answered.

'Never?'

'Mother's allergic.'

'Not even fish?' he laughed.

'Oh. We have a koi pond in the garden, but if I can't cuddle it, it's not a pet.' She shrugged, matter-of-factly, and took a sip of Coke from her plastic cup.

'Koi? When I said fish, I was thinking more like . . . gold.' Vincent laughed.

'I . . . er . . . my family are . . . '

'Rich?' he helped, with a kind smile.

'I was going to say fancy, but yes,' she said apologetically.

'Why do you sound sad about that? Lots of people would give their right arm to grow up wanting for nothing.'

'I know, and I guess that's what makes me sad. I appreciate everything I've had in life, but my parents have tried very hard to keep our wealth . . . contained. Sharing it with those in need is almost disapproved of. They think money makes them happy, but really it just makes them . . . secure. Happiness has nothing to do with it. In fact, they're probably the unhappiest people I know.'

'Does this have anything to do with you roughing it at the local newspaper?' Vincent fiddled with a chip, hoping this conversation wasn't making Evie uncomfortable.

'It does, yes. I'm twenty-seven and this is my first job. Not ever having to work sounds glorious, but not when you feel like you're being kept captive in your own house. Having money doesn't mean anything if you don't use it in the right way.'

'And what's the right way?' Vincent looked intrigued.

Evie shrugged. 'Helping people? Animals? The earth? Having adventures? I could think of a hundred better ways to use my family's money than what it's being used for now. Which is nothing.' She looked troubled. Agitated. She'd picked away at the foil wrapping of her burger and created silver confetti on the tablecloth. Vincent decided this wasn't the time to delve into her family issues and changed the subject.

'So not even so much as a hamster?'

He shook his head in disbelief, she smiled and his heart swelled just a little.

'No, not even a hamster!' She smiled again.

'Fair enough.' He nodded, curling his bottom lip out into a sort of approving pout. Evie couldn't help but look at his mouth then, but she caught herself before she let her mind wander.

'And you? No fish of your own?' She was making fun, but he didn't seem to realise, and Evie quite liked that.

'Just a family mutt called Max, but he died a few years back. I don't think I've ever cried so hard in my life as the day we lost him. Mum too. Since then she's not been able to get another dog. Can't handle losing them.' Vincent

75

suddenly felt himself being swept away by grief so he shook his head sadly.

'Can I be honest with you?' Evie smiled at her own cheeky thoughts which made Vincent wonder where she was taking this conversation.

'Of course.' He opened his own burger, removed the gherkins and passed them across to her.

'These questions are awful,' she revealed.

'Oh are they now? And why is that?' Vincent leaned his chin on his hand again, smiling.

'You're not finding out anything . . . meaningful. Whether I have siblings or pets doesn't tell you anything about . . . well, *me*.'

'Yes it does! It tells me you have a brother. And that you're heartless towards fish and most likely amphibians!'

Evie rolled her eyes. 'You know what I mean. They're things I'd expect to be asked in an interview by someone who doesn't need to know my personality. My . . . ins and outs.' She hadn't intended to sound provocative, but all the same, the slight tilt of Vincent's head and the sudden raise of his left eyebrow pleased her. 'Ask me something that will make me think. Something I'll have to wonder whether I should tell you the answer to or not.' She leaned forward on her elbows, fascinated to see what he'd come up with.

Vincent thought hard, looking directly into her eyes. She didn't shy away from his gaze. She just wanted to know what he was seeing when he looked at her.

Vincent, however, suddenly felt her stare was too much.

76

Her eyes weren't full of anything other than happiness, something Vincent had known very little of in his life and he feared they were like the sun; beautiful and necessary but looking at them directly might hurt you. He averted his eyes down to his large, calloused hands and wondered what he was doing. No, in fact, he wondered what *she* was doing, this brilliant girl who wanted for nothing, whose nimble hands could create brilliant worlds on a page in mere minutes, with an oafish man who bumbled about the underground with a violin barely scraping together enough pennies to buy two burgers, fries and two Cokes. He was a giant who had caught a butterfly and knew he'd only kill it if he kept it but was so reluctant to let it go for its beauty made him something he wouldn't be without it: happy.

'All right,' he said eventually. 'I have a question.'

'Go for it.'

'It's a doozy.'

'Go on . . .'

'Seriously. Brace yourself. It's amazing.'

'Tell me!' Evie giggled.

He took a deep breath. 'OK.' He paused for dramatic effect just long enough to wind her up a little bit more. She looked at an imaginary watch, unamused. He brought his hand to his mouth as if he was holding a microphone. 'If you could undo one thing from your past, what would it be?' He quickly moved the microphone over to Evie so she could answer, and she tapped the top of it to make sure it was on.

'*That's* your question?' she asked, humorously exasperated.

'What?' He couldn't help but laugh. 'It's a very interesting question. Could reveal a lot about your . . . ins and outs.' He smirked. Evie felt her cheeks flush and hoped she hadn't gone red.

'Well. My answer is . . . I wouldn't.' She sat back, feeling her mother possess her again as she clasped her hands in her lap in a no-nonsense manner which was utterly ridiculous considering how much Evie liked nonsense.

'Wouldn't what?' He picked up the remaining half of his burger and halved it again in one bite.

'Undo anything. I believe that everything I've done and everything that's happened in my life has happened for a reason, and if I changed anything, I wouldn't be the same person I am now.'

'Have you been asked this before?' He narrowed his eyes at her. 'That was a very practised answer.'

'I just think about stuff like that a lot. Don't you?'

Vincent stuffed the last of his burger into his mouth and shook his head.

'I think about it all the time,' Evie continued, 'about what makes everyone who they are, and if we went back in time and changed anything, whether or not it would make a difference. Would it make us better or worse, or would we just stay exactly the same because we were always destined to end up this way no matter what happened throughout our lives?' Evie was no longer looking at Vincent. Her burger had become far more interesting. She was relaxed, almost spaced out, lost in a world of her own. Vincent took a sip of his drink and although he tried to stop it, he couldn't; he grinned at her even though she wasn't looking.

'And what's your conclusion?' he asked gently.

'Ugh, I don't know.' She took a deep breath and snapped out of her trance, glancing up at Vincent then back down at the mess she'd made of the foil wrapper. She swept the pieces off the table into her hand, then instead of scattering them onto the train station floor, dropped the tiny traces of foil into her coat pocket. 'If I had an answer to that, I think I'd be far more sought-after than I am.'

She glanced at Vincent again and noticed the way he was gazing at her. It was the way she'd seen movie stars look at each other. Like nothing else in the world mattered except them existing in that moment. Evie had watched many romantic movies, and enjoyed them, but she never wept with happiness when the couple finally kissed, and she'd never understood the force a look like that could have. She realised now that that was because she'd never been looked at that way before today.

'What about you?' she asked, trying to stop the mood from becoming too intense. 'What's the one thing from your past that you'd change?'

Vincent scrunched up his face like he'd been hoping she wouldn't ask the same question in return. 'Urgh, can I only pick one?' He laughed nervously.

'They're your rules, Winters, not mine!' She ate one final chip and then wiped her hands together, signalling she was done with food. Now she was hungry for more conversation.

'I think I would go back to when I was learning the violin and figure out how to play with my eyes open. That way I would have met you sooner.' He tried to give her a confident smile but as soon as the words had come out he'd second guessed himself and it showed.

'I quite like the way we met,' Evie confessed. 'Even if it did take you forever to finally say hello.'

'OK,' Vincent said, the awful underground lights reflecting in his eyes. 'I have one more question.'

'Go on.' Evie tilted her head.

'And forgive me if I'm being forward.' He was suddenly bashful, his hair flopping over his eyes again, a tinge of red in his cheeks.

'Go on,' Evie nudged, feeling a jolt in her stomach.

'No, really, I don't want to make you uncomfortable . . .'

'Vincent,' Evie said, a little more seriously than she'd intended. She dipped her head to meet his eyes. 'Just ask.'

He pursed his lips but still managed to smile through them. 'Is there a . . . Mr Snow?'

Evie laughed. 'Even if I was married he wouldn't be a Snow. I'd be a . . . well, whatever *he* was.'

'Oh. Yes. I didn't quite think that through.' He brushed his hair out of his eyes, the red hue now covering his whole face again, right to the tips of his ears.

'No.' She held up her left hand to show him her ring finger. 'Not married. And not involved, either. I've never really been one for romance. Much to my mother's horror. If anything, I've avoided it to spite her.' She laughed, but then felt mean. 'I love her, she's my mum, but we have very different ideas about how I should be living my life.'

'I'm guessing working at *The Teller* wasn't her idea?' Vincent scrunched up the wrapper of his burger along with the paper plate and stuffed it back into the bag it had come in. Evie did the same.

Even though she hadn't quite finished her burger, she'd lost her appetite.

'Definitely not.' She laughed at what an understatement that was. Eleanor Snow couldn't have been more against this endeavour; in fact Evie was still pinching herself that she'd been able to get this far. 'And I can only continue living my life how I want to live it as long as I progress as an artist professionally, beyond the pages of *The Teller*, within the next year.'

'And if you don't?' Vincent didn't look too troubled by her story. Evie supposed it sounded like an empty threat to him – a fairy story about an evil queen keeping her daughter in a tower – but she herself knew only too well just how serious her mother was.

'If I don't, I get married to whomever she chooses and spend the rest of my days as a wife and mother. Nothing more, nothing less.'

'Wow. We'd better start getting your artwork out there

then. It needs to be seen by the right people if you want to animate for motion pictures.' Vincent took her rubbish from her and stood up.

'*We?*' Evie asked, taken aback, looking up at him.

'I don't want to jump to any conclusions, Evie,' he said, walking across to the bin, 'but I think we're friends now, and friends help each other out.' He gave her his most adorable smile.

'I suppose we are, Mr Winters.' She nodded, grinning. She'd been living on her own for just over a month, and this was the first friend she'd made. Preconceptions had been the undoing of any potential friendships at the office (if Grayson called her 'Princess' one more time, she vowed she'd buy a tiara, wear it to work every day and be done with it), except maybe with the receptionist but that may have been due to the fact she was also female and fed up of the misogynistic work environment rather than through any real connection to Evie, herself. Then again, Evie hadn't been very responsive to friendly advances either as she always had her head in her sketchbook, searching for some way to progress further than the newspaper.

'Evie?' Vincent ventured.

'Another question?' She stood to take her coat from underneath her. The evening was drawing to a close, and the air was chilly. 'Better make it a good one. All the others have been a bit of a let-down!'

He walked back over to her, but kept his distance. His hands suddenly felt like two useless lumps that he didn't know what to do with, so he shoved them deep into his coat pockets.

'I was just wondering ... Seeing as it's only' – he checked his watch – 'eight o'clock, would you like to go for a walk? With me. Somewhere.'

Evie thought about getting up for work early the next morning, and then had the glorious realisation that tomorrow was Saturday.

'Now that, Vincent, was a brilliant question,' she said, smiling.

Vincent, the brilliant violinist, had never met his father but his mother, Violet Winters, had worked hard to bring her two children up on her own. When the time came for his sister, eight years his senior, to go to university, Violet realised that by seeing one of her children all the way through higher education, she was taking the opportunity away from the other. There was no money left to send Vincent any further than college, and she knew she wouldn't be able to put aside enough by the time he was eighteen, even if she worked three jobs. Instead, she scrimped and saved for a whole year to buy him a violin for his tenth birthday. She'd seen the way he looked at them when they passed the music shop on the way to school, and how his fingers twitched, desperate to try one.

83

'If you get really good,' she told him, 'that violin will pay for whatever you need.'

At ten years old, he'd believed this to be true, but now, eighteen years later, he wasn't so sure it was that simple. He'd practised until his fingers were numb, and as the commuters at the station would confirm, he was the best there was. The problem was that he had taught himself from books and from nagging people he knew who also played. In the process, he'd picked up bad habits, and his unusual technique and lack of knowledge of music theory made him unacceptable to every music school in town, especially when he was also looking for a scholarship. He'd filled in application after application, every time having to leave questions about qualifications blank, and he knew it was useless. Even though he could outplay the greats, the best schools were looking for the best musicians, and to be considered one of the best, you had to have had a formal education.

Through busking and his part-time job at the very music shop where his mother had bought the violin he still played, he made enough money to pay half of the rent on a small flat in a seedy part of town, but that was about all. He shared the flat with a guy he'd gone to college with who called himself a musician too but who was nowhere near as talented as Vincent, although he was a great deal more deluded: he'd even gone as far as giving himself a stage name, though he wouldn't divulge how many times he'd actually been on a stage, other than trying to crash one. Sonny Shine was a wannabe rock star, and although Vincent loved him like a brother, he thought he was a moron. Sonny was usually late with the rent, but Vincent couldn't kick him out because he couldn't afford the place on his own and he knew no one else was stupid enough to live there with him. So, Sonny and Vincent lived together as harmoniously as they could, Vincent on the violin and Sonny on the electric guitar.

Vincent had managed to put a sweet spin on burgers and chips with his romantic meal for two in the station, but if he planned to see Evie again, he needed some new ideas. He didn't have a lot of experience with girls. He was bisexual and he'd had as many relationships with men as women which, at the age of twenty-eight, was the grand total of two. Two *serious* relationships, at least. The first, for six months when he was nineteen, had been with a red-headed, fierce-tempered girl called Tallulah Holly. She was beautiful to look at, like a mermaid from a lagoon, and she was very sweet in small doses, but behind closed doors she was bitter and left a bad taste in your mouth for days. She worked in a café serving coffee and fried breakfasts to construction workers, but she wanted to be an actress, and Vincent had become completely besotted with her when he saw her play Portia in an amateur production of *The Merchant of Venice* and just *had* to go to the stage door to speak to her.

Tallulah was high and mighty right from the off, and she signed Vincent's programme even when he hadn't asked her to but Vincent was convinced she could do no wrong. After six months, during which his life revolved around her and she made things as difficult for him as possible, he decided to introduce her to his mother. They dropped by unannounced (because Vincent knew Tallulah would find an excuse not to go if he told her), and even though Violet thought she was far too big for her boots and was aware of Tallulah looking down her nose at the tiny house that smelt slightly damp and the makeshift meal she had rustled up at short notice, she could see how happy she made her son and so was as nice as the pie she had served them. It was only when they were back at Tallulah's flat (because she always refused to go to Vincent's as she thought Sonny was a moron – though that was a fair opinion because everybody did, and he was) and Tallulah said, 'She's a sweet woman but it's obvious why your father left. She's not really much to look at, and that *cooking*! My *God*!' that Vincent's rose-tinted glasses cracked and he saw her as everyone else did: a bitter girl whose life hadn't turned out the way she'd wanted it to, so she tried to make every-one else's just as sour as her own. He'd ended it there and then, as gently as he could, mind you, but the actress in Tallulah *had* to make a scene. She broke most of her own crockery that night.

Vincent's second relationship was with a guy called Will Johnson. It too only lasted six months, but it ended as amicably as it had started. Will worked behind the bar at a club Vincent's college friends liked to go to. They'd dance the night away getting sweaty and terribly drunk, but that wasn't really Vincent's thing, so instead he assigned himself as the group's designated driver. Like a parent at a children's birthday party, he would watch his friends run off to the dance floor and inevitably embarrass themselves before the evening was out while he'd wait at the bar and drink as few of the tiny bottles of overpriced Coke as he could without getting chucked out. It took Will two weeks of serving Vincent to pluck up the nerve to offer him a drink on the house. It took him another week to ask his name and another for his number. Will worked in a club with loud music because he wasn't very good at talking to people, and as Vincent was the first person he'd ever wanted to speak to, it made him think he must be special. (Will also worked in a club with bright lights because he was ginger and hoped all the strobes and lasers made it impossible to tell.) As it turned out, he went to the same college as Vincent, taking English literature and art, and was working at the club to make a bit of extra money for art supplies. They spent most of their time together discussing books and making out on Vincent's sofa to vinyl records. In the end, the relationship simply fizzled out. As Will put it, *life happened* and a relationship wasn't what either of them needed or, in all honesty, wanted but a great fondness remained.

Vincent had had flings, random kisses and on one occasion a one-night stand, but he was by no means a Casanova. He also felt that Evie had an odd vibe. He felt intimidated by her, even though she was incredibly warm and friendly, and he couldn't quite put his finger on why.

They had folded up the table and the camping stools and left them in Vincent's busking spot. *I'll sort that out tomorrow,* he thought, imagining the angry station staff member who would be waiting for him when he started his busking shift the following day. For now, though, Evie was his sole concern. When they emerged from the station, it was drizzling slightly, but not enough for it to be unpleasant, and it made the river that ran through the town ripple and glisten. Evie ran across the street and leaned over the black-painted railings, looking down into the water. She leaned over as far as she could without her toes leaving the ground so she could see her reflection – but raindrops kept making it wobble. Vincent appeared beside her in the water but he was facing away, leaning his back against the railings.

'What *are* you doing?' he asked.

'What does it look like I'm doing?' Evie replied. Vincent turned to look at the river to try to see what she saw.

'You're . . . looking for the Loch Ness monster?'

'Nope. I doubt Nessie would pick such a dirty river.'

Vincent nodded in agreement. 'OK. Maybe you're . . . you're trying to see your future and using the river as your crystal ball?' He waved his hands around mysteriously.

'No,' Evie said, laughing. 'I've tried that before, though. Never works!'

'You're . . . you're . . . trying to make me think too hard. I give up. What *are* you doing?'

'I wasn't doing *anything*,' she teased. 'I was just looking.'

'Why didn't you say that in the first place?' He prodded her arm playfully.

'You wanted there to be an answer and I didn't have one. I thought you'd have fun creating your own theories.'

'Is that what you do every time you don't have an answer? You make one up?' Vincent started to walk along the pavement, hoping she'd follow, but she didn't.

'Why not? It's more fun to imagine that I'm searching for my future in the water rather than knowing I was just looking for no real reason, right?'

'I suppose.' Vincent was a good ten feet away from her now and was having to raise his voice a little for it to reach her. A light went on in a house nearby and he wondered if she was going to close the gap between them, but she was showing no signs of moving.

'There you go! Why should I shatter your wonderful fantasy with my boring reality?'

What a brilliant thing to say, Vincent thought. Then he thought a little more and . . .

'What a brilliant thing to say,' he said.

'It's true, though, isn't it?' Evie was gazing into the river again.

Vincent had had enough of the distance. He wanted to be closer to her and started to wander back, trying to look casual but knowing he didn't. There were rules that told him he was supposed to wait three days before he called her again after tonight, and that he was supposed to seem uninterested to make her want him more, but he had never liked playing games that involved manipulating how people felt. Feelings were confusing enough without people toying with them to make them fit their own needs. Even if he had been an advocate of manipulation, something told him that Evie wouldn't fall prey to it anyway. Her mind worked in ways beyond that kind of silliness.

'Look over there.' Evie pointed to a woman crossing the bridge over the river. She was wearing a khaki coat with a hood that was pulled all the way over her head, shielding the majority of her face. She was alone and struggling with two plastic bags of shopping. 'What's her story, do you suppose? What do you *want* her story to be?'

Vincent thought for a moment. The woman looked quite ordinary, if a little bedraggled and melancholy. She was prob-ably just on her way home from her weekly grocery shop.

'She's on the run,' he said seriously.

'You think?' Evie whispered.

'Yeah. She's just escaped from her house with all her possessions in carrier bags, moments before the police broke in to find her brother murdered.'

'And why did she murder her brother?'

'Because *he* murdered her husband.'

'And now she has no one,' Evie said in tragic tones.

'And she's hiding.'

'In plain sight.' Evie shook her head, playing along.

Vincent shot her a mischievous look. 'We'd better catch her and turn her in.' And with that he was running.

'What? VINCENT!' Evie chased after him, not knowing whether to laugh at his silliness or be terrified of his potential seriousness. She caught up with him, grabbed his arm with both her hands and started to pull him back the other way. 'Stop it!' Now that she could see he was stifling laughter, she was also giggling.

'No, Evie! We've got to stop this criminal mastermind!' By now he was laughing so hard he could barely get the words out. The woman was walking straight towards them. 'Excuse me!' he called, hushed enough for her not to hear what he had said but loud enough for Evie to clamp her hand over his mouth.

'SHUSH!' Evie's giggles had sapped her strength and Vincent turned his head away to free his mouth. By now the woman was much too far down the street to hear their conversation, presumably because she quickened her pace when she saw Evie and Vincent wrestling in the middle of the road, but the pair hadn't noticed and nor did it matter.

'Excuse me, ma'am, we have reason to believe you're on the run . . . '

She tried to put her hand over his mouth again, but he held her wrist at a distance.

' . . . from the police!'

'VINCENT!' Evie tried to put her other hand over his mouth, but he stopped that one too, holding both her wrists out to the sides away from his face, only gently but her giggles meant she had no strength to fight back. Her little hands flapped about, all the while she was laughing near the point of bursting.

'. . . FOR KILLING YOUR BROTHER!' Vincent yelled.

Evie quickly yanked her wrists behind her so that he was pulled in towards her, his arms around her waist, fingers still circling her wrists. He looked at her, trying to read her face, as they'd both become very quiet and serious all of a sudden, like a blanket of snow had fallen over the world around them. He felt big and oafish in comparison to her. She wasn't small, she was of average height and seemed healthily put together with broad shoulders, and even though her skirt was cinched in at the waist, she had large hips and thighs from her love of bread and cheese. He was merely too tall and too big and he felt that just by having his arms around her, he engulfed her entirely. Evie however felt like she fitted there perfectly. She'd always been broader than other girls, never graceful and elegant, and Vincent made her feel delicate and dainty, for once. Vincent wanted, more than anything, to close the gap between them, but his uncertainty about how she felt made him falter.

'Evie,' he said, his mouth dry and his voice husky.

'Yes,' she whispered back, a slight smell of gherkins on her breath.

'One more question.' He wasn't able to look anywhere other than at her eyes. Her make-up had smudged slightly, softening the black lines around her eyes, but the chocolate centres still swam with tears of laughter.

'Make it a good one,' she warned, edging a little closer. Vincent didn't move a muscle.

'Feel free to say no . . .'

'OK . . .'

Evie's heels had left the ground. Vincent seemed to have turned to marble, his words only escaping the tiny gap between his lips, his arms rigid around her. He let his hands soften, and her wrists slipped easily out of his grip; then, as if it was entirely natural, she brought them up and rested her palms on his chest. For the second time that night, he didn't know what to do with his hands so he linked his own fingers and rested them on the small of her back. Evie saw the uncertainty in his eyes and that little nervous flicker of his eyebrows was back. She wished she didn't make him so nervous and yet she was a little glad that she did because her own pet butterflies were back. The ends of their noses bumped, and Vincent breathed out the words, 'Can I kiss you?'

Before he knew it, she had closed the distance. Evie's mind raced a mile a minute while Vincent's turned to sponge. There was so much uncertainty in the way he kissed her and yet none of her kisses had ever been so sure. She held onto the lapels of his coat as if the speed of her life had just gone nought to sixty. The whole world vanished and it was just Evie and Vincent floating into nothingness, maybe never to return, but that was OK because they had each other.

They parted, only slightly.

'I promised myself I wouldn't do that,' Vincent whispered.

'Why would you make such a promise?' Evie pulled away, searching for an answer in his expression.

'I don't want you to think I do this all the time and that

I'm confident with this kind of thing, because I'm really, *really* not,' he confessed.

'I know you're not. Your eyebrows keep twitching.' She smiled up at him, which just made them twitch more.

'And I don't want to rush . . . this. Whatever *this* is.'

'Neither do I, but maybe this isn't rushing. Do you feel rushed?'

'No.' He pecked her lips with his.

'Do you feel uncomfortable, or like this shouldn't have happened?'

'I don't.' He kissed her again.

'Then it's not rushing. It's right.' And again they were lost to the world, or rather, the world was lost to them.

There were only two train stops between where Vincent busked and where Evie lived, so they strolled the twenty-minute walk to her block, making it last for forty. Even though they'd already kissed, Vincent didn't hold her hand until halfway home, when their fingers brushed accidentally and he instinctively held on. They paused as they both acknowledged their entwined fingers, and Evie took the chance to reach up on tiptoes for what she expected to be just a peck, but he moved his other hand to her face and held her there a little longer. She noted how much she enjoyed how shy he looked after each kiss they shared.

They arrived outside Evie's apartment building and came to a reluctant stop.

'This is me.' She gestured upwards. 'Mine is that one, just there.' She pointed out a flat with a bare balcony, a light on inside and a small window flung wide open.

'I see.' Vincent shoved his spare hand into his pocket and scrunched up his shoulders.

'Do you want to . . . ' She gestured again, not knowing how to invite him in without it sounding like an invitation for more than just coffee.

'Erm . . . ' Even though it was dark, with only the street lights to illuminate them, Evie could see that red tinge sweeping over his face.

'Just coffee, I mean. Nothing else.' *Oh Evie*, she thought.

'Right. Of course.' He couldn't meet her eyes. *Vincent, you're twenty-eight, stop blushing*, he scolded himself.

'It's only the first date. I'm not quite so easily conquered.' She was trying to be nonchalant, picturing Audrey Hepburn or Marilyn Monroe, but she doubted Audrey or Marilyn had had to deal with racing hearts and dizzy minds as they recited their lines.

'You make it sound like you're a country.'

'One whose terrain no one explores on a first date!' *OK, that was a pretty good line.*

'So this was a date?' A smile crept across his lips.

'Well . . . we had dinner, got to know each other better and kissed towards the end. If that's not a date, then I need to re-evaluate my romantic knowledge.'

95

'When you put it like that, I suppose it was.' Vincent's eyes filled with warmth.

'Only a *first* date, mind you,' she said, very tentatively, hoping he'd catch on.

'The first of many.' He took her right hand in his and kissed it. 'I shall leave you to the rest of your night, Evie. When can I see you again?'

'Tomorrow?' She jumped in too quickly, but Vincent shot back immediately with 'Yes, tomorrow. Midday?'

'Midday,' she confirmed, and with one final lingering kiss, they parted, already eager to see each other again.

Evie climbed the stone steps, let herself in through the main entrance of the building and looked back through the glass doors to see Vincent watching her from the bottom of the steps, still not quite wanting the evening to end. She gave him a little wave, and as he eventually turned away, she felt something inside her chest tugging her back in his direction. Reluctantly, he started to walk back towards his own home in the dodgy part of town.

'And who is that, may I ask?' Evie hadn't noticed that Lieffe had crept up behind her and she realised that seeing him must have been why Vincent had decided to leave.

'Lieffe, you made me jump!' She swatted his arm, and the little man laughed.

'I wouldn't have done if you weren't up to mischief! Go on. Who's the dish?'

'Dish!' Evie tutted. 'He's called Vincent Winters and he's a very respectable man. He's a classical musician,' she said pointedly, her nose in the air.

'Wonderful! Well don't leave it too long before you invite him in. I want to meet him.'

'I did invite him in, but it was only our first date, and like I said, he's a respectable man.'

'What does that say about you if you invited him up to your flat on the first date?' Lieffe raised his eyebrows playfully as Evie struggled for words. In the end, she just swatted him again, laughing, and then retreated to her apartment to spend the night dreaming of the evening she'd just had.

December

The Second Date

Vincent awoke the next morning to find Sonny's feet in his face. He'd fallen asleep on the sofa, only for Sonny to come home roaring drunk at 3 a.m. and cuddle up beside him. It was just another thing to add to the list Vincent was racking up to prove that the previous night had indeed been a dream. But it hadn't been.

At midday, Evie emerged from her apartment building wearing a burgundy dress, brown boots and her green coat. A loaf of bread, still in its plastic packaging, was dangling from her hand. Vincent, in his skinny black jeans, almost-not-purple T-shirt and black coat with almost-not-purple piping, felt underdressed.

'You look gorgeous.' He felt silly as he said it.

'You look the same as yesterday!' Evie laughed. 'Which is wonderful, by the way,' she added with a kiss hello on the cheek.

'Where to?' Vincent asked, indicating the bread.

'I was thinking the park?' She shrugged.

'To feed the ducks?' He raised an eyebrow.

'Precisely.'

'Perfect.' He took the bread from her and offered her his arm, which she happily took, and off they went.

'Vincent, I am *so* sorry!' Evie flung the door of her flat open and ran straight to the bathroom to fetch a towel as Vincent stood dripping on the doormat.

'It's fine!' he laughed, taking the yellow towel from her and mopping his face and sopping hair as best he could.

'Come in, come in! Don't worry about getting anything wet!'

Vincent slipped off his squelching shoes and left them outside the door. He slipped off his wet socks too, tucked them into his shoes and closed the door behind him.

They had been having a lovely day by the pond in a nearby park, which was filled with birds and old people, when Evie had started talking about her love of ducks.

'They're your favourite animal? Really?'

'Mm-hmm,' Evie had answered, watching as a duck nipped breadcrumbs from her cupped hands.

'Not something majestic or fearsome, like a lion, or a—'

'Dragon?' she'd said, quite serious, and Vincent had smiled. 'Ducks are silly. I like silly,' she had argued.

'Like you?' Vincent had said, teasingly. He'd stepped closer to the edge of the pond, his hands in his pockets as usual. Evie had taken a whole slice of bread out of the bag and thrown it like a Frisbee, aiming for his face. He'd batted it out of the way with ease and it had landed in the pond, but as he had taken a step backwards to dodge the slice, he hadn't bargained on a goose being right behind him. The back of his knees had hit the bird, which had squawked and nipped his left leg, causing him to lose his balance and fall backwards straight into the pond. Luckily it hadn't been very deep, and Evie had laughed rather hard, though her laughter quickly turned to guilt as she watched Vincent turn crimson with embarrassment.

Now, although Vincent was soaked to the skin, it was an excuse for him to see where Evie lived, and for that he was grateful.

'The bathroom's through there. I'll ... er ... I'll leave you to get undressed and have a shower if you like.' Evie reached over and pulled a piece of green pond slime from his hair. 'There's a dressing gown in there. It's not ... short or anything. It'll cover everything ... I'll er ... put the kettle on.' Flustered, she handed him yet another yellow towel and pointed the way, not quite meeting his eye.

Vincent emerged fifteen minutes later wearing the dressing gown, which did, indeed, cover everything. Evie took his clothes from him and put them in the washing machine.

'It'll probably take an hour or two to wash and dry everything.' She bit her lip apologetically, but his eyes lit up.

'That sounds great.'

She grinned and handed him a cup of tea. 'I don't have a sofa, I'm afraid. Just a chair and a mattress.'

'So I see. You just have an empty bedroom, then?' He moved one of the pieces of her bed frame away from the wall and looked at it, befuddled.

'I've just not had the time to put it together yet, and to be honest, I quite like the mattress in the living room. The windows are much nicer in here.' Evie went to move her coat from the green armchair so that Vincent could sit down, but he touched her arm.

'Don't worry about that. I've got a better idea.'

Together they took a blanket out on to the balcony, huddling underneath it as they watched people down below on the streets, driving past in their cars. Some of them had their windows wound down and were playing loud music, which Evie and Vincent sang along to, badly.

'I can play the violin but I really, *really* can't sing,' he confessed.

'I can't sing *or* play the violin! You're one up on me,' Evie said, laughing.

They talked for hours, long after the tumble dryer had beeped to tell them that Vincent's clothes were dry. They shared childhood stories of mishaps and mayhem, made each other laugh with tales of mad family members, and confided memories of tough times. Afternoon quickly turned into evening, and thoughts of going home started to enter Vincent's head.

'What's the time?' he asked.

'I'm not sure.' Evie shrugged, willing him not to go just yet.

He looked into his empty mug. 'I should probably . . .' He left the sentence hanging in the air.

'Stay longer?' she finished for him, trying to sound like she was joking but meaning every word.

'I've intruded for long enough. Not to mention that I've made your flat much damper than it was before!'

'It was my fault for making you go for a swim today.' She smiled, then laughed again as the image of him sitting in the pond flashed back into her head. 'I'm sorry,' she said between snorts. 'You just looked so helpless!'

This time Vincent didn't turn red with embarrassment. He just gave her that look again. The one where the romantic leads get tunnel vision and all they can see is that one person they want.

'You've looked at me like that before,' Evie said quietly.

'Like what?'

'You *know* what.' She prodded his shoulder with a finger. 'What are you thinking when your face does that?

What does that look mean?' Although she wasn't fishing for compliments or in need of a declaration of true love, she was hoping that he was feeling the same way she was.

'Aren't you suddenly full of questions?' Vincent said, his voice dropping to match hers.

'No point in being coy. We've kissed already.' She winked playfully, trying to lighten the mood, but she felt her stomach flip all the same. 'And I don't like games. Being straightforward makes everything easier.'

'I agree,' Vincent said, nodding.

'So, what's the look for?' Evie repeated.

Vincent could see he'd backed himself into a corner and she wasn't going to let up until she had an answer and he had no reason not to be honest.

'I don't have a mirror so I can't be entirely sure, but . . . I'm pretty certain it's my "I'd really like to kiss her again" face. Then again, it could be my "I can't quite believe my luck" face. Or my "she's totally bonkers and I really quite like that" face. Take your pick.'

He hadn't looked at her once. Instead he'd been looking at his hands as he fiddled with the stitching on the end of the blanket. Evie set her mug down beside her on the floor and took both of his nervous hands in hers. They were twice the size of hers, solid and rough, but she smoothed them out so that she could hold them. She shuffled a little closer as elegantly as she could. The twitch of his lips told her she wasn't being graceful at all, but then his expression stilled as she leaned her face towards his until their noses were touching. She gently pressed the tip of her nose on to the bridge of his and traced the outline of it all the way down to the end, before tilting her head in further so she could reach his lips and kiss him.

Her hands slipped out of his and she reached up to the nape of his neck, where she entwined her fingers in his shaggy hair and held on as she felt the speed of her life accelerate once more. Vincent slid his arms around her waist, aware that this was more of her than he'd ever dared think of holding, and he pulled her towards him. She was still kissing him as she climbed into his lap and his arms encompassed her entirely. Their kisses became deeper, full of longing, and being that close suddenly wasn't quite close enough.

Their hands became heavier and while Vincent was still trying to hold on to some of his inhibitions, Evie's had floated away in the evening breeze, long forgotten and happily lost. Evie pulled away fast and clambered to her feet, taking his hand in both of hers and tugging him into the flat. She paused by the mattress, asking him with her eyes whether this was what he wanted. He responded by scooping her up in his arms. She wrapped her legs around his waist and one thought filled her head as they sank down on to her makeshift bed: *It's not the first date any more, after all.*

Evie's hands trembled as she dragged the blanket back on to the mattress while trying not to be seen by the outside world. She pulled it over herself immediately, not from embarrassment at being seen by Vincent – it was far too late for that – but because the balcony doors were still flung wide open and now the winter air was crisp. She curled up next to Vincent, whose eyes were closed, and rested her head against his chest, which was moving in time to his heavy breathing. As soon as her cheek pressed against his skin, his arm instinctively curled round her, and it felt so right that she couldn't imagine having his arms too far from her ever again.

'Evie?' Vincent mumbled.

'Mmm,' she whispered back.

'Don't go away.'

She tilted her head to look at him. He still had his eyes closed, but his brows had knitted together above them.

'What do you mean?' She was entirely worn out and couldn't keep her own eyes from shutting.

His arm pulled her in closer and Evie's body stretched out and pressed against the outline of his side. 'You're spectacular.' He felt her lightly shake her head and exhaled in disbelief. 'I mean it.' He opened his eyes and tilted her head with a finger on her chin. 'You're like . . . that single firework that makes everyone gasp in a display that would otherwise have been quite disappointing.' Evie enjoyed his silly spontaneity while Vincent felt the relief of finally saying what he'd thought up hours ago and dared not say.

He took a deep breath and watched Evie's head rise and fall with it. 'I'm just a little . . . I don't know. We've known each other two days and it already feels like I've been here with you, like this, a million times before.' He twirled a strand of her hair around his finger and her closed eyes crept open a little.

'I know,' she said. 'And you're just as worried as I am that it'll disappear as quickly as it happened?' Vincent nodded and kissed her forehead, warm against his lips. 'Neither of us are kids, Vincent. I know what I want out of life and I know how I feel.' Evie twisted so that she was lying on her stomach, leaning on her elbows to look at him.

'Of course you do.' He gently brushed her cheek with his thumb, concern etched on his face. 'But things change over time.'

'Then let's worry about that when the time comes. For now, I'm happy, and I don't see that changing.'

'Me neither.'

Despite his words, Evie could see that Vincent's worry wasn't going anywhere. All she could do was prove to him that whatever this was between them, it wasn't a fickle, childish fling. It felt honest and uncomplicated, like nothing else had ever been in either of their lives, although in very different ways. Evie moved forward, putting her weight on his chest, and gave him a long, lazy kiss, during which a tear containing reflections of all his fears escaped his eye but he wiped it away before she could see it. Eventually she pulled away, her eyes full of happiness, and they settled down under the cover, sleepily talking about nothing until they both drifted seamlessly into sleep.

Neither of them could have known that this was the calm before the storm.

This December was much the same as every year Evie had experienced it, except that now mulled wine tasted sweeter, she noticed the smell of cinnamon wherever she went, and carollers found lots of hard boiled sweets in their instrument cases and hats.

'Evie! EVIE!'

Lieffe rushed to the doors of the apartment building and looked to the left to see a man standing on the pavement underneath Evie's window, wearing thick gardening gloves, with a large and very real Christmas tree lying on its side at his feet.

'You must be Vincent,' he said. 'Do you need some help with that?'

Vincent looked sheepish. It was New Year's Eve, and Evie had spent Christmas without a tree. Although it had been an extremely romantic idea in Vincent's head, it had turned out to be rather impractical. Lugging the tree across town without a car had worn him out, and although the wind was biting and snow was most certainly on its way, he'd sweated through his T-shirt, presumably his coat too, and his face was redder than Rudolph's nose.

'Vincent? What's going on?' Evie had run out on to the balcony after scrambling to find half-decent clothes to throw on. Vincent was out of sight, hauling the tree through the doors to the building, but he heard her and called back, 'I'll be up in a minute!'

Lieffe helped Vincent stand the tree in the lift but only Vincent could fit in beside it. 'Good luck!' Lieffe wished him with a little two-fingered salute as the doors closed.

Evie was waiting as the doors opened on the seventh floor, laughing at the sight of the lift filled entirely with tree and Vincent squashed up against the wall. Together they dragged it along the corridor, leaving a trail of pine needles, and manoeuvred it through the door of Apartment 72. Once Vincent had got it upright in the corner of Evie's living room, they both stood back to admire it. It was a little lopsided, but they both loved it all the same.

'Gives it character,' Evie said, smiling.

Vincent produced from his pocket the tree's first ornament. It was a hard boiled sweet made out of orange glass, with a piece of green ribbon attached to the centre so Evie could hang it from a branch.

'Wherever did you find it?' Evie asked, as she marvelled at it, holding it between her fingers and up to the light.

'It just appeared in my pocket one day.' He held up his hands and she hit him with a tea towel she'd been using in the kitchen while he'd been sorting out the tree. 'I figured it was meant for you.'

Evie had got out of having Christmas with her family by

telling them she was ill. Eleanor Snow hated anyone being sick in any way, and even more so when she had guests to entertain, so as soon as she knew her daughter had the sniffles, she insisted that she didn't come home for Christmas dinner or the annual Snow and Summer festive party. She even cut the conversation short and put the phone down faster than usual, just in case she caught Evie's 'illness' through the handset.

All in all, Eleanor didn't seem too upset and Evie couldn't have been happier. She and Vincent went to Violet's house for Christmas dinner instead, taking along with them a box of mince pies Evie had made on Christmas Eve, although several of them had disappeared into Vincent's mouth before Christmas morning arrived. During dinner, Vincent was pleased to see how genuinely taken Evie and Violet were with each other. Afterwards, Evie had insisted on clearing the table, and when she was out of sight, Violet placed a hand on her son's arm.

'She's truly wonderful,' she said, her eyes glistening.

'I know,' Vincent beamed.

Vincent hadn't been back to his flat for days, but Sonny hadn't been in contact so he was unsure if he'd even noticed. More and more of his clothes and belongings had ended up at Evie's place as he stayed over increasingly frequently and they settled into a routine of sorts. They'd pinned up bunting and fairy lights, and as Evie drew sketch after sketch at her newly bought desk, Vincent would pin those to the walls too. They'd assembled the pieces of her bed and were actually using the bedroom to sleep in, but they often took a blanket out on to the balcony at night to talk through their day over tea before sleeping. As the new year drew closer, both Evie and Vincent were looking forward to new beginnings together. The life they'd created in the month they'd known each other was ideal, but it was something they knew they'd need to work hard to keep.

Their plan for January was for Vincent to apply to music schools and to try and find some gigs bigger than playing underground tunnels to disgruntled commuters, while Evie was going to send copies of her portfolio to publishers and animation studios. All she needed was one person to give her a chance to change the future her mother had planned for her. Just one person had to say yes for her to be able to spend her life with Vincent, and she was determined that that was going to happen.

As midnight approached on New Year's Eve, Evie and Vincent were in her living room, taking it in turns to throw chocolate chips into each other's mouths. Whenever either of them succeeded, it resulted in hands being flung into the air in triumph, and lots of cheering. When they heard a neighbour's party start the countdown, they ran to the balcony.

'. . . FOUR . . . THREE . . . TWO . . . ONE!'

Fireworks erupted, lighting up the sky around them. Vincent lifted Evie off the floor and into his arms, and even though he was kissing her, she could feel his smile. When he returned her to the floor, she leaned over the balcony and yelled, 'HAPPY NEW YEAR!' at the people in the street below, many of whom shouted it back. Then a very calm voice from the balcony to her left said, 'I hope it's a wonderful year for you both.' A man in a tweed jacket, with suede elbow patches, raised a glass of whisky in a toast to them.

'Oh, it will be,' Evie said, smiling back at her neighbour. 'And for you too.'

July

Sonny

Evie hadn't heard from her mother in months, and she wondered if Eleanor thought it would be easier if she spent the rest of her life pretending she didn't have a daughter. She felt a little cruel for wishing that could be true, but her time with Vincent had been near-perfect and she didn't want anything to ruin it. And Eleanor Snow would undoubtedly ruin it. Right now, the only problem with Vincent was that Evie was completely and utterly in love with him.

'Vincent. What do we do if I don't get any further than the newspaper?' Evie had just finished clearing up after dinner, and she stood in the kitchen doorway, tea towel in hand. She was having another of the moments that had been occurring all too often recently, when she would

113

remember her mother's conditions about her living in this flat and having the job at the paper and would feel like she was going to be sick.

'Is your mother actually going to force you to marry someone you don't want to?' Vincent asked gently.

Even though she knew Eleanor was extremely cold, Vincent's question did make Evie wonder whether her mother would be that heartless, especially if she met Vincent for herself.

'You're twenty-seven,' Vincent continued. 'You can make your own decisions . . . can't you?' He was reading a book in the green armchair, which they'd moved further into the living room now that the mattress was on the bed where it belonged. Evie dried her hands on the tea towel, then slid into the living room in her socks, stopping at the armchair, where she collapsed dramatically into Vincent's lap.

'Of course I can make my own decisions. But what if they're decisions that make me happy, but upset, embarrass and shame the rest of my family to the point where they disown me entirely?'

'Am I *that* awful?' He pouted, but she kissed him and said, 'Not at all. You're wonderful, and that's just the problem. They like boring and bland.'

'I can be boring! Look.' Vincent's face became completely expressionless and he swept his hair into a sort of neat comb-over.

The phone rang, and as Evie ran to it, Vincent followed

her, putting his boring, serious face as close to hers as possible, making it very hard for Evie not to laugh as she picked up the receiver.

'Hello? *No one ever rings this phone,*' she mouthed to Vincent who was messing up his hair once more.

'Hello, is that Evelyn Snow?' The voice on the other end was well-spoken and full of charm, and Evie would have known it anywhere.

'It *is* Evelyn Snow, yes. Is that James Summer, of Snow and Summer Ltd? The most dashing man in all the land, with the world's wealthiest ladies falling at his feet, day in and day out?' Evie had adopted her mother's tone of voice, clipped and posh, which she'd perfected as a child in order to amuse her little brother.

Jim laughed. 'It's good to hear your voice. I visited your parents' house today and it's like you never existed! How's the job and the flat?'

Vincent was back in the armchair with his open book in his hand, but he'd read the same sentence four times because he was too distracted, trying so hard not to eavesdrop on Evie's conversation.

'I'm not surprised,' she said. 'I'm a bit of a family embarrassment at the moment. The job is fine ... sort of. But hey, I'm drawing and getting paid to do it, and that's a thrill in itself.' She let her chest swell with pride.

'And your mother's *letting* you? Has she gone completely *sane*?' Jim couldn't keep the shock out of his voice.

'No, she's just as awful as ever. I'm not here

without conditions, of course.' Evie's pride quickly sank and drowned.

'Well, I was just calling to tell you your presence was missed. I thought you would have at least come home for Christmas. You missed the famous Snow party, and we always have a dance or two.'

'Jim, you only ever dance with me to avoid Nelly Weathersby.' Nelly was the daughter of a lawyer who worked at the firm, and she was completely besotted with Jim. She was an attractive girl, but whenever she looked at Jim she had a glint in her eyes that made her look psychotic, and he had once overheard her saying she was desperate to know what their children would look like. 'And it's always more than a dance or two and you know it!'

There was a pause on Jim's end of the line. He thought about all the times he and Evie had danced together at that same festive party every year and how it was only partly because of Nelly Weathersby but mostly because it was the only time he could be close to the girl who had never loved him back.

'Well,' he said after a moment, and Evie could sense the tinge of sadness breaking through the charm, 'I was just hoping that I might see you soon, that's all, but it's enough to know you're well.'

'I am.' Evie glanced at Vincent, who was still pretending to read.

'Good. Don't ever be a stranger, Evie. It gets tiresome around here without you.'

'I won't. I'll visit soon. Oh, and Jim, could you do me a favour? Keep an eye on Eddie for me.'

'Always do. Speak soon.'

As Evie put the phone down, she couldn't explain the feeling of unease that made her skin prickle all over. Maybe it was a strange kind of homesickness after having spent months away from the place she'd been kept captive, or maybe it was knowing that the man she'd just spoken to might one day be her husband out of family obligation. She turned to Vincent.

'I need a better job. We both do.'

'We've done as much as we can.'

And they had. As soon as the new year had begun, they'd bought paper and envelopes and Evie had sneakily scanned her artwork at the newspaper offices and printed off copies of her best drawings. Together they'd written letters to publishers and animation studios. Vincent had filled out applications to every music school he could think of, and Evie helped him fill in the boxes he usually left blank. Someone had to reply with *something*.

'It's been months,' Evie said. 'I'm not so sure.'

'Schools won't be taking on new students until September.'

'But it's already July and when September rolls around, I'll only have two months left before my mother puts her foot down and this has to end.' Evie rushed the end of her sentence, feeling a lump build in her throat.

'Hey now.' Vincent put his book down and held out his

arms to her, and she let him pull her on to his lap. 'Even though you've made your mother sound like a pterodactyl ready to kill at a moment's notice, I'm not scared of her. If you want to marry someone you love, then you'll just need to tell her she can stick her arranged marriage where the sun very clearly doesn't shine!'

Evie liked the sound of his words but she knew it wasn't that easy and she didn't have the heart or the energy to fight it. Instead she nodded and nuzzled into his shoulder, pretending he was right. 'Cup of tea?' she asked, taking a deep breath and deciding to plough on with a positive outlook on what could be a very grim situation.

'Yes please.' Vincent kissed the top of her head and she hopped off his lap and wandered into the kitchen.

'Can you hear that?' Vincent's ears had pricked up at a noise intruding through the open balcony windows. It sounded familiar, but he couldn't put his finger on why he knew it.

'Are you hearing voices again?' Evie teased from the kitchen.

'They're a constant,' Vincent called back. 'This is different.' He went to the balcony and spotted a man staggering along in the centre of the road. He was dressed in ripped grey jeans and a long baggy top that was hanging off one shoulder. Slung on his back by its strap like a rucksack was a guitar, and he had a beer in either hand. A car came up behind him and beeped, but he only sang louder, and suddenly Vincent knew why that slightly out-of-tune drone had sounded so familiar.

'Sonny!' he shouted. The shaggy blond-haired man stopped singing and whipped around to find out who was calling his name. 'Up here, Sonny!' Vincent would have laughed if he hadn't had to take care of a drunk Sonny before, but he knew just how unpleasant it could be and he certainly wasn't up for it tonight. Not with Evie around.

'HEEEYYYYY!' Sonny yelled, finally spotting Vincent.

'What the hell are you doing here?' Vincent whisper-shouted back. 'This is a nice area and you're making the property prices decrease just by passing through!'

'RUDE! You are RUDE!' Sonny flung his arm out to point at Vincent but lost his grip on one of the beer bottles, which slid from his hand and smashed on the concrete. 'Awwww, no!' He dropped to his knees in front of it, and Vincent thought for a moment he might start lapping the beer up like a cat.

'Go home, Sonny.'

'I . . . er . . . I have a gig.'

'Very funny. You never have gigs.'

'No. I'm abso . . . absolutely . . . deadly serious.' Sonny waved a hand in front of his face in a downwards motion and his expression turned very stern. He held it for a second and then burst out laughing.

'Then why are you here?' Vincent looked back into the flat. Evie was standing in the doorway between the kitchen and the living room, her eyebrows raised and a slightly confused smile playing on her lips.

'Well, y'see, I've always wanted to play a proper concert, and now that I am, I'm a bit . . . nervous. Eight beers' worth of nervous. If we're being . . . y'know . . . honest 'n' stuff.' Sonny took a swig from his remaining beer. 'Nine if you count this one. But not ten . . . ' He gestured to the puddle of beer and broken glass in front of him.

'Right. Better get going then!' Vincent pointed down the street, like he was telling a dog to go home after it had followed him to school.

'Yup. OK. On my way!' Sonny got up off the concrete and almost fell over immediately. 'Bye, Vinny!'

'Goodbye, Sonny.' Vincent turned back into the flat. Evie still looked a little confused, but mostly amused. She'd not seen Vincent anywhere close to angry before.

'Vincent!' Sonny called out.

'WHAT NOW?' Vincent yelled properly this time. Evie jumped, and he instantly mouthed *Sorry* to her, but her eyebrows had furrowed and her lips had melded into a single thin line.

'Vinny, I don't know where I'm going.' Sonny sounded helpless.

Vincent rubbed his temples. 'How do you not know where the gig is?' he said wearily, turning back to the balcony.

'I know where it is!' Sonny had been looking up at the balcony for too long, and now he stumbled backwards. 'I just don't know how . . . ' He made two fingers on his empty hand walk like a pair of legs in the air in front of him, and then he shrugged.

'You don't know how to get there?' Vincent asked, and Sonny nodded, pouted and then giggled. 'Well, it's your own fault for getting so inordinately pissed.'

'I know,' Sonny said matter-of-factly.

'I think it's probably best if you skip the gig and go home.'

Vincent was about to head back inside when Sonny said, 'But they're paying me for it!'

'A paid gig, Sonny? How've you managed that?'

'It's a school. A prom. The actual band they had was better.'

'What happened to the actual band?'

'They pulled out. So they pulled me in! Yaaayyy!' Sonny cheered, gagged and then vomited over the broken beer bottle.

Evie came out on to the balcony and looked down. Sonny was trying to hold back his hair, but his long T-shirt was dangling in the stream of sick coming from his mouth.

'We've got to help him,' she said, looking up at Vincent. 'A paid gig means he can afford his rent, and that means neither of you gets evicted. Let's try to sober him up on the way, then we'll keep an eye on him at the school, pretend we're his entourage or something, and get him home safely again.' Evie ran back into the flat and was already pulling on her boots before Vincent had said a word. 'Well?' she asked, shrugging on her coat.

Vincent could see she was looking at this whole endeavour like a quest or an adventure and Evie wasn't the sort of person to leave a friend – or a friend of a friend – in need, let alone standing in a puddle of his own vomit in the middle of the street. He looked down at Sonny once more and huffed.

'OK,' he said. 'But I still hate him.'

Sonny hadn't been too far off track when he'd been looking for the venue of the gig so Evie and Vincent hadn't had to drag him that far. The school was in a nice part of town, only fifteen minutes' walk from Evie's flat. Sonny had been sick again in a bin on the way, but they'd stopped to get him coffee, and he'd started to make a little bit more sense by the time they reached the school gates. The only problem was that he smelt very strongly of booze and vomit. Vincent had brought along one of his own T-shirts to replace the one Sonny had been sick on, but he wouldn't let Sonny put it on until he was sure it was safe. It wasn't perfect, but at least it would mean that the smell wouldn't knock out the kids at the front.

'He'll have to do. It's his own fault.' Vincent stood back, his face contorting at the odour. Evie brushed down a swaying Sonny and pulled strands of his hair back behind his ears.

'Stop being so mean. He's just nervous, that's all.'

'You're way out of your league with this one, Vinny. She's marvellous!' Sonny winked at Evie, and she smiled with her lips tightly shut, trying not to breathe in sweet Sonny's stench.

They went in through the front gates and were directed by a bemused receptionist to the headmaster's office. Mr Glass was a very skittish man, who was constantly wringing his hands and smoothing down what was left of his greying hair. When he saw Sonny, he almost keeled over.

'And who are you two?' he barked, wiping sweat away from his stubbly upper lip.

'We're his friends,' Evie said smoothly. 'We're here for moral support, but we're also happy to chaperone the kids if you need us to.'

Vincent looked at her, impressed by how well she thought on her feet.

'We *are* down by a few teachers,' Mr Glass muttered. 'And without *him*, all we have is outdated records . . . ' He looked Sonny up and down once more, and Sonny gave him a weak, apologetic smile. At this point, Sonny was secretly hoping to have the gig taken away from him. He felt too drunk, too sick and too nervous to be able to strum a guitar and sing without his voice wobbling, but he would never turn it down himself out of pride.

Mr Glass let out a long sigh. 'Fine. You're on in ten. Half

an hour of whatever you've got. Oh, and the press are here. We haven't told them yet that the Dream Catchers have pulled out. They've got quite a big following, and *The Teller* wanted it to be on their front page, but I'm hoping we'll get a small article at least. We need all the good press we can get for this wretched school!' He stalked out of his office, slamming the door behind him.

As soon as he was gone, Sonny collapsed into a desk chair, dry-heaving. 'I can't . . . do . . . this,' he said between retches.

'He *really* can't,' Vincent said, shaking his head.

'He *can*! You *can* do this, Sonny.' Evie knelt by the chair and stroked Sonny's hair back into place, breathing only through her mouth. 'We'll be right there in the audience. Just look at us and play to us. It's only a few songs. And I know the people from *The Teller*, so I'll make sure they only get good pictures and say nice things.'

Sonny looked at Evie with his wide grey eyes. 'Seriously, Vinny.' He shook his head. 'Where did you find her, and can you take me there?'

The 'Down the Rabbit Hole' theme seemed to be going down a treat with the kids. The school hall had been decorated with red roses and white rabbits, and several couples were already furiously making out on the dance floor (to what really were extremely outdated records), while sullen singletons sat on the sidelines gorging themselves on cookies labelled 'Eat Me'. Evie and Vincent left Sonny by the side of the stage and made their way to the back of the hall, where the photographer and journalist from *The Teller* were standing.

'Well, hello, Princess. What are you doing here?' Terry Lark was a squat man who looked older than his thirty-four years.

'No tiara today?' asked Harrison Feather, a lanky chap whom Evie had never seen without his beanie hat on his head. He claimed it helped him focus when taking his photos, but that didn't explain why he *never* took it off. Evie felt Vincent's hand tighten around hers.

'Not today, gentlemen. I'm here for Sonny Shine.' She was met with blank faces as she leaned against the wall in an attempt to be nonchalant, but slipped a little further down than she'd have liked, making her a good foot shorter than Harrison and awkwardly at Terry's eyeline. 'Surely you've heard of him? He's a real rebel. I thought that's why you were here. He's certainly front-page news.' She caught Vincent's eye and winked. He looked back at her like a rabbit caught in headlights.

'We were here to report on the Dream Catchers playing at the school that the lead singer used to go to before the band became a big hit,' Harrison explained. 'But seeing as they're not here, we might as well call it a day. C'mon, Terry.'

'Your loss, boys,' Evie said, shrugging her shoulders. 'Sonny's a brilliant musician.'

'Evie . . . ' Vincent whispered.

'Not to mention a bit mischievous,' she went on. 'Who knows what he's got up his sleeve to make tonight special?'

'*Evie*.' Vincent nudged her and pointed to the stage. She hadn't realised that the outdated records had stopped and a spotlight was shining directly on Sonny. If Vincent had looked like a rabbit caught in headlights a moment ago, there was no way to describe the expression of terror on Sonny's face as he gazed out into the crowd of judgemental teens.

'*That*'s your brilliant musician?' Terry snorted, while Harrison clicked his camera furiously, capturing every single one of Sonny's most unflattering angles.

Sonny had changed into the garment Vincent had thrust at him before he and Evie had left him by the stage, but in their haste to leave the apartment, Vincent had managed to pick up Evie's purple dress instead of one of his own purple T-shirts. Sonny might have got away with it if he'd just put it on over his jeans, but in his drunken state, he'd thought far too literally. It was a dress, therefore he wore it like a dress. He had removed his jeans as well as his own vomit-stained T-shirt, and was now standing on the stage wearing a dress that stopped midway down his thighs, showing off orange boxers, chunky black leather boots and bare hairy legs. Evie and Vincent were more than open-minded enough to accept Sonny wholeheartedly had he naturally felt more comfortable in women's clothing, but seeing as this was unintentional (thanks to the amount of

126

alcohol coursing through his bloodstream), they both felt embarrassment flush into their cheeks.

'That's my dress . . . ' Evie whispered out of the side of her mouth.

'I thought it was one of my T-shirts. I am *so* sorry.'

'It's not me you need to apologise to.'

Sonny was standing at the microphone with his eyes closed, his breathing echoing around the hall through the speakers.

'Play something, then!' shouted a burly kid who barely fitted into his borrowed tuxedo.

Sonny's eyes snapped open and searched the crowd for the boy. He strummed one chord, hard. 'Happy?' he snapped.

'Oh no,' Vincent groaned, his voice cracking.

Teenagers were awkwardly giggling left, right and centre, and Sonny held his hand up to shield his eyes from the spotlight to better see his heckler.

'You think this is easy?' He brought the mic close to his face, so his words were loud and harsh. 'Coming up here. Putting yourself out there.'

'You're putting more of yourself out there than we wanna see!' shouted the boy. 'Where's the dress from anyway, Sluts R Us?'

'Hey now!' Evie said, a little louder than she'd bargained for, and a few teenagers at the back of the crowd turned to look at her. Some of the girls even pointed, whispered and laughed, and Evie thanked whoever was watching over her that her high school days were long gone.

127

'It *is* quite low cut . . . ' muttered Vincent, and Evie bashed him on the arm.

'Now I know why you liked it so much!'

'If I wanna wear a dress, I'm gonna wear a dress!' Sonny swayed away from the mic and belched quietly. 'Do you know how many beers I had to drink to pluck up enough courage to even get on this stage?'

'Beers?' Mr Glass appeared beside Evie and Vincent. His brow had started to drip with sweat. 'We need to get him down from there!' Vincent went to stop the headmaster as he rushed to the side of the stage, but Evie put a hand on his arm and pulled him back.

'It's best we don't get involved. Let him get Sonny and we'll just go home.'

'Yeah, best get back to the castle, Princess,' Harrison quipped, still taking pictures.

'Maybe Prince Charming here will let you climb his tower.' Terry leaned back to give a dirty laugh, but it was hardly out of his mouth when Vincent's fist connected with his nose and the noise that erupted out of Terry's mouth wasn't any kind of laugh.

'Vincent!' Evie squeaked. Vincent pulled his hand back, which was covered in blood from Terry's undoubtedly broken nose and Harrison snapped the winning shot. Vincent didn't know what had come over him but as he looked at Terry's bloody nose, rightly or wrongly, he certainly wasn't sorry for what he'd done. All the kids in the hall had flocked towards them at the back when they heard

Terry's yelp and had started to chant, 'FIGHT! FIGHT! FIGHT!'

Understandably, the incident seemed to have riled Terry. He looked ready to swing for Vincent, but the blood pouring from his nostrils and his watering eyes were preventing him from acting on his urges. Evie saw their chance.

'Go, go, go!' She grabbed Vincent's hand, then turned and yelled, 'SONNY!'

Sonny didn't need telling twice. He jumped down from the stage, ran to the heckling boy and hugged him, then skipped after Evie and Vincent.

'Evie . . . ' Vincent began.

'Don't,' she snapped.

The three of them were walking back to her flat, even though Evie had wanted Vincent to take Sonny home immediately and stay there with him. She hadn't looked at either of them since they'd left the school.

Sonny was still wearing her dress. He'd left his jeans and his puke-stained T-shirt behind.

'I'm not going to apologise,' Vincent said.

'Then we're not going to talk for a very long time.'

'You heard what he said, Evie! You shouldn't have to put up with that!' Vincent was still enraged by the way Terry had spoken to Evie. He couldn't believe she'd not mentioned how vile her colleagues at the paper really were. He'd had no idea what she had to put up with every day.

'You're right, I shouldn't have to, but do you know why I do?'

Vincent threw his hands in the air. 'I honestly have no idea.'

'To keep my job!' Evie spun round so quickly that Vincent bumped into her. Sonny in turn bumped into the back of Vincent, slipped and landed on the pavement. 'I put up with their vile remarks and my weird, creepy boss, I bite my tongue and get on with my job, because guess what, Vincent? I love you and I want to stay with you, and if I lose this job, I have no chance of getting a better one, and that is the *only* way we can stay together. And now you've ruined it. You've completely ballsed it up.'

It was only at that moment that Vincent realised the gravity of what he'd done. Evie was certain to be fired from *The Teller* after Terry and Harrison printed their article, along with the picture that would make Vincent look like a hooligan. Especially as there would clearly be no mention of how vile Terry had been.

'Oh shit,' he muttered, the blood draining from his face.

'Language!' Sonny scolded.

'Shut up, Sonny,' Evie said.

'Hey, I thought you were nice,' Sonny mumbled, picking flowers from someone's front garden next to where he sat.

'Evie, I didn't think,' Vincent said, ignoring Sonny.

'No, I know you didn't.'

130

'We *can* fix this.' He didn't know how, but if she gave him a chance, he'd do all he could to try.

'I don't see how, Vincent. I don't have any friends at *The Teller*. There's no one there to fight my corner.' Evie felt helpless and drained. Vincent had sped up her life, but now the joyride had crashed she needed it to halt, just for an evening, so she could properly survey the damage. *How could I have been so careless?* she thought. She'd been so happy that she'd forgotten what was at stake. She looked at Vincent, and for a moment she saw him through her mother's eyes, and all she saw was trouble. 'I just think it'd be best if you took Sonny home.'

'I would quite like to go home now.' Sonny hugged Vincent's right leg, but Vincent was too concerned about Evie's cold, glistening eyes to think about anything else. He realised that her twinkle had dulled, and his heart cracked knowing that it was his doing.

'Evie . . . I'm *so* sorry.'

'So am I.' Her voice wobbled.

'We will figure this out,' Vincent said, determinedly.

He wanted to take her hands, hold her close, but she was radiating a vibe that told him to stay where he was. The lump in Evie's throat was too big to talk through so she just nodded and let the tears spill over. When Vincent saw them glistening on her cheek, though, he couldn't help himself. He took a step towards her with one hand out-stretched, but she moved backwards, away from him, and his heart split perfectly in two.

July

A Visitor

There are times in life when two people who want to talk do not do so for no other reason than each of them fearing that the other person does not want to talk to them. Evie and Vincent found themselves in that situation for eight days after the school prom. Evie had taken a night to herself to figure out exactly what to do should she be fired, which come Monday morning she was, unequivocally and without ceremony. The only conclusion she had come to was that she had to prevent her mother from finding out. Besides that, she needed to find a new job that was better than the one she'd had at *The Teller*.

While Evie busied herself writing more letters to publishers who might be looking for illustrators and animation studios that might be in need of artists, Vincent was sitting by the phone, willing it to ring – to be specific, willing Evie to call. The waiting drove him (and Sonny) mad, so eventually he decided it was time to take matters into his own hands.

Evie had returned home after trying her luck at another newspaper. She had attempted to speak to the editor so she could show him her work in person, but she'd been turned away and almost thrown from the building when she'd refused to leave until someone, anyone, looked at her drawings. It was then that a woman from the offices upstairs came to explain that Terry Lark had called every newspaper in town to tell them what had happened at the school prom. Although he didn't have the power to have her blacklisted, who would want to work with someone who'd encouraged her drunk musician friend to play in front of schoolchildren and then let her aggressive boyfriend break her colleague's nose?

Evie plonked herself down in the green armchair, still wearing her coat and shoes, and put her head in her hands as she felt the familiar prickle of tears. She didn't know how long she'd been sitting there before she heard the flutter of wings. She looked up. Through the window she could see a dove perched on the railings of her balcony. It was impeccably white, bar one little streak of black along its right wing. Leaving her troubles in the armchair, she opened the balcony doors very slowly, careful not to scare the bird, hoping she could get just a little closer and while away some time watching it. The dove didn't flap or fuss when she clunked the windows open. In fact, it came closer, shuffling along the railings and bobbing its head towards her.

'Hello there, little one,' Evie sniffed.

The bird cooed and stretched its neck in her direction. Evie held out a hand, and the bird happily let her stroke it with a finger. It closed its eyes and cooed a little more, like a cat would purr when tickled behind its ears. 'You're a funny one, aren't you?' Evie's cheeks ached as they took on a shape they hadn't experienced in over a week, and she remembered that was what smiling felt like. The bird turned away from her, balancing expertly on the metal railings with its scratchy feet, and stretched out its right wing. Evie thought for a moment that it was just normal bird behaviour; they flapped and stretched their wings all the time when she saw them in the park and on the street. It was only when it dropped its wing, turned its head to her, squawked and extended the wing again that she realised it was trying to show her something. She got down on her knees and finally saw what it wanted her to see. What she had thought was a black streak, natural bird colouring, was in fact ink. Ink forming words written in Vincent's hand:

Eight days of your silence has convinced me that your voice is the most beautiful sound I will ever hear.

Evie read the sentence, and then she read it a dozen times more, until the bird's wing started to droop a little, tired from holding it out for so long.

'Thank you, Little One.'

The bird tucked its wing away and turned to face her, and she could have sworn there was a smile upon its beak as it puffed its chest out proudly.

'May I ask a favour?' Evie was already writing a reply in her mind. She wondered if the bird might let her use its other wing and its powers of flight to deliver the message on her behalf. The little white dove turned around once more and produced its left wing happily, displaying its blank canvas. She scrambled back inside the flat to get a pen from her pencil case, excitement bubbling in her stomach as she wrote:

Eight days of my silence has meant eight days of Sonny's singing. No wonder you miss me.

She thought it would probably be best to keep things light-hearted.

Her mind wandered back to the last time they had spoken, when she'd practically shouted at Vincent in the street. A small flush of embarrassment rushed through her body, but then she remembered that Vincent *had* lost her her job that night, and felt the justification of her actions restored. That didn't prevent her from loving him, though, nor did it mean she hadn't missed him. Waking up thinking he might be there and remembering why he wasn't had been a stab in the chest every morning. All she'd wanted to do was call him and ask him to come home, but she'd feared he might have been angry at her for the way she'd spoken to him, even if he had deserved it.

'Thank you,' she said to the bird once she'd finished writing.

It bobbed its head once, like a nod, then flew away. To Vincent, she hoped, though she wasn't exactly an expert on the reliability of doves delivering private messages. She was still kneeling on the balcony with the pen in her hand, a few blobs of ink on the tips of her fingers, when a furiously fast knock on the door interrupted her thoughts.

'Evie, if you're in there, please open the door, and do it quickly. We don't have much time.'

Evie knew that voice, but . . . surely not? It was muffled through the door, so she might have been mistaken.

'Evie, *please.*'

This time there was no mistaking.

'Jim?'

Evie ran to the door and opened it to find Jim Summer standing on her doormat. Even though she had always thought of him like a brother, it didn't stop her from going slightly weak at the knees at the sight of his handsome face. He looked like a sculpture of a man, too perfect to really exist, but then he moved and spoke and you realised why men and women alike drooled over him daily.

Although Jim had turned up unexpectedly and urgently, he couldn't help but smile when he saw Evie, and pulled her in for a tight hug.

'Can I come in?' He was jittery and spoke quickly.

'What's got you spooked?' Evie laughed, but she was still a little worried. She'd never seen Jim so flustered.

'Your mother's on her way. She's just seen this.' Jim produced a newspaper from his pocket. Not just any paper. *The Teller*. He flipped it open to page 5, and there it was.

Evie had avoided reading the newspaper since the prom. She'd thought maybe Terry wouldn't be so cruel as to submit the story, let alone allow it to be published, but if he had, she couldn't face seeing it in print. Now that she had, it was worse than she could ever have imagined. Vincent's angry face and clenched fist, and Terry's bloody nose. Complete with Evie in the background, wide-eyed and reaching out for Vincent. She found the armchair with the back of her knees and sank down into it.

'Eleanor's furious, Evie. She's coming to take you home.'

'This *is* my home.' Evie looked up at Jim pleadingly.

Jim knelt down beside her and put a hand on her arm. 'Eleanor won't see it that way, and you know it. To you, this was the start of a new life. To her ... it was a silly escapade that had an expiry date, and that was only if it hadn't ended in tears before then.'

Evie was stung. She felt herself shrink inwards, seeing herself as her family saw her: a stupid little girl with stupid little dreams, and they were laughing at her pointless attempts to reach them. Like a toddler stretching for the cookie jar on the highest shelf.

'You know I don't think that, Evie,' Jim said, more gently this time. 'Don't look at me like that. But with a mother like Eleanor, how long was this really going to last?'

The weight of reality crushed Evie's heart. Up until now she'd been trying her best to be optimistic, to think positively about the life she had in this flat with Vincent. Now she realised that it had all been make-believe, and the hope she had felt just moments ago was gone. She and Vincent had spent months pretending that life could continue the way they'd come to love it, but the last few days had proved that it wasn't that simple. And Jim was right: Eleanor Snow was never going to let it work.

'How long do we have before she gets here?' Evie's heart had started to pump harder, her breath short.

'Maybe half an hour? I overheard her talking to my mother. I came straight away to warn you that she was on her way.'

'Your mother? Why was she talking to your mother?' Panic and anger formed a tight knot in Evie's stomach.

'Eleanor's insisting that I ... that we ...' Jim's voice trailed off.

Tears of rage spilled over on to Evie's cheeks.

'She wants me to propose. To you,' Jim said finally. 'And she wants you to say yes. No matter how ... we feel.' He couldn't look at her.

Marrying Evie was all he had ever wanted. But not like this. He'd fallen in love with probably the only girl he knew didn't want to be his girlfriend, let alone his wife, but then again, perhaps that was why *he'd* fallen for *her*. Evie *knew* Jim. From the day they'd met as children, Evie made sure there were no pretences, no silly family traditions masking who they really were and no secrets. She'd always hated secrets. If she felt like he was hiding something, she coaxed it out of him one way or another and then didn't speak to him for days simply because he'd kept something from her and shut her out. She had trained him to be honest but Jim *knew* Evie, too. He knew she wanted more from a relationship than swooning each time she saw him. She wanted conversations. Adventures. *Love*. Jim knew this and it was exactly the reason he didn't want to marry the woman he'd already given his heart to.

'I can't . . . ' Evie whispered.

'I know,' Jim said. 'That's why I'm here. I didn't want you to have to face her alone.' He took her hand and squeezed it.

'Thank you.' She squeezed back.

Jim hesitated for a second before saying, 'So, I have to ask . . . '

Of course he does, Evie thought.

'He's called Vincent,' Evie answered, even before he was able to voice the inevitable question. Jim looked at her, dumbfounded. 'He's a violinist. He busks on the

140

underground to pay the rent on a flat he shares with a wannabe rock star who can't actually sing.'

'Well,' Jim said with a small, sad smile, 'you couldn't have picked someone better to piss off your mother.'

Evie laughed through her tears and Jim's smile grew wider because he'd made her laugh despite everything. Jim didn't need to ask whether she truly loved Vincent or not. He could see it clearly and after all, the only secret Evie had ever let Jim keep all these years was what she'd known all along: that he loved her. They never spoke about *that*. The least he could do was repay that kind gesture.

'You need to be with him, this Vincent,' he said simply. 'And I will do all I can to make that happen.'

Evie shook her head. This man had the kindest heart she'd ever known. Part of her wanted to love him as she knew he loved her, but the simple fact remained that he wasn't Vincent, her full-of-flaws and terribly unsuitable Vincent.

Just the thought of him and how far away he was made her body ache.

'And here's another thing. I've also essentially been barred from working for any newspaper in town, because who wants to work with the crazy girl with the angry friends who punch people in the face?' Evie laughed at how ridiculous it sounded, but the look of pity that Jim gave her made a sob escape her throat.

There was the clipped clicking of heels along the corridor

outside, and Evie's hand instinctively tightened around Jim's fingers. Her stomach somersaulted as knuckles rapped on the door with three precise, evenly spaced knocks, each one making her flinch.

'I'll answer it,' Jim said.

'No. Let me.' Evie stood up, wiped the tears from her face and straightened her dress. The few steps to the door felt like miles, and when she opened it and saw her mother's cold eyes fixed into a hard stare that cut through Evie like she wasn't even there, she wished she had let Jim do the honours after all.

'Pack your bags. You're coming home.' To Eleanor, it really was that simple, but to Evie, those words meant the end of everything she'd always wanted.

'This *is* my home,' she said, feeling like a child stamping her feet. She wondered how many other twenty-seven-year-olds had to fight their mothers this hard for their freedom.

'Don't be ridiculous. I said you had a year to climb to a higher position in your . . . ' she turned up her nose, '*chosen field*, and not only have you failed to get a better job, but you've lost the one you had!'

'Mother, please—'

'It serves you right for consorting with ruffians such as *this* one.' Eleanor held up her own copy of *The Teller*. She'd even taken the liberty of circling Evie's face and crossing out Vincent's in hard lines with a red pen.

'Mrs Snow, with all due respect . . . ' Jim began, coming

to the door, but when Eleanor pierced him with her stare, he couldn't help but stop mid-sentence.

'What are *you* doing here?' she asked.

'Evie and I are old friends, Mrs Snow. You know that. I . . . came to see how she was.'

'How *convenient* that you happened to turn up mere moments, it seems, before I did.' She eyed Jim's attire, coat and shoes still on, much like Evie. Jim straightened, and in his mind Evie went from being his friend to his client and he adopted the tone he used in court.

'Mrs Snow, with all due respect, last November you said Evie could have a year to make this life she's created work. It's not even August yet.'

'Precisely. It is nowhere near the end of the year and look what a mess she's already made!' Eleanor declared.

Evie hated that they were talking about her like she wasn't stood beside them but she could barely speak. She wished her tears weren't directly triggered by her anger. It made her look hysterical, and she was less likely to make sense to whoever she was arguing against. When that person was her mother, she stood very little chance as it was.

'Surely you're not going back on your word before Evie's had a proper chance to prove herself?'

'She's proved that she's more of an embarrassment than I first thought.'

Jim was stunned into silence. How could a mother be so cruel towards her own flesh and blood?

'You can't mean that,' Evie muttered.

Evie's relationship with her mother had never been warm. She and her brother had been raised by nannies and hadn't seen all that much of their parents during their childhood, but Evie had always believed that, at the heart of it all, her mother loved her and wanted what was best for her. She didn't believe that any longer. How could she, when her mother was trying to take away from her the only thing she'd ever asked for or had truly wanted?

Eleanor fixed Evie with her unflinching stare, her lips barely a line, but there was something there. A flicker of uncertainty. A moment of doubt. A hint of panic that maybe she was wrong. Evie saw it, took a breath and seized her moment.

'I'm not coming with you, Mother. I can't be married off to someone I don't love, nor can you do that to Jim. I don't care what family traditions say, nor do I care that the man I want to be with isn't what you'd call a smart match.'

'You can't mean this . . . this . . . ' Eleanor fluttered the newspaper around, hoping to catch her words with it.

'What? This what?' Evie said, her anger flowing faster than her tears. 'He's a *person*. He's a good man and he makes me happy, and as my mother, that is all you should want for me!'

'Do *not* tell me what I should and shouldn't want for you. I know exactly what is best for both you and Eddie, and—'

'Not this time, Mother,' Evie interrupted. 'This time

you're wrong, and I'm not coming home until I've seen this through.'

If Evie didn't know Eleanor, the look on her face would have been enough to scare her – but she did know Eleanor and, knowing what was behind that look, despite her outward defiance, she was terrified. Looking at the expression on her mother's face, she knew she was going to have to compromise somewhere, otherwise Eleanor would drag her out of the apartment by her hair, and even though Evie knew that was entirely wrong, she was still a daughter crying out for her mother's approval, and, more importantly, for her mother's love.

'All I'm asking is that you give me until November to try to make this work. Like you promised. If I get a new job, a better one than the one I had at *The Teller*, a job that pays for this flat and for the life I want to live, then that's the end of you controlling me. I'll marry a man of my choosing and you won't even have to come to the wedding.'

Eleanor was silent, taking in Evie's words. Finally she sniffed her agreement and Evie's heart lurched downwards. *You didn't even fight for me*, she thought sadly.

'If you insist on playing this foolish game, then go ahead,' Eleanor said, her face set in stone. 'But I want to make it known that you won't hear from me or your father again should you continue in this manner after November. Neither will you be entitled to any inheritance.'

'Mrs Snow—' Jim interjected, but Evie stopped him.

'Fine,' she said, a tear escaping.

145

'And you'll never see Eddie again.'

'No,' Evie whispered. 'You can't—'

'You can't honestly think I'll have you anywhere near him, influencing him with your silly ideas?' Eleanor looked incredulous. 'No. If you make this life work, as far as Eddie's concerned, he doesn't have a sister.'

Evie was stunned, and Eleanor took her silence as agreement.

'So what happens when you fail?'

'*When?* Mrs Snow, I don't think you're being entirely fair—' Jim started, but Evie held out her hand, stopping him again.

'*If* it doesn't work out, then . . . I will come home without a fuss,' she said quietly. 'I'll stay in the house, locked away so I can't cause you any further embarrassment, and . . . and I will marry whomever you wish. My only request is that you don't force Jim into anything. You're *my* mother. Jim can make his own choices. Or rather . . . *his* mother can.'

'Evie . . . ' Jim whispered.

'Done.' Eleanor sniffed her approval once more, then turned on her heel and left.

As soon as the door to the flat slammed shut, Evie fell sobbing into Jim's arms. As he held her, the sound of wings returned and made her heart lift out of her shoes just an inch. She ran to the balcony, where Little One proudly displayed the new message on his right wing.

Would it be terrible of me if I asked to see you? I miss you. And your flat. It doesn't smell like Sonny.

146

'Evie? Is that a dove?' said Jim, following her out on to the balcony, where Evie was kneeling on the floor, gently holding the bird's wing between her fingers.

'He's a messenger,' she said, absent-mindedly, her attention focused on the words in front of her and how she would reply.

'Evie, look at me for a moment.'

Reluctantly she turned her tear-stained face to Jim's, which was etched with lines of concern. She hadn't noticed before, but although Jim was still handsome, he was ageing. She'd always thought of him as that eight-year-old boy she'd met almost twenty years ago, but now she saw the lines that were starting to appear around his eyes and mouth. He was getting older. As was she.

'How are you going to find another job?' Jim looked awkward, like he wanted to go to her and hold her, maybe more for his sake than hers, judging by the amount of worry filling the wrinkles on his face.

'I have no idea. I don't even think I will.' Her eyes glazed over and she felt everything going numb again.

'Then why did you fight so hard to make your mother let you have three more months?'

'Because it means three more months with Vincent. Saying goodbye to him today was just too soon.'

Evie turned back to the dove, with no more tears to cry, and wrote:

Come to me now.

Jim left Evie after giving her a long and lingering hug good-bye. Once on the street, he got in his car and angled the rear view mirror so that he could see the balcony of her flat but she wasn't there. Not long afterwards, Vincent arrived, dressed more smartly than Evie had ever seen him. He'd even ironed his black jeans and had run his fingers through his hair in an attempt to make it look a little less 'mad scientist'. Evie had laid a cold wet flannel over her face to try to make it less red and blotchy but Vincent wouldn't have noticed anyway. As soon as she opened the door to him, he held up a crisp cream envelope that had clearly been ripped open at the top. The return address in the corner told her it was from a music school. A good one.

'Someone's replied?' Evie snatched it from him and started to take out the letter.

'A couple of months ago,' he said excitedly. Evie looked puzzled. 'I was invited to audition. I didn't want to tell you because I didn't want to disappoint you if it didn't go well, and I knew it would make me nervous too. But then this arrived yesterday. Read it!'

Evie grinned and hurriedly pulled out the letter, scanning it for one word and one word only: *scholarship*. When she saw it, she burst into tears and threw her arms around Vincent.

'Congratulations,' she whispered.

'I've missed you.' Vincent brushed her cheek with the back of his fingers and smiled as if all was right with his world again now that they were together. Evie's stomach twisted. She couldn't find the words to tell him what had happened, so instead she kissed him like it might change their future.

Life resumed. To Vincent, those eight days had merely been a pause in their indefinitely long life together. Evie had decided against telling him that things had already come to an end, and that these last three months were merely a prolonged goodbye. Knowing it made her miserable but what good would come from making him miserable too? Without her realising it, Evie had become more distant as she prepared for their inevitable goodbye, which confused Vincent no end and was the cause of many an argument. She pushed him away when she used to invite him in and she held back when she used to gush. Vincent went back home to his own flat every few nights, when they argued, and the next morning, Little One would turn up on Evie's balcony so that Vincent could find out from a respectful distance how she felt, and whether she wanted to see him. The answer to which was always *of course*.

The dove's wings had become almost entirely black, so he'd started carrying their messages on his back and his chest, but he welcomed them with open wings. No one wanted their love to work more than he did. Their messages of love and kindness gave him strength and a purpose. When he flew past strangers, they felt an inexplicable sense of happiness. He'd become a beacon of hope, and Evie and Vincent's messages were the flames, but as much as Little One would read their notes, he could never know the thoughts in Evie's head nor could he see her mother's serious face as Evie did every time she closed her eyes. Evie knew her time with Vincent was limited but Little One, poor Little One, was as much in the dark as Vincent and the winged messenger couldn't know that he was rooting for a love that had been doomed from the very beginning.

6

august

Evie found herself looking up at the music school building on the campus of the university her son had attended.
The building was old and majestic, and its tall clock
tower stood ominous against the grey sky. The rain was
icy and harsh and prickled her face if she looked directly
upwards, so she pulled her coat collar up around her neck
and skittered up the steps to the school.

She wasn't sure how she was supposed to behave in this
world. She assumed, after having already crossed through
one wall, that walking through doors and walls came
with the package, but as a living, breathing woman, she
had always knocked before she entered a room, and she
didn't feel like that should change now that she was dead.
Lieffe had said she wouldn't be able to make an impact

on the world around her so opening a door wouldn't be possible, so she waited for a few minutes in the downpour until finally, a man with a trilby, a beautiful grey suede waistcoat and a briefcase exited the building. While he fiddled with his umbrella, Evie slipped through the open door, and the man put the chill he'd felt down to the dreadful weather, though he couldn't explain the whiff of treacle he'd caught as the door closed behind him.

Inside was a reception desk, behind which a striking red-headed woman sat fiddling with the cord on the telephone as she talked in low tones. Evie had visited the university only once before, when she'd come to watch her son's recital. She'd wept so loudly that the mother of another student sitting in front of her had turned to offer her a tissue. Evie couldn't help it. August had played so beautifully. He had taken to music almost as soon as he was born into existence, and she had made sure to nurture it. She swore her children would have the chances she'd never had, to do exactly what they wanted to do. Whether they succeeded or not, she was there beside them every step of the way.

When August had said he wanted to study music, Evie did everything in her power to help. She bought him his first violin, paid for his piano lessons and asked to hear him play almost every evening. August studied night and day all through school until he got a scholarship to the second best university in town (the best didn't have a basketball team, and August's passion for basketball at the time of applying was insatiable). He'd gone on to win composing competitions with his classical piano pieces, one of which brought the opportunity for one of his songs to be played on the credits of an independent movie, and his career in composing film scores was born. Now, at the age of fifty-two, his days of studying far behind him, the university welcomed him whenever he wanted to play the pianos in the music rooms he used to practise in, but August would usually only visit when he needed the space to think.

Evie walked down every corridor on every floor, peeping in through the windows, hoping to see her son's greying auburn hair and his fingers darting up and down the keys. When she finally found him, his hands were still, and his head rested against the ivories. He was snoring gently. The shadows under his eyes told her this was probably the most sleep he'd had in days.

Since their second daughter had left home, something between August and his wife, Daphne, had been lost in amongst the emptiness and stillness of the house. A flame that had once burned with the heat of a thousand suns was now merely an ember, and the memory of what they had once felt for each other taunted them both. August still loved Daphne more than anything. The only women that competed for his affections were his two daughters, Gwen and Winifred, and Evie herself when she'd been alive, but August knew his and Daphne's love wasn't the same as it had once been, that something had been lost and he had no idea how to find it again. It was like something was blocking his heart. Like part of a machine had come unhinged and all the things he usually used to communicate perfectly had slipped out of the assembly line and got lost. Somewhere inside him, all the wonderful things he thought were piling up, left to fester in their own beauty. August and Daphne didn't argue. They barely even spoke, because August had forgotten how, and their maddening silence had resulted in trips to the practice rooms at his old university where he would sit for hours at a time, usually until he fell asleep on the keys.

Evie thought maybe she'd need to walk through this door in particular, just one, in order to speak to her son. It could take hours for someone to come this way and open the door so she could walk through. She stood back and surveyed the door carefully. She guessed it was just a case of aiming and walking. She sucked in a breath and stepped forward, and although it was only a short distance, she still shut her eyes tightly just as her head should have hit the door, but instead, her whole body went cold and rigid, almost like she had become the door itself for a moment, and then she felt herself softening into her own flesh again and she was on the other side. August's shoulders shifted as the temperature of the room dropped slightly and the skin of his forearms prickled. Evie's motherly instinct took over and she hushed him as she knelt down by his side. She wanted to stroke his hair, put her arms around him, but if her entering the room had caused his sleep to be disrupted, she didn't want to find out what effect touching him could have.

'August?'

She wasn't sure what he could hear or whether he would respond. She just had to believe what Lieffe had told her. She had to believe this would work.

'August. My darling boy. In all that time we had together, in all those years bringing you up and watching you grow into a fine man, I was never entirely honest with you.'

Evie's ghostly heart raced. Saying these words in life would have killed her, and yet now that she was beyond the grave, she *had* to divulge the secrets she'd kept so securely or else her soul would never rest. She looked for some sign that August was listening, but there was nothing she could do except keep talking.

'When I was younger, before you were born, I used to send love notes to ... someone. I don't suppose it matters who. We sent our messages on the wings of a bird I called Little One. When I first saw him, the bird, he was as white as snow and so beautiful but there was so much of our love for him to carry that his feathers soon turned as black as ink. I've heard rumours that he's still out there somewhere, and that to this very day he still sits on the balcony of my old home, waiting for our story to be finished. If the rumours are true, then Little One hasn't rested all these years. He's just been ready and waiting.'

Evie's eyes glistened with guilt. She'd been so concerned about telling Vincent that things had to end, and how he would react, that she'd forgotten to tell Little One. He'd been so sure of their love that he'd waited for Evie and Vincent to return and while he'd waited, he'd continued to spread the love he carried on his wings to anyone he could. He'd grown tired and sometimes felt like giving up but he'd continued on all the same, always hopeful. Evie had always wanted to find him, but she had been a coward and just couldn't bring herself to go looking for her past. She knew that asking August to do it for her would mean revealing the stories she'd spent most of her life hiding, but she also knew it was time to concede. It was time to set Little One free.

'August, you must find him. Let your heart call to him, and when he comes to you, wash his wings. Relieve him of the duties he carried out so diligently when I was still alive. And tell him from me ...' she whispered, 'thank you.'

A tear spilled over and splattered on to the back of August's right hand. It shimmered for a moment, like a pearl, and then sank into his skin, and he stirred. Evie held her breath and watched his eyes open just a crack. There was a moment of recognition before she felt herself being pulled by her heart backwards, and she didn't have the strength to fight it. She closed her eyes and let her limbs go heavy as a force gently picked her up and pulled her from the room. There was a sucking noise as she felt the atmosphere turn as thick as treacle, and then she thudded abruptly on to her backside on solid ground.

Evie opened her glazed eyes and saw the vague shape of Lieffe's concerned face peering down at her.

'How did it go?'

She blinked a few times until it no longer felt like she was looking through frosted glass. 'OK, I think. I'm not really sure.'

'You found him, then?' Lieffe took one of her arms and helped her into the desk chair.

'Yes, I found him. He was asleep, so I told him what I needed to tell him. Just as he was waking up, I felt myself being dragged back here, but there was a moment . . . a split second where he opened his eyes and it was almost like he could see me.' Evie sniffed, not wanting to get emotional again.

'Oh Evie. You've done well. Do you want to rest? Visit the others tomorrow? Time is at our disposal here, after all.' Lieffe started to walk to the door, looking exhausted himself having spent his time wringing his hands with worry while Evie was on the other side of the wall.

'No, I want to keep going, but—'

'What is it?' Lieffe spun to face her, his worries clear

in his eyes: *Was she having second thoughts? Was this all too much for her? Too painful to relive?*

'What are the chances of a cup of tea first?'

When August awoke, he had the feeling he wasn't alone. He thought he'd seen a familiar face watching over him, but when he rubbed the sleep from the corners of his eyes, there was no one to be seen, and he put it down to the strange dream he'd been having. He massaged his temples as he remembered a bird flying across his mind's eye. It was black, but as it flew, words written in ink fell from its feathers and tumbled down, splashing to the floor, creating puddles, revealing the bird's natural white colour beneath. He could still hear a soft but haunting voice repeating, *Let your heart call to him ... Wash his wings ... Tell him ... thank you.*

August shook his head to shake the thoughts away, but they clung to him as he trudged home later that night. They niggled in his head when he saw the look of longing on his wife's face turn to disappointment when he didn't kiss her goodnight, not because he didn't want to, but because he'd forgotten how. And when he climbed into bed beside Daphne, those thoughts continued to whir and clunk like cogs in his brain. He got out of bed only moments after he'd gotten in. Daphne sat up.

'Where are you going, August?'

'Just downstairs. My brain won't shut off.'

'Will you ever tell me what's going on in there?' Even though the moon was shining through the window, August couldn't see her because the sadness in her voice was sucking all of the light out of the room.

'I'm just stuck on a melody for this new score,' he lied, feeling the bird's wings flap behind his eyes. 'Get some sleep. I'll be back soon.' And August left before her sadness could reach him.

There weren't any silver stars stippling the still black sky, but there weren't any rain clouds either, and August was thankful for that. He didn't like rain, although the strange tree at the bottom of the garden drank it up like there was no tomorrow and instead of bearing new fruit, seasonally, it always ripened after a thunderstorm. He and his sister discovered as children how awful the fruit tasted, so they never picked it, just left it to fall and rot in the grass at its roots.

August stood at the back door of the Snows' house, a mug of decaf coffee in his hand, looking out at the tree garden. They'd moved into the Snow house shortly after Evie had passed away, in order to take care of August's Uncle Eddie and his partner, now in their late seventies and in need of an extra helping hand. It was the house Evie had grown up in, and August had thought it could be a new start for him and Daphne. But although things hadn't become any worse, they hadn't become better either. August thought maybe they could find what they had lost in this house but all they found were more of his awkward silences and more of her longing sadness. August thought about how much he loved his wife, and wondered how he'd lost the way to tell her. How had he derailed that train, and how would he ever get it back on its tracks?

He walked out on to the patio and sat down on one of the metal garden chairs, only remembering how heavily it had been raining earlier that day when the water started to soak into his flannel pyjama bottoms. He stood up abruptly, catching his mug on the edge of the garden table. The mug splintered from its handle, plummeting to the ground, and hot coffee erupted over his bare feet. He yelped and did a little dance until the coffee cooled and when it had, he sank back down into the seat, not caring about the water any more, and cried. August hung his head and cried out the feelings that remained in his heart until his tears had mixed with the puddles of rain on the table. His heart cracked cleanly in two and he could have sworn it made a sound that vibrated through the air, rustling the leaves on the strange tree at the end of the garden.

'August?'

Daphne's voice was timid and shy, very unlike the voice he'd heard when they'd first met at university. She'd been singing so loudly in the practice room next to August that he'd gone in to tell her to keep the noise down, but when he'd flung the door open only to see this tiny mouse of a girl singing louder and better than most stage stars he'd heard, he'd fallen for her on the spot. He'd ended up inviting her to sing with him while he accompanied her on the piano, something they continued to do every lunch break they could spare for the next five weeks, before he eventually asked her out to dinner. She had always been so tiny and *so* loud.

'You're my little oxymoron,' August would say to her.

'And you're just my moron,' she'd respond playfully, and reach up on tiptoe to kiss him on the cheek.

Over the years, however, her voice had quietened. She barely sang any more, and when she spoke, she sounded drained and meek, her boisterousness dried out.

'Oh August.' She rushed to him and enveloped him in her arms as best she could but her hands didn't meet around his shoulders. 'What happened?' she asked, glancing at the broken pieces of ceramic lying on the paving, but he just shook his head.

'What happened to us?' he asked, looking at her through tear-shrunken eyes.

She gazed back at him completely flabbergasted. 'I thought you'd never ask. I thought you didn't want to talk about it. I thought you . . . ' She trailed off.

'Thought I what?' He hesitated, hoping she wasn't going to say what he thought she was going to say.

She took a deep shaky breath. 'I thought you didn't care.'

August collapsed into her arms once more and sobbed

and Daphne held on to him tightly, almost as though she was trying to stop him from slipping away. After a while, she shook him gently.

'August,' she whispered. 'August, look.'

Neither of them had heard the thump of wings or the scratching of feet on the table because their hearts were beating so loudly in their ears but when Daphne had opened her eyes she saw him, and she wanted her husband to see him too: a blackbird sitting boldly close to August on the garden table. August pushed himself quickly out of his seat and took a few steps towards the house, almost knocking over a plant pot, but the bird cooed softly as if to reassure him.

'Ssshh! You'll wake your uncle!' Daphne hushed.

'It can't be . . . ' August whispered, tears still spilling down his cheeks. Daphne instinctively stretched out her fingers to the bird, but August took her hand and pulled her towards him.

'What is it? What's wrong?' she asked.

'That bird. I dreamed about that bird today when I fell asleep in the practice room.'

He caught himself too late and looked sheepish but Daphne already knew. She knew he returned to the old university practice rooms when he felt stressed because the red-headed receptionist often called the telephone number they had on file, which was for his mother's house that they now lived in, just to let Daphne know he'd fallen asleep in one of the practice rooms again and would probably be home late. It wasn't quite the big secret he thought it was.

'*This* bird?' Daphne asked, sceptically.

'Yes.'

'This *exact* bird?'

August nodded, and the look on his face had Daphne convinced. 'He must be a very special blackbird, then.'

'I don't think it is a blackbird.' August recalled his dream, letting the memories run free and they rushed around his mind and through his veins, happy that he'd stopped resisting.

Cautiously he took a step towards the bird, and Little One took a step towards him. They continued in single steps until Little One was sitting on the edge of the table at the height of August's belly button, looking straight up at him. August knelt down so they were eye to eye and carefully stroked the top of the bird's head with his index finger. Then he looked at his finger. Right on the tip was the word *home*, written in black ink. He looked back at the bird, who now had a little white patch on the top of his head.

'Well would you look at that?' He sat back on his heels and beckoned Daphne over to take a look and she noted in her head that it was the first time she'd felt included in years.

'It's ink?' she gasped, not believing she was seeing the perfectly written little word. 'May I?' She'd spoken directly to the bird, who nodded and spread the feathers of one of his wings. Daphne swiped her little finger across a feather, but the wing remained as black as night. She reached across and took August's hand in hers, gently pressing his index finger against Little One's wing. Together they caught the words *I've never loved anyone.* She frowned, and this time used August's little finger to see if there was more to that sad sentence. When she looked at his hand again, she saw *like I love you, Evie.* She laughed and shook her head in sheer disbelief. More tears sprang to August's eyes and spilled over, flowing through the tracks his previous tears had made.

'Your mother? That Evie?' Daphne managed to get the words out without sobbing.

'I dreamed about her today too. It must be.' August didn't care about sobbing. 'Why don't your fingers work?'

'Don't you see? He's a flying book, full of love notes. Your mother's *secret* love notes, and what good are secret notes if everyone can read them? You've got Evie's blood running through your veins, and this little one' – the bird cocked his head in recognition – 'must know that.'

Daphne held August's hand and read the words over and over, more so that she could just feel his warmth for a little longer.

'We need to wash his wings. He's been carrying these notes around for years. It's time he rested.' August held out his cupped palms, and Little One hopped, happily and trustingly, into them.

Together Daphne and August cleaned the 'blackbird'.

Daphne fetched warm water and towels, and dug out a blank notebook she had been saving. August removed the ink carefully, word by word, and together they placed them in order in the book. They dropped a few here and there and they spattered onto the kitchen tiles, lost. They worked until the small hours of the morning, until finally Little One was clean. His wings had been restored to their glorious creamy white, his feathers glowed and he was a dove once more. The notebook was full, bursting to the brim with Evie and Vincent's story, as told through their letters.

'What are you going to do with it?' Daphne asked August after they'd let Little One outside, intending to set him free, but he'd only wanted to go as far as the tree at the bottom of the garden.

He stared at the book lying open on the table, his urge to read it fighting with thoughts of honouring his mother's well-kept secrets.

'What do *you* think?' he finally said and, again, Daphne noted that this was the first time in a long time that they'd had a conversation at all let alone one in which he'd asked her what she thought. Daphne took the open book in her hands and flipped it open to the first page. She placed it gently in August's hands.

'August, I think you were led to this book for a reason. Please don't tell me we just worked *that* hard to recover a story that we'll never even know.'

That night, they climbed into bed and started to

read, and even though they'd been married for years, they behaved like teenagers on a first date. When their hands accidentally brushed, Daphne blushed and August wouldn't look her in the eye. They started out reading to themselves, but the further into the story they got, the more of it they read aloud to each other, and as they read, the cold that had gripped their marriage for so long seemed to magically melt away. August even put his arm around his wife and held her close to him, and Daphne's sadness lifted like rain evaporating into the clouds.

Evie had to set her tea down on the floor as an odd sensation gripped her chest. Something had started to rattle in there, like a hummingbird beating its wings, and she gripped the arms of the desk chair because she thought she might take off. Then almost as soon as it had started, it stopped. Lieffe looked at her, as if he knew something she didn't.

'How do you feel?' he asked.

She caught her breath, collected herself and smiled. 'Lighter.'

Her first journey was over at last. Her son had always shown empathy, more so than her analytical, academic daughter, which was why she'd known this secret was meant for him. He also had a strange awareness of the supernatural. Of course when August had woken in the night as a child, scared of shadows that he claimed were ghosts and monsters, and Evie had cradled him back to sleep, she had assured him there were no such things. Had anyone else found a scraggly blackbird in their garden, they would have shooed it away, despite any odd dreams they might have had – but not August. August was a man who believed that everything happened for a reason, and that certain things were meant to be. He believed in fate and destiny, and Evie somehow knew that he'd fit the pieces of the puzzle together.

Now she was glad his imaginative streak had continued into adulthood because, against all the odds, the supernatural *did* exist and Evie was very much a part of it.

7

horace

Over tea, Evie told Lieffe the story of Little One. It felt odd to talk about it in such detail, but it didn't feel difficult any more. Now that August knew, she'd unlocked that door for good. *Now to unlock the others*, she thought.

'Little One is resting at last. It's time you did too, so who's next?' Lieffe asked.

Evie rubbed her hands together to generate a bit of warmth. The thunderstorm had left the room ever so slightly chilled and damp.

'My daughter,' she said with a nod and a stifled smile as she thought of the little girl at four years old, stubborn and pouting with her arms crossed.

'OK,' Lieffe said, 'but first, I must warn you before you

cross the wall again that time works differently here than it does on the other side. While we move at a leisurely stroll, time on the other side sprints. That's why life feels so short and death feels ... everlasting.' He sighed.

'How long have you been here, Lieffe?' Evie asked.

'Oh, I've lost count of the years – and the cups of tea,' he said good-naturedly. 'Would you like another?'

Evie shook her head. 'Could I borrow a pencil?' she asked, wheeling the chair over to the desk in the corner with her heels. She opened its drawers and found a few odd items: three buttons, a box of paper clips, a safety pin – and a pencil. It wasn't sharp, but it wasn't entirely blunt either, so it would do.

'Of course, but why?' Lieffe called from up the stairs as he put the mugs in the sink of the kitchenette behind his office.

'It's the next key!' she shouted, wheeling herself back over towards the wall.

Lieffe returned to find Evie scratching her pencil against the plaster of the wall, her tongue sticking out of the side of her mouth in concentration. She was covering her drawing with her hands, so Lieffe couldn't see what it was. He stood behind her at a distance, curiosity making him crane his neck. Finally she pulled back to reveal a cartoon, no bigger than her palm, of a cat wearing a waistcoat and a monocle.

'Ta-da!' she said, holding out her hands to frame the masterpiece.

Lieffe chuckled. 'Now who's he when he's at home?' He scrunched his face and squinted at the drawing, but it was no use, so he just moved closer, until his nose was almost against the wall, to get a better look.

'That's Horace. He was a real cat, but he died when my daughter was only seven. She didn't take it well at all. She cried and cried and would sleep in the spot Horace used to sleep and refuse to move. So I started drawing him for her, and my husband made up stories to go with the pictures. She lived for those stories when she was younger, and we talked about Horace so often that in time she started drawing him for her son, too. In that way, Horace never really died. He lived on for longer than most cats ever do!'

'Is this what will help you find your daughter?'

'Absolutely. Horace was one of the last things we talked about before I died.'

'Looks like you did need to summon the family cat after all!' Lieffe tapped the Lost Box with the tip of his shoe.

'Yes, but not in quite such a brutal way. This is far more humane.' Evie laughed and turned back to the wall, but the drawing had gone. She touched the place she'd seen it only moments ago, and the wall responded to her touch by growing fur.

Actual fur.

From Evie's fingers outwards, the whole wall rippled and sprouted ginger fur, right to its edges. Evie couldn't help but laugh and stroke the soft fluff underneath her hands. She even threw caution to the wind and pressed her cheek into it, enjoying the warmth and the soft purring she could feel reverberating inside the ginger wall.

'Evie. I'd step away from there if I were you.'

Evie glanced behind her. Lieffe looked slightly concerned, but his glinting eyes gave away his amusement. She took a few steps back to get a good look at the wall, which was now starting to protrude in the centre and turn black and rubbery. Above the protrusion, two holes appeared and were filled by giant yellow eyes. The fur folded and moulded until eventually the wall had transformed itself into a larger-than-life cat's face.

'Horace!' Evie gasped, and laughed. Horace's eyes widened and he sniffed about the room in recognition. Then he licked his lips and his tongue almost hit the desk chair. 'I can't believe this!'

'Neither can I. I can assure you the wall has never pulled anything like this before. This is very ... new.' Lieffe rubbed his stubbly chin and eyed the enormous cat, but Horace just smiled back with his big feline teeth.

'So ...' Evie said, stroking Horace's nose, 'how am I supposed to get through the wall with this great cat blocking the way?'

Horace twitched his nose to shake off Evie's hand. When she stepped back, he opened his mouth as wide as he possibly could, showing all his teeth and his rough tongue. Lieffe let out a great laugh.

'What? No! No, no, no! I'm not getting in there!' Evie's reluctance just made Lieffe laugh harder.

'I don't think you have a choice, my dear girl. This is how the wall wants you to travel, and I fear it might not take your refusal too kindly.' He wiped away a tear and gave Evie a reassuring squeeze on the shoulder. Horace looked down at her disapprovingly.

'All right, all right,' she huffed. She dragged her feet to Horace's bottom teeth. 'I suppose there's no other way ... is there?' She looked at Lieffe, hoping maybe he was pulling her leg and she wouldn't have to go through with this after all.

'It's through the wall or not at all!' Lieffe continued to laugh as he sat down in the desk chair, ready to watch the show. It felt like forever since he'd enjoyed himself this much.

Evie poked her head into the great gaping mouth and shouted, 'Hello!' The sound of her voice echoed right the way down Horace's throat. Horace rolled his tongue into a tight bundle and then flung it over his bottom teeth so that it unravelled on the basement floor like a red carpet.

'He must think highly of you, Evie. This looks like VIP treatment!' Lieffe could barely keep his voice steady and his face straight.

'That's enough from you,' Evie said sternly. She took a step on to Horace's tongue, trying to be careful not to hurt him. Horace lifted her a few inches off the ground and slowly started to pull her into his open mouth. Evie turned her head to Lieffe, keeping her balance. 'If I come out Horace's . . . other end, there will be hell to pay when I get back.' She ducked as she passed through the cat's teeth, then sucked in a breath and held it as he gently closed his mouth around her.

Horace winked at Lieffe, who was watching in fascination, then closed his eyes and the giant face melted back into the wall, which turned from ginger back to cream. If it wasn't for the few stray hairs left behind on the concrete floor, he might never have been there at all.

the second
secret

the shoe
box

October

Jim

James 'Jim' Summer was a respectable man from a well-connected family. When his father retired, he would take over the family business, and when his parents finally passed on, he would inherit the Summer fortune and estate. Until then, his father and mother, James and Jane Summer, controlled every move Jim made. His mother even went so far as to lay out his clothes for him each morning.

Although he knew no different, he was aware that there was something wrong with the way the Snows and Summers functioned. From the way they picked their partners to the way they named their children, everything was too coordinated, too pristine. Neither family had any warmth, not even an ember, which led to them being terribly sinister and avoided by most. If it weren't for the fact that they were incredibly well off, Jim supposed, they probably would have been isolated from society altogether. And the only reason he knew all of this was because one person opened his eyes to the madness when he was eight years old, and that person happened to be a Snow: Evie.

Although Evie might have literally been the girl next door, she was far from that stereotype. When she was younger, she was round and gawky. She never wore glasses or braces, and she always had quite a pretty face, but she couldn't hold herself properly. She looked uncomfortable in everything she wore and out of place in every setting, and when she ran, which she did often, she looked like a newborn giraffe trying to find its feet. Her mother tried to encourage her to be ladylike, but Evie resented the idea that to be considered a lady you couldn't behave the same way as all the young boys were encouraged to do. Her brother Eddie and Jim were almost forced to play and be boisterous, while Evie had to sit still and be boring and pretend she was elegant when clearly she was itching to gallop as fast as possible through as many muddy puddles she could find. She saw nothing wrong in being elegant if that was what you wanted, but it wasn't what *she* wanted.

As she got older, she lost most of the gawk but kept most of the round, and even though she grew into an odd but beautiful young woman, to her family she was the ugly duckling. However, unlike most women who were partial to cake and cups of tea with three sugars, she embraced her extra weight. Partly because she knew those few extra pounds annoyed her mother, but mainly because she was healthy as she was and couldn't stand the thought of exercising any more than walking up the seven flights of stairs to her flat on the occasions when the lift broke down – though luckily this very rarely happened as Lieffe kept the building in such good order.

As children, Jim and Evie were pushed together, their families set on them getting married when they were older, but then as they *did* get older, their friendship suddenly became 'inappropriate'. They were now *too* close, according to their parents, so their time together was cut down and limited to the weekends. Jim didn't understand why, but Evie did. It was because Jim had fallen in love with her and it was plain for everyone to see. Neither set of parents understood love, or marrying someone you had fallen for, because neither pairing had any affection for their spouse whatsoever. They'd been married off because it was smart and strategic and made the most sense. Jim and Evie had been paired together for the same reasons, so watching Jim fall in love with the woman they'd chosen for him to marry, something they didn't understand, terrified them and they tried to put a stop to it. But all that really did was made Jim love Evie more. And all would have been well if Evie had fallen for Jim too, but her heart didn't long for him the way his called out for her. She often wished it did, but Jim just wasn't the man for her and they both knew it.

Evie often wondered whether she should keep her distance from Jim, to avoid giving him the wrong idea and getting his hopes up, but even though she didn't love him, it was clear to both of them that their souls were made of the same stuff, and no matter what, at every stiff upper-lipped gathering, at every family event and even just for the weekends, they ended up side by side. He was the best friend she'd ever had. Maybe even the *only* friend she'd ever had, and because of that she couldn't let him go, nor did he want her to. Jim might not have been very good at communicating how he felt, but that didn't mean he didn't understand. He knew full well that Evie would probably never love him, but it was enough just to be near her and to hold her affections in one way, if never in the other.

Now, however, Jim sat in the drawing room of the Summer family home, in his father's armchair by the lit fireplace, holding a small green velvet box in his palm. He opened it, took out the engagement ring and examined it in the light of the fire. A white-gold band held a large glinting emerald at its centre, with smaller diamonds surrounding it shining just as brightly. Jim sighed. It was the perfect ring and he knew Evie would love it, but even just the act of giving it to her could be the end of any affection between them. If she said yes, she would be doing so out of obligation rather than choice, and if she said no, her family would disown her. His would most probably disown him too, for embarrassing them. Whether he asked or whether he didn't and whether she said yes or whether she said no, both Jim and Evie weren't destined for happiness. No, now it was simply a case of deciding which path would cause the least damage to their hearts.

Jim heard the front door close and voices twittering. He snapped the ring box shut and slid it into his trouser pocket. He'd started to feel light-headed, so he doused the flames of the fire and went to fetch his jacket to go for a walk, but when he got closer to the door, the conversation out in the hall started to become audible. He pulled lightly on the doorknob and saw his mother, Jane, and Eleanor Snow taking off their coats and hats after a walk with the dogs. Jim didn't make a habit of eavesdropping on conversations – it wasn't the gentlemanly thing to do – but he knew that what he overheard might be of use to Evie, and he wanted to help her in any way possible.

'Jane, you know as well as I do that my daughter will be home by the first of November,' Eleanor said, unbuttoning her coat and hanging her scarf on the coat stand.

'But what if she *does* find a new job, Eleanor? What then? We'll have to marry Jim off to that ghastly Nelly Weathersby!'

Jim shuddered at the thought, then straightened his shoulders and took a deep, silent breath. If he had to marry Nelly Weathersby to let Evie live the life she wanted, then so be it.

'Don't be dense, Jane. I've given Evie three months of delusion, but she's coming home at the end of it whether she's found a job or not. I'm not having her roaming about making a mess of things all of her life. Especially not with that *stray* she's taken in. A musician, of all things! I knew my daughter was stupid, but my God! And Eddie's been

181

acting strangely recently too. I do hope she's not rubbed off on him too much . . . '

The two women disappeared further into the house, their conversation fading with them, but Jim had heard enough. His heart was bouncing around his chest as he flew out of the front door, not bothering to grab his coat on the way.

The flat had been wallpapered with Evie's art. There wasn't an inch of space that hadn't been covered in pages from her sketchbooks. She had poured herself into her ink pot and tried to push her worries for the future aside by drawing sketches and sending them to anyone who might potentially need an artist. Even companies she'd sent her drawings to before received more of them, just in case the first lot had been missed. Vincent lounged on the sofa filing sheet music into folders and writing music notes on the staves in his exercise books. He was now a mature student at quite a decent music school, and he was loving it. Learning was something he'd not done much of when he was younger, especially not of what he loved the most, so now that he had the chance, he had leapt at it and he wasn't going to let it go. Evie, however, had started to resemble a parrot who had been pulling out its feathers, and there was little Vincent could do to console her, but today was one of their better days. She was consumed by her drawing and he quietly went about his business, occasionally playing a piece on his violin which entranced Evie, but like all storms, this was just the calm that came before.

The door to the flat rattled under Jim's hand. Vincent looked at the back of Evie's head, her curls barely contained by the hairband she'd used to tie them back from her face, out of the way of her artwork as she scrawled away at her desk. She hadn't heard the door, so Vincent flipped his books closed and opened it himself, coming face to face with a man who looked like a model from a clothing advert. The ones that strangely often have no clothes *on*. Vincent felt a little warm under the collar for thinking that and instead turned his attention to what exactly this insanely gorgeous specimen was doing on his girlfriend's doorstep.

'Oh. Hello. Are you . . . ?' said the man, a little flustered. He knew Evie was still spending time with Vincent but he hadn't ever thought about how he would feel should he meet him. Nor did he expect Vincent to be so *tall*. Evie looked up at the sound of his voice and ran to the door.

'Can I help?' Vincent said pleasantly.

'Jim? What's wrong?' Evie knew that Jim wouldn't make house calls unless it was urgent. He was part of the life she didn't want but a life that was still on the cards and so until she'd had the chance to prove she was capable of getting a job and living with the man she loved, Jim would stay away. That was until he had learned that Eleanor never intended to let Evie keep this life whether she made it work or not.

'Can I come in?' Jim asked, looking down the hallway, convinced he'd find Eleanor at the bottom of the corridor, coming after them with a torch and a pitchfork.

183

'Of course. Jim, this is—'

'Vincent? It's truly a pleasure to meet you.' The two men shook hands.

Vincent stood protectively close to Evie, his shoulder slightly in front of hers. From the worry in his brow and the warmth in his eyes it was clear to Jim that Vincent really did love her, and although he knew that Evie had never needed taking care of, he felt comforted knowing someone good was keeping her company at the very least.

'Vincent, this is Jim.' Evie paused, trying to find a way to explain exactly who Jim was. A way to encompass everything Jim had been to her over the years and what he may still become in place of Vincent. After far too long of a pause, she settled for, 'He's my best friend,' and Jim liked that a lot.

Vincent relaxed slightly, but he eyed Evie, wondering why she'd never properly talked about this Jim before.

'Evie, we need to talk. I overheard my mother and Eleanor earlier.'

'You need to stop eavesdropping, Jim.' She tried to sound humorous, but her gut was churning and it sounded more like she was telling him off.

'If it wasn't for my overactive ears, I wouldn't be able to warn you like this.'

'Warn me?'

Jim looked uncomfortable. He subtly shifted his eyes towards Vincent.

'Vincent, could you make us some tea?' Evie said, taking the hint. 'We'll be on the balcony.'

184

Vincent didn't take offence. He'd known for a while she was hiding something, and the sudden appearance of this childhood friend, whom she'd failed to mention looked like a demigod, made him a little nervous. He wished she'd just talk to him, though. Whatever it was, they could figure it out together.

Vincent disappeared out of sight, and Evie took Jim by the arm and led him out on to the balcony.

'What's going on?'

'Evie . . . I hate to be the one to tell you this,' his hands were shaking, 'but I heard Eleanor saying to my mother that even if you do find a better job than the one you had at *The Teller*, she's still going to make you come home and put a stop to all of this.' He gestured inside to the flat – and to Vincent in the kitchen. Evie thought she might be sick over the balcony.

'No. No, she promised . . .'

'I think Eleanor's surprised us all with how cold she can be.'

'She *wouldn't*.' Evie could barely breathe.

'If you fight her, you'll lose everything. You'll never see your parents again, which, arguably, wouldn't be a huge loss . . . but you'll lose Eddie too, whether you find a new job or not. If you do find work, you'll still lose it all. And, this is nowhere near as important as the rest of it but, I doubt your mother will make it easy for me to see you either.'

Evie looked at him, wide-eyed and breathing heavily.

Not seeing Jim any more would be like removing her life-line. Through everything, Jim had always been there and she'd always turned to him when things were going right as often as when they were going wrong.

'Look at me, Evie.' He ducked a little so he could catch her eye. 'If you choose not to come home, you'll lose all of that, yes, but if anyone can make it work, you can.'

Evie shook her head but no tears came. She'd cried them all out every time she thought Vincent wasn't looking but he'd always known. Her eyes were too big for him not to know that the happiness in them he'd fallen in love with had been, temporarily he hoped, replaced by sadness. Vincent appeared in the doorway, having abandoned the idea of making tea that no one would end up drinking.

'Evie?' He looked at the shivering woman on the balcony and even though he knew something was terribly awry, she still looked strong. She still had some fight left in her yet. 'Talk to me.'

Jim didn't want to, but he knew he needed to leave. He stood up. 'I'm going to leave you to it. It really was a pleasure to meet you, Vincent.' Vincent could see he meant it but he looked back to the almost unrecognisable, considerably less bouncy Evie, and wondered if he really had made her happy.

Jim looked back to Evie. 'Think about what I said?' he asked, before he let himself out.

Once Jim had gone, Evie went to Vincent and let him take her in his arms. She just needed a few moments of being held by the man she loved before she made him entirely miserable.

Evie made tea, sat Vincent down and told him everything. She told him about her mother's visit to the flat, and about the promise Eleanor had made to let her try to find a better job by the time November rolled around. She also reminded him that no one had responded to her letters and her artwork and said she doubted anyone would in the time she had left. And then she told him how, despite all that, her mother was going to go back on her word anyway, whether she found a job or not. Eleanor would be the fatal gust of wind to their house of cards.

'You don't truly believe she'll do that, do you?' Vincent said, a little hysterically.

'Absolutely I do. If you'd met her, you'd know. We've talked about some of this before.'

'I know, but I never . . . This is ridiculous!' He raised his voice. 'You are a twenty-seven-year-old woman!'

'I *know*, Vincent. But I come from a family of traditions. Arranged marriages. Business over pleasure. In my family, personal choices have always been limited, and if I don't follow suit, I lose everything.' Evie held on to her cup of tea as though it was a piece of floating driftwood in the middle of the ocean.

'Can't you see how twisted that is?' Vincent had risen to

his feet and was pacing the floor around her as she sat on the rug. He ran his hands through his black hair over and over.

'Of course I can. Believe me, I know how wrong it all is, but being able to see that doesn't change it.'

Vincent stopped pacing and looked at her, completely lost. Then a spark flashed behind his eyes like a firework going off in his brain.

'Let's run away,' he said.

'Oh Vincent. Be serious.' Evie swatted at the air like she was batting away his idea, but her heart had heard it and was holding on to it.

'I *am* serious. Why not? What's stopping us?' He knelt down by her side and took hold of her shoulders.

'Your education, for a start. It's taken you how long to secure a scholarship? I'm not going to let you throw that away.'

'But I would, Evie. *We* are more important. We'll go somewhere else, somewhere new, somewhere your mother can't find us, and I'll apply to schools there. I'll . . . I'll see if I can transfer!' He was grabbing at anything if it meant they could stay together.

'You'd really do that?' Evie said, stroking his cheek.

'For you, Evie,' he mirrored her action, touching her cheek with his thumb, and she felt exhaustion overcome her, 'I'd do anything.'

30 October

Eddie

Halloween had taken over in mid-September. Skeletons could be seen hanging in windows, it seemed everyone was adorned in something either orange or black, and everywhere smelled like pumpkin. Evie loved Halloween for two reasons. She'd never been allowed to dress up as a child, nor was she allowed to join Jim and her brother when her father took them trick-or-treating, so it became like forbidden fruit. Everything looked far more desirable and more fun than it probably was, simply because she wasn't allowed to participate. As an adult, she felt too old to join in, but she loved watching all that fun from the outside. The other reason she loved Halloween so much was that Eleanor Snow just happened to have given birth to her daughter on the spookiest day of the year. However, the

Snows weren't big on birthdays so if it weren't for Halloween marking the occasion, Evie doubted she would have
noticed the day come and go at all. Evie had been worried that the festivities had started so far in advance this
year that everyone would have Halloweened themselves
out by the time her birthday rolled around, but now that
the day was nearly upon them, excitement only seemed to
be increasing. A few well-aimed eggs caught her balcony,
but she had escaped the reams of toilet paper that now
festooned the balconies of floors one to four. The world
felt a little more hostile the night before Halloween, and
for Evie things were about to get far scarier than she'd ever
imagined.

At 3 a.m. on the 30th, her phone rang. It was so loud in
the silent apartment that she sat bolt upright in bed, wide
awake. Vincent had gone home the evening before after
yet another argument. She'd eventually agreed to the idea
of running away – it really seemed like it was their only
hope – but thoughts of Eddie, Jim, Violet and Vincent's
scholarship had racked her with guilt, and she'd changed
her mind again. It wasn't the first time, and each time Vincent would try to bring her round and they'd argue.

Evie scrambled out of bed, registering it was only the
phone and not an alarm of any kind, but her heart was still
pounding when she picked up the receiver.

'Hello?' she croaked, her voice still thick with sleep.

'Evie? This *is* Evie, right?' said the shaky voice on the
other end.

'Er, yes. This is Evie Snow. Who is this? It's really, really quite early.' She rubbed at the prickly sleep that was stopping her eyelids from opening properly.

'Evie, it's Eddie.'

Her breath caught. 'Eddie? What's wrong? Why are you calling at . . . ' she took a few steps backwards so she could check the clock on the kitchen wall, 'three in the morning?'

'You live at flat seventy-two, yes?' Eddie asked.

'Yeah . . . why?'

There was a knock on the door. Without hesitation, Evie put the receiver back on the cradle, cutting the line dead, and opened the door to her little brother, the hood of a sodden navy blue raincoat pulled around him and his phone jammed against his cheek. He was only twenty years old but Evie looked at him with the eyes of a big sister and all she could ever see was a young boy that she needed to protect and take care of. He looked up at Evie through the strands of mousy blond hair that hung limply around his face.

'Thank God for that.' Eddie, forgetting just how damp he was, hugged his sister with the force of a stampeding elephant, knocking the wind right out of her. Had she not been so overwhelmingly pleased to see him, she would have told him off, but instead she fetched him a towel and put his wet shoes and coat in the bathtub, then sat him down on the sofa and made him a cup of tea.

'I'm really sorry for coming over this late, but it was the only time I could sneak out without anyone knowing.

Mother's given me strict orders not to see you.' Eddie sniffed through his pointy nose. He was tall and thin, all angles, and looked more like their mother. Evie, with her rounded edges, had more in common with their father.

'That sounds about right.' Evie shook her head. 'Is something wrong?' Eddie stared forlornly into his mug of tea. 'I know you wouldn't risk the wrath of Eleanor Snow for nothing.' She touched his arm. He was still cold from the rain but he also tensed up at her touch. The Snows weren't prone to affection, so hugging and kissing was foreign in their household, and although Evie had shunned all of that nonsense and was now used to showing love with physical gestures, Eddie wasn't so practised.

He sighed, avoiding her eyes. 'Isla was fired yesterday.'

'What?' Evie snatched her hand away to cover her mouth. 'Why? She's always been brilliant at her job!'

'She was . . . caught kissing someone at the back door. She was sneaking in after she'd been out drinking.'

Evie cast her mind back to when she was sixteen and the thirty-year-old Isla had let her tag along on one of her adventures. The night she'd watched Isla kiss not only boys, but girls too. The night Evie had been taught a valuable lesson in love. When she'd seen Isla dancing very closely with a woman, she had thought it was odd, but maybe it was the lack of physical affection Evie had experienced growing up that made it seem that way to her. But when she'd seen Isla leaning in for a kiss with this strange woman, Evie had marched right up to them and dragged Isla outside, where she had demanded an explanation. When Evie was sixteen, the ideas she had in her head about relationships were limited. Her parents had taught her that love could *only* exist between a man and a woman. Any variations on that were wrong. Unnatural. *Disturbing.* So when Isla, someone she held in such high regard, did something she believed to be wrong, she needed to know why. She had felt let down by Isla's actions.

'Evie, oh Evie. Your mother's really filled your head with nonsense, hasn't she?' Isla had shaken her head, making her glossy hair bounce around her long face. Her eyebrows were beautifully neat and her dark eyes were soul-seeing. But standing there with her hands on her hips, she had looked like a mother scolding a child.

'What do you mean?' Evie had crossed her arms, faltering.

'Do you truly believe only men can love women and only women can love men?'

'Well . . . what other way is there?' Evie's anger had slowly been replaced by curiosity.

'Let me make it simple. Let me tell you how I see it. When you eat a chocolate bar . . . ' Evie had raised an eyebrow. 'Don't give me that. Let me finish. When you eat a chocolate bar, sure, the wrapper might be pretty, full of bold colours and fancy details . . . but ultimately, what do you care about? The wrapper? Or what's *inside* the wrapper?'

'The chocolate,' Evie had answered immediately, knowing her mind and her stomach well. 'I care about the chocolate inside the wrapper.'

'Exactly!' Isla had said, nodding. 'For me, it's the same with people. I don't care about what's on the outside. I care about what's on the inside. Someone's mind. Their heart and soul. For me, it doesn't matter whether they're a man or a woman. That's only the wrapper they come in. What I really care about is the chocolate. It's called being pan-*sexual*.' She had wriggled her shoulders with the joy of it all and thrown up her hands, not knowing that what she'd just said had completely changed Evie's way of thinking for ever.

'Wait a second,' Evie had said, touching Isla's shoulder just as she'd been about to head back inside. 'I didn't see you talk to that woman much before you went to kiss her. How did you know you liked her . . . chocolate . . . before you kissed the wrapper?'

'We've been meeting here for a while now.' Isla had laughed then, a loud and happy laugh. 'I like her bold colours and . . . *fancy details*!' And with that, she had winked and gone back inside, leaving Evie with a whole new world of thoughts.

Now, back in the flat and remembering that night, Evie suddenly had more than an inkling as to why Isla had been fired.

'She was caught kissing a woman, wasn't she?' she asked.

Eddie nodded. 'How did you know?' His thin eyebrows wrinkled.

194

'I've been friends with Isla for a very long time. I confided in her a lot as a teenager and there was a lot she told me too. She kept my secrets and I kept hers. I knew Mother would have kicked her out immediately should she ever have found out that Isla differed so drastically from what she thought a woman should be.' Evie made a note to remember to try to get in contact with Isla in the morning.

'She's hired someone new already! A little thing called Clementine Frost. It's almost as if Isla never existed,' Eddie said, sniffing.

'Clementine Frost,' Evie said. 'Is she a redhead?' she asked hopefully.

'Yes!' Eddie laughed, despite the situation. 'It's fantastically curly too, but Mother makes her wear a hair net. She looks ridiculous.' Even though he was clearly upset about Isla, Evie couldn't help but notice that Eddie seemed to warm at the thought of Clementine and didn't appear to harbour any ill feeling towards her.

'What's that cheeky smile for? Are you smitten?' Evie prodded her brother playfully, but her playfulness quickly turned to concern when he burst into seemingly inconsolable tears. She'd only ever seen him sob like that once before, and that was when he was six years old and their father had found him trying on Eleanor's high heels.

'Eddie, whatever's the matter?' She no longer cared about her brother's aversion to human affection. She set down her tea, pulled him into her arms and rocked him gently. They sat like that for a long time, until his breathing calmed and he mumbled something into the flannel of Evie's pyjama top.

'What was that?' Evie asked softly.

Eddie lifted his face. 'If Mother fired Isla, then she's bound to kick me out too . . . when she finds out.' He sniffed hard and sank his head back against her chest.

'When she finds out what, Eddie?' But Evie knew exactly what he was talking about. Of course she did. She was his big sister. She had grown up looking out for him, learning his little tells for when things weren't right. She had guessed, but she and Eddie had never spoken about it, so for a long time Eddie had been struggling alone with something he wouldn't dare reveal to anyone. Anyone except for Isla, it seemed.

'Nothing,' he said, firmly. 'I should go.' He pushed away from Evie trying to leave the flat as fast as he could but she caught his hand and squeezed it.

'Eddie, whatever it is, you don't have to deal with this alone. Mother and I are two very different people. I won't ever betray your trust and tell her.'

Eddie couldn't look at his sister. He thought he was being stronger and braver if he kept silent and hid who he was for the sake of peace and acceptance in his family but what was the price? His own sanity? His own happiness? When he realised the answer was all of the above he sank back down onto the sofa next to his worried sister. Eddie knew he had to say something now or he never would. It was time. 'I . . . I like men,' he whispered eventually, calm rivers of tears flowing down his face, catching at the sides of his lips. 'I'm gay.' In two words, the weight on his shoulders lessened considerably and his muscles visibly relaxed.

'I know,' said Evie, squeezing his hands.

Eddie should have been shocked but he knew his sister and *of course* she'd seen it coming. He didn't know anyone who was as observant or anyone who cared as much to look for what was making someone sad or out of sorts.

'You never said anything.'

'I knew you'd tell me in your own time,' Evie said, stroking his hair. 'It had to come from you, not me.'

Eddie nodded, but the weight of another thought started pushing down on his chest. 'Mother's going to find out,' he whimpered.

'She doesn't have to,' Evie reassured him.

'She does.' He shrugged. 'I need to tell her. I can't hide who I am. She's already picked out my perfect wife, so if I don't tell her soon, I'll be married before you are.'

'Who?!' Evie was gobsmacked. She'd not yet been married off and her mother was already picking mates for her younger brother? Eleanor must have started to panic that Evie's resistance would scupper her plans so had made an early start on ruining Eddie's life too.

'Nelly Weathersby,' Eddie said with a roll of his eyes. Evie had never hated her mother more than in that moment.

'What! She's far too old for you! She's older than *me*!'

197

'And she's a *she*,' Eddie pointed out.

'Yes, and clearly that's far more important.' Evie put her arm around his shoulders and gave him a firm squeeze, and although the tears still flowed, she could see the vague hint of a smile on Eddie's face.

'I can't tell you how good it feels to say things like that.' He covered his mouth to stifle an emotional laugh. Evie could only imagine what it felt like to keep a secret that big for so long. 'But how do I tell Mother?' His face fell, the weight starting to press against him again.

'Well,' Evie said, trying to remain light-hearted, 'she's not going to take it well. We both know that.' She suspected that Eleanor would throw Eddie out of the house and spend the rest of her life pretending she'd never given birth to a son.

Eleanor would probably even succeed in forgetting.

'But I *have* to tell her, Evie. I refuse to live my whole life pretending I'm someone I'm not.' Eddie could picture the life he might lead were he free to, and his whole body longed for it to become a reality. He knew he had to tell his family, no matter what that meant.

'Then you need to prepare for the worst,' Evie said. 'But I'll be here for you, every step of the way.'

'But where will I go?'

Eddie looked at Evie, his eyes filled with tears that were full of fear and hope for the future, and in that moment, Evie saw clearly what her own choices in life would do to her brother. If Eleanor Snow was prepared to abandon her daughter for marrying the man she loved, goodness knows what she'd do to Eddie for wanting to marry a man at all. She would kick him out on the street, not caring that he had nowhere to go, and it would be Evie's job as his sister to look after him. But if Evie didn't do what her mother wanted, she wouldn't be able to provide Eddie with the safety and security he would need to live his life.

If Evie married Jim Summer, she'd have a house and a fortune to provide for Eddie when he inevitably lost everything. She could look after him without any problems. Yet if she married Vincent and was cut off from her family, they'd barely be able to afford rent and food for themselves, let alone Eddie too. Evie thought about her packed bags and the empty cupboards in her bedroom. She thought about Vincent's face when she'd said she'd run away, and then when she'd changed her mind. Then she thought about how it would crumple when she told him she really did have to stay, that she wouldn't be changing her mind back again this time. When she told him she'd have to marry Jim to help her brother. When she told him that this was the end.

'You'll come to me,' she said, keeping her voice calm and her face expressionless. 'I will look after you. When I marry Jim, Mother will be so happy that she might turn a blind eye to me making sure you're OK. She wouldn't even have to know that you're with me at all. You could actually come out to her and Father. You could make a show, tell her where to stick her arranged marriage and leave! Then you'd come straight to me and Jim, and they'd never have to know where you are if you didn't want them to.'

Even though it killed Evie to think of marrying anyone other than Vincent, the look of relief on Eddie's face made the thought of her sacrifice worth it all. *The chances of successfully running away had been low anyway*, she thought. *Mother would have found us one way or another.* For the first time, she prayed for that to be true.

'You'd really do that for me? You'd let me stay?' Eddie looked like the child Evie always saw him as. It wasn't that she thought him feeble or immature. It was just that he was her baby brother. Even though he was six-foot-stupid and more than capable of looking after himself, she still felt the sisterly urge to hold an umbrella over him in the rain, check he had a hanky in his pocket before school and leave mugs of tea outside his room when he'd argued with Father. It was an older sibling's job to be overprotective, whether the younger sibling was more than capable of looking after themselves or not.

'Eddie, for you,' Evie stroked a strand of hair off his cheek, and tears gleamed at him from her dulled brown eyes as she repeated the words Vincent had said to her, 'I'd do anything.'

31 October

Dreaming

The balcony doors were flung wide open and the drawings pinned to the walls fluttered in the breeze. After Eddie's visit, she couldn't get back to sleep so had asked Vincent via Little One to come over and had spent the day in a state of numbness, not knowing how to think or feel. Vincent could tell something wasn't right, but something in his gut told him not to open that can of worms. Instead he just cuddled her when she let him and read when she got anxious and paced.

Now it was ten in the morning of the 31st and Evie had left Vincent snoring in bed while she made tea and sat on the cold concrete in her pyjamas, staring through the bars, her birthday entirely forgotten. Her jumper didn't do much to fend off the wind's biting teeth, but she didn't care all that much. She was numb already, without the wind's help. Today was her last day of freedom. She laughed inwardly at how she'd ever considered it freedom; how she'd really thought her mother was giving her a chance to do what she wanted to do, be who she wanted to be, when all it had really been was a temporary adventure. Eleanor had shown her a full bucket of water, given her a drop and then tipped the rest into the gutter. And Vincent still didn't know.

Evie heard him stir in the bedroom and snapped back to life, wiping the tears away from her face with the back of her fingers and draining the last of her tea, even though it was now ice cold.

'Evie? Where've you gone?' Vincent was barely awake and yet he already sounded playful.

'I'm out here.'

'Are you kidding? It's freezing!' He emerged on to the balcony with a blanket wrapped around him. 'Happy birthday,' he smiled as he draped it around her shoulders and sat down on the floor with her, his body heat sinking into her clothes and skin immediately. 'Is everything OK?' He could see it wasn't, but he needed her to tell him of her own free will. And yet at the same time he didn't want her to tell him, because he had a horrible feeling that he already knew what she was going to say.

Evie looked at him and saw the world spinning in his eyes. Losing him meant losing everything she'd ever wanted, and yet having him meant losing everything she'd ever had. She had to tell him.

'Vincent . . . ' She couldn't bear to take his hand.

'It's over, isn't it?' he whispered.

He knew, but he didn't want to hear her voice say the words he'd been dreading to hear since he'd learned the truth about Eleanor Snow's ultimatum.

Of course he knows, she thought.

'Am I that transparent?' Evie felt tiredness set in, deep within her bones. She knew she'd been acting strangely, differently, distant. How could she not when her heart felt like an anvil, so heavy she could barely lift herself out of bed each morning?

'Why?' Vincent asked. He'd promised himself he wouldn't cry should things end like this but now that he was faced with the reality of losing her, he couldn't stop himself.

'Eddie snuck out in the early hours of the morning last night and came here. We talked and he admitted to me . . . well, he told me that he's gay. I've sort of known for years, but it was the first time he actually said the words. He wants to tell Mother and Father the truth, but when he does . . . ' Evie paused, 'Mother will throw him out. He'll be alone, so I need to take care of him.'

'Right,' Vincent said, pulling the blanket tighter around them both.

'If we run away, if I'm not here to help him, he'll carry on pretending he's something he's not because he'll have nowhere else to go. He can't live like that. Even if we did leave and I tried to stay in touch, it wouldn't be enough.

203

Mother would put a stop to me seeing him, and she's already pegged Nelly Weathersby for his wife.' She took a deep breath that stung the back of her throat. 'If I stay, I'll have to marry Jim ... but that means I could look after Eddie. I could give him a place to stay and the life he deserves, and Mother would never have to know. Jim would agree to that, I know he would, and even if she did find out, she'll probably just be glad that Eddie is no longer her problem.'

Vincent listened in silence. When had something so simple turned into this impossible situation? Once Evie had finished, he placed a hooked finger underneath her chin and lifted her face to look at him.

'Evie,' he whispered, 'I ... I understand.' Evie felt her lip tremble. 'Being apart is going to break our hearts, but being together, having the life *we* want, will cause more trouble for more people. Marrying Jim ... ' he paused, giving his heart a moment to start again, 'is the lesser of two evils.'

'You couldn't be evil if you tried.' Evie placed a hand on Vincent's chest. She could feel his heart whirring inside him. She needed to give him hope; she needed to give herself hope. 'Maybe, after some time has passed, we'll find a way to keep going, even if it is without each other.' And with those words, the tears came.

Vincent caught Evie as she crumbled into him and he caved in over her. Together they held the broken pieces of each other in place while the glue came unstuck and the ribbons unravelled. Once their tears had been cried out and what was left of their energy had been spent, they fell asleep, huddled against each other under the blanket.

Evie was startled awake by sirens in the street below. 'What's happening?' she asked.

There was no reply, and when Evie looked around blearily, she saw that Vincent wasn't there to answer. The blanket had been neatly tucked around her before he'd left.

'Vincent?' she called, panic rising in her chest when no answer came. She scrambled to her feet to see an ambulance below, paramedics clad in green spilling into the building.

'Vincent!'

A voice in her head told her that something had happened, that Vincent was the one the ambulance was here for, but when she ran back into the flat and found his toothbrush missing from the bathroom, his mug gone from the kitchen cupboard and his packed suitcase gone from beside the front door, she knew he'd simply left.

She ran back outside and saw Little One swoop down and land on the balcony to her left. The balcony that belonged to Mr Autumn, her quiet neighbour. It was then that her tired, sunken stare fell on the figure sprawled on his back in his blue-and-white-striped pyjamas. A glass of

205

whisky was still in his lifeless hand, but the contents had pooled and poured off the edge of the balcony and into the road below.

Little One was perched on the railings, his feathers entirely ink-ridden. He looked from Autumn to Snow, from Snow to Autumn, lost. Evie stood there, lost herself, and although the paramedics hadn't yet reached him, she knew that Colin Autumn was already dead.

Vincent didn't own enough for his possessions to clutter up Evie's flat, but even so, the place felt empty without them there. Evie sat cross-legged on the rug, staring at the walls around her, her sketches glaring back. The day's last light seeped in through the windows and moved around the room, touching every sketch and engulfing Evie. Then it passed and faded, and a slow, solemn knock at the door shuddered through her bones. Without thinking or feeling, she got up and opened the door to a sombre Jim Summer, with a beady-eyed Eleanor close behind, ogling Evie's pyjamas.

'No fuss, Evie,' Eleanor said in clipped tones, and Jim flinched.

'I'm so sorry,' Jim whispered, wishing he had just one moment alone with Evie before what was to come next.

Wordlessly Evie stood back so they could enter. Jim

was reluctant, but Eleanor nudged him through the door. Once it was closed behind them, the silence was suffocating.

'Well, Jim?' said Eleanor. 'Don't you have something to ask Evie?'

'Not out of choice,' he said, his gaze steady.

Jim had never seen Evie like this. She wore no make-up and she was still in her pyjamas, but she didn't look defeated or tired or ill. She looked like a woman who was ready for war. A woman who knew her fate and was willing to face it with every ounce of strength and bravery she could muster. A woman who would make the best of a future she hadn't chosen.

'I want to say something first,' he continued, and Evie's eyes flicked up to meet his for the first time since the visitors had arrived. 'I know this isn't what you want. I know you will never love me in the way you love him, or . . . or in the way I love you.' Evie felt her breath catch. It was the first time he'd ever said that. The first time he'd acknowledged what they all already knew. 'And I know I can't give you everything you've dreamed of.'

'Jim, this isn't the time for sentimental rubbish—'

'Eleanor,' he snapped. 'Quite frankly, I don't care what you think.'

Eleanor looked startled for a moment, and then her face resumed its usual impassive state, a hint of disdain lingering on her lips.

'You're forcing us into a future neither of us wants, so

you can afford us a little sentimentality at the very least,' Jim said sharply.

Eleanor simply nodded once, so quickly it would easily have been missed if you'd blinked.

Jim turned back to Evie, his face and tone softening. 'I can't give you everything you've dreamed of.' He swallowed and dropped his voice to a whisper, even though he knew Eleanor could still hear him. 'I know I'm not *him*, Evie. But marrying your best friend is the next best thing. I will do everything in my power to make sure you feel safe from every evil.' He glanced at Eleanor. 'And I will try to make you as happy as you can be under the circumstances. I know you've never needed it, but I *will* protect and take care of you.'

Evie thought she must have been exceptional at pretending, because all she wanted in that moment was to be taken care of. *Properly* taken care of as opposed to the way her mother tried to take care of her, by forcing things on her and ignoring all protest. She didn't let her face change. The tears she'd cried had washed away everything she was and all the hope she'd held for a future that was never to be. She was an empty slate, ready for her mother to draw on and map out her life. Jim deserved more than this, more than her. She didn't have anything left to give him. She mustered up a small smile and nodded. Jim lifted the ring box out of his pocket and opened it.

'You're *supposed* to be down on one knee,' said Eleanor, pointing to the floor.

'You're *supposed* to be able to marry who you want,' Jim snapped.

He cautiously walked forward with the box out in front of him. Evie peered inside. The ring was beautiful, if a little extravagant. The emerald was on the large side – undoubtedly Eleanor's choice – but aside from that, the colour, the cut and the band were all perfect. The only thing that wasn't was the fact that it was for her.

'Evie.' Jim swallowed, his mouth dry and his palms sweaty. 'Will you marry me?' The situation was awful and Jim wished it wasn't happening like this, but (and he hated himself for feeling this way) a part of him jumped for joy that he was finally asking Evie the question he'd wanted to ask for years.

'Well?' Eleanor asked, eyebrows raised.

She wasn't at all remorseful and she appeared to have no real understanding of what was really taking place: that the Evie they'd always known was disappearing.

Evie looked at Jim's kind, warm face, etched with worry. Her drawings seemed to stare down at her with scared eyes, all desperately hoping she would find the courage to do what her heart was telling her to do. *Don't do it, Evie,* they whispered. *Eddie will find another way. Do what* you *feel is right.*

When faced with the choice between what is right and what is easy, we are encouraged to choose what is right, even if it puts us in a difficult situation. But what happens when you're faced with the choice between what is right for you and what is right for those you love, and *neither* choice is easy? Evie had thought about this far more than many people do or should, and had decided that choosing what was right for those she loved was right for her too. How could she put her own happiness above that of her brother?

She took a deep, steadying breath, not taking her eyes off Jim. Her heart had curled up into a ball in her chest, and she nodded her head in rhythm to its sobbing.

'Is that a yes, then?' Eleanor's tone was that of an unimpressed schoolteacher.

'Yes,' Evie snapped, showing her true feelings for the first time that evening. Her eyes were full of hate, and Eleanor couldn't help but be taken aback by her daughter's sudden outburst. 'It's a yes,' Evie said, softening as she turned to Jim.

'Well? Put the ring on her finger! Hurry! We need to get home and tell Jane the good news.' Eleanor strode out of the room, not bothering even to congratulate her daughter and her new fiancé.

Jim took the ring out of the box and Evie held out her hand, not wanting to look. The cold band slid along her ring finger.

'There,' Jim said, kissing the back of her hand. 'I'm so sorry, Evie,' he whispered.

'We'll be OK,' she said. She tried to smile reassuringly, but she wasn't sure it came across as anything other than a grimace. Jim pulled her towards him and held her in his embrace, stroking her hair. Evie wasn't sure what to do. Her hands hung limply by her sides and her head rested against his shoulder.

'I know that everything you've dreamed of until now has been taken from you,' Jim said. 'But you must keep dreaming, Evie. You *must*.'

An image popped into Evie's head. It was the image of an eight-year-old Jim standing in her garden dressed as a dragon. He'd handed her a wooden spoon and a saucepan to be used as a sword and shield, then he'd roared and snorted until she'd realised she had to slay him.

That image was replaced by another: Jim teaching her to ride his bike in the woods when she turned twelve because her mother hadn't got her the bike she'd so desperately wanted. She'd felt so unsteady on the saddle, but Jim hadn't let go until she'd told him to.

Next she saw Jim's face through the flames of the eighteen candles on the birthday cake he'd baked for her himself because Eleanor had said that eighteen was too old to be made a fuss of and Evie's birthday was just another day of the year. Her mind shifted through all the birthdays she'd shared with Jim, frame by frame, a flick book of the kindness and love he'd shown her over the years.

Then her memory spanned through all those ordinary days when they'd simply spent time in each other's company. At every moment, Evie realised, Jim had put her first. He'd always made sure that she was happy and had done everything he could to be there for her, and now not only was he doing that again, but he was vowing to do it for ever more. It was the greatest birthday gift he could and would ever give her.

Evie felt overcome with sorrow and gratitude. She flung her arms around him and held on to him as tightly as she could, and in that moment, all her drawings turned to glass and fell from the walls, shattering around her, lost for ever.

1 November

The Shoebox

Jim had planned to stay the night in the armchair, unwilling to leave Evie on her own, but she had taken his hand and led him to her bed, where she'd curled up in his arms. The resolution to her predicament, although an unwanted one, had brought her some kind of peace, and sleep had found her at last. But Jim stayed awake, trying not to let his tears fall into Evie's hair or on her face. God forbid she woke up and found him in such a state. Jim may have been less stiff-upper-lipped than his family but crying in front of Evie was something he just couldn't do. He'd promised to be strong for her, and he wasn't going to go back on that promise on the night of their engagement.

Before Evie awoke, Jim had shifted her under the covers and started to pack up her things as best he could. It would be too upsetting for her, he thought, to have to put the life she loved so much into boxes, to be taken away from the one place she truly felt she belonged. But what to do with her drawings, which were now just shards of glass scattered about the floor?

He searched the flat and finally found an old shoebox in the cupboard by the front door. He swept every last piece of glass into it, even the little bits that had found their way under the rug and hidden behind the armchair. By the time Evie shuffled yawning into the living room, most of her things had disappeared from their rightful places and were in the very same boxes she'd used to move them into the flat in the first place.

'We could have done this together.' She squeezed Jim's shoulder as he crouched to reach under the coffee table to retrieve the last sliver of glass.

'I know. But I didn't want you to have to put yourself through it.' He picked up the shard and dropped it into the shoebox. 'I thought you might want to keep these.' He put the lid on and handed her the box, and although she took it, she shook her head.

'No. I have no use for them now.' She smiled. It was getting easier to pretend her smiles were real. 'They should stay here. This is where they belong.'

She crouched down next to him and started to push the coffee table over to one side of the room, and when Jim realised what she was doing, he moved to help her. Together they rolled up the rug, then Jim fetched a sturdy butter knife from the kitchen and slid it between two floorboards, prising one of them up so that it came out completely. Evie knelt down next to him, holding the box in her hands like it contained something living. He slid his arm around her shoulders, waiting for her to crumble, but she didn't. Instead she kissed the closed lid of the box and carefully placed it in the hole in the floor.

'Bye, dreams,' she said. 'I hope one day someone else finds you and uses you better than I did.'

8

isla

Evie rocketed down Horace's throat as though it was a slide and was catapulted into the air in a huge gush of water. Like a cat, she landed squarely on her feet in a burst of ginger fur, and opened her eyes to see that she was standing by the blue front door of her own house. This was the place she had lived after she left her flat. It was a house she knew well, but it seemed different now. The paint on the door looked dull, and the chandelier in the hallway that she could see through the window didn't shine as brightly as it used to. It felt as though the house had lost its soul, its magic – everything that had made it a home and not just a structure containing a family and their belongings.

There was movement from an upstairs window, and

Evie saw the blonde waves of her daughter's hair. Isla. Evie had named her after the woman who had taught her far more than her own mother ever had. Isla had a husband, Chester, and son, Percy, and their house was a two-hour drive from Evie's, but she had been staying here while she was getting the place in order after her mother's death. She also knew that leaving her father on his own in such a big house was out of the question.

The front door of the house opened with a creak that Evie had never heard it make before, and out came an old man in his mid-seventies. He took a deep breath and looked around at the overgrown front garden; then, just for a split second, he glanced at Evie, and her breath caught, but his gaze flitted away again and Evie felt silly for thinking he'd seen her. Even though his age was apparent from the wrinkles in his skin and his stooped posture, his eyes still shone like he was twenty-something, and Evie would have known their glint anywhere.

'Uncle Eddie? Where've you disappeared to?' Isla called from inside the house. She appeared next to the man and linked her arm through his. 'I know you hate housework, but these boxes need to be sorted. And don't think your age will get you out of it either. I've seen how you chase after Oliver.' She winked at him, to which he gave a throaty laugh, and she pulled him gently back into the house.

Eddie had lived with his partner in the Snows' house

ever since he was in his thirties (after his parents had passed away, of course. They never would have allowed it had they been alive and able to intervene and Eddie took great joy in the big middle finger it was to his parents each and every day they lived there). However, now that they were in their seventies and having trouble doing all the things they used to do so easily, August and Daphne had moved in with them shortly after Evie had passed away and each of them benefited from the extra company in many ways.

Evie took her chance before the door shut her out, and slipped in behind them into the hallway of the house she'd lived in since her wedding. Cardboard boxes were scattered about, filled with objects she recognised as her own. She knelt down, not sure why she was careful not to touch anything. Her jewellery box, her books, her trinkets and treasures all sat in boxes marked with words such as *Charity* and *Storage*. Other boxes had her children's names on them. These were filled with things that August and Isla associated with their mother so strongly that they wanted to keep them for themselves.

'August!' Isla called from upstairs.

August leapt up from the sofa where he'd undoubtedly been snoozing, then clutched his lower back with a wince. 'That woman,' he muttered as he hobbled to the bottom of the stairs. 'She'll be the death of me, I'm sure of it.'

'August!' Isla shouted even louder, and came to the banister on the landing above. 'You were asleep, weren't you?' she asked, catching sight of her bedraggled, squinting brother climbing the stairs.

'No,' August said through a yawn.

'You're infuriating,' she said, matter-of-factly.

'You're annoying,' he retorted without even looking at her.

It was a routine they'd played out many times over the years. Isla poked her tongue out at him, August poked his out at her, and just for a moment they regressed to their childhood years and forgot their real ages of forty-seven and fifty-two. Isla couldn't help but smile at her silly older brother.

'Come on,' she said. 'These boxes won't pack themselves, and Uncle Eddie keeps popping the bubble wrap.'

There was little Evie could do while her daughter was buzzing about the house trying to get Eddie and August to behave, but despite her family not being able to see her, she enjoyed spending time in their company. They sat in her old bedroom, emptying cupboards and drawers and talking and laughing, and Evie laughed along with them. Together Eddie and August found many new ways to annoy Isla, but her brilliant debating skills always defeated them, and sheepishly they'd turn back to the task at hand. They found belongings Evie ached to hold once more, and others that she couldn't even remember owning; they kept almost everything she wanted them to keep but also chose to hold on to things Evie would have thrown away in a heartbeat.

'What about this?' Isla pulled out an ornate lamp. A miniature statue of a woman was leaning against the lamp's stand, her flowing dress draped off one shoulder, almost revealing all. One wrist was pressed against her forehead, as if she was about to faint; the other hand rested saucily on her hip, and she had a come-hither look in her eyes.

'Keep it?' suggested Eddie with a shrug.

It was now almost nine o'clock in the evening and seventy-five-year-old Eddie was getting tired so his answers were becoming more and more half-hearted.

'Really? I don't remember seeing it around the house ... ever,' said August, eyeing the lamp.

'No, me neither, but Mum must have kept it this long for a reason,' Isla pointed out.

'I hated that lamp,' Evie said, even though none of them could hear her. 'Aunt Esme gave it to me, and I hid it so well that I'd forgotten about it until now!'

'Keep it, then. But I'm not having it!' August said, refusing to take it from Isla as she tried to pass it to him.

'Well I don't want it!' Isla said, now wishing she wasn't the one holding it.

'Look, if you think Mum would have wanted us to keep this ... thing, then that's your call. But I am not going to be the one taking the God-awful thing home!'

The sound of a car on the gravel in the driveway interrupted the siblings' quarrel. August got up and went to the window. Isla looked at the lamp and huffed as she slid it into a box marked with her own name, and Evie couldn't help but smile with affection for her daughter.

'Dad's home,' August said with a furrowed brow, beckoning Isla and Eddie over to the window. Evie followed, unsure if she wanted to see what they were seeing. She knew that her death, even though it wasn't a surprise, would have taken its toll on her husband. He'd loved her and taken care of her until the end, and watching him look up at the house and see three faces at the window instead of four made her wish she could reach out to him. But that would have been selfish, because Evie had no secrets to share with him. She had told her husband everything in life and so had no need to reveal anything to him in the afterlife.

'Come on. We'd better go and make sure he's OK,' Eddie said, and ushered them downstairs.

He opened the door to greet Jim.

Jim Summer looked weathered and worn now, but he was still as handsome as the day he'd married Evie, and he'd lost none of his charm either.

'Hello, all,' he said, just as he used to every time he walked through the door, although lately it had been with much less gusto.

'Hello, Dad,' Isla said, greeting him with a kiss on the cheek. August simply hugged his father with closed eyes and a held breath, and Eddie shook Jim's hand firmly.

Hello, Jim, whispered Evie, hoping he'd hear, though she knew that of course he couldn't.

'How was she?' Isla asked.

'Quiet.' Jim's expression changed quickly to that of a person who'd just got a paper cut. 'I hate leaving her alone.' A sob escaped before he could cover his mouth, and August rushed to put his arms around his father again and hold him upright before his old, rickety legs caused him to stumble. 'I'm fine. I'm fine,' Jim reassured them. He patted August's back, took a deep breath and collected himself.

'The cemetery is lovely and peaceful, and you can visit as often as you like. We all can,' Isla said, and it was only then that Evie realised Jim had been to her grave. Tears rolled down her cheeks without her being aware of them.

'I know. I'm being silly. I'm just tired. I think I'm going to call it a day.' Jim gave everyone a smile to let them know he really was going to be OK, but their eyes were still worried.

'Here,' Isla said. 'Let me help you.' She took her father's hand and helped him climb the stairs.

'Did they behave today?' Jim asked, squeezing his daughter's hand.

'Do they ever?' she said with a sigh, and Jim laughed. 'Are you sure you don't want to help us go through her things?' she continued. 'We're worried we're throwing away things we should keep.' Isla opened the door to the spare room, and Evie could see Jim's possessions scattered about. *He's been sleeping in here*, she thought.

'It's more likely that you're keeping things she would

223

have thrown away,' he said. He knew her so well. After fifty-four years of marriage, how could he not? 'No. I can't. I trust your judgement. Besides, I've already got everything of hers I wanted to keep.' He walked slowly into the spare room and carefully plonked himself down on the bed.

'OK,' Isla said reluctantly, not wanting to leave her father alone with his grief.

'I'm fine, Isla. Really. Just ... missing your mother, that's all.' He smiled. 'Mind you,' he looked around the room, eyeing every corner, 'knowing Evie, she's probably still here somewhere, trying to make sure we're all doing OK.' He smiled to himself, and Evie laughed with him, feeling more present and alive than she had in a while. She knew Jim could feel her near, and she was glad about that.

'You're probably right,' Isla said, feeling a little surer he would be all right for tonight. 'You get some sleep.' She closed the door slowly, not quite yet wanting to leave him in his own company, but knowing deep down that he was stronger than the rest of them combined, and that he really would be fine. Evie slipped out of the room with her.

Isla had never been a troublesome child, but she had been feisty, stubborn and seemingly always ready for an argument, which meant that letters from school were sent home every now and then about her tendency to talk back to teachers. While Evie tended to August's creativity, Jim homed in on Isla's need for debate, and taught her how to structure her arguments so that she'd never lose, much to her older brother's dismay. August couldn't bear that his little sister, five years his junior, could outsmart him by the age of seven. Evie would raise her eyebrows at Jim across the dinner table, to which Jim would simply shrug, but after dinner he'd ruffle Isla's hair and congratulate her on a calm and reasonable execution of her case for why she should be allowed to stay up just as late as August. Isla grew up loving discussion and asking a million questions just to understand things better. Although she was very much Jim's protégée, Evie made sure she taught the little girl compassion, love and tolerance; all the things her own mother had never taught her. Their relationship was built on all these qualities, but most of all it was based on honesty. At least Isla thought it was.

The moment Evie had accepted Jim's proposal, she'd made a vow never to talk of her old life again. Her flat, her drawings and Vincent were in the past, and it served no purpose resurrecting them and hurting all over again, so she had simply buried it all and denied its existence entirely. So when Isla's inevitable artistic streak manifested itself in drawings all over her school books when she was sixteen, Evie started to panic. She avoided long conversations with her daughter for a whole week before Jim found her at the dining room table holding one of Isla's drawings that had slipped out of her school bag.

'She's good, isn't she?' he said, sitting down across from Evie.

'She is.' Evie nodded, stroking the drawing with a finger.

'As good as you were.'

She held up a hand to stop him talking about things she wanted to forget.

'You draw Horace for her all the time,' Jim said tentatively, hoping not to upset her.

'That's different. All mothers draw with their children, but this . . . ' Evie set down the sketch and put her head in her hands.

'You're worried that if she keeps drawing and nurturing this talent, it's going to feel more and more like you're lying to her,' Jim said, and Evie looked up through her fingers and nodded. 'Then talk to her.'

'No,' Evie snapped, and Jim looked taken aback. 'I'm sorry. Sorry. I just . . . I can't open that door. I just can't.' Evie's voice wobbled and she took a deep breath to stave off the burst of emotion she felt in her chest. 'I want her to be whatever she wants to be, and if that is an artist, then I will completely support that, but . . . I'll need your help more than ever to hide that part of my life. If I tell her about how, all those years ago, I worked as an artist at a newspaper, or about how hard I fought to keep that career alive, one thing will lead to another and I'll have to tell her everything. And I can't, I can't relive it all again, I can't relive losing . . . '

Jim had leapt up from his seat and walked briskly around the table to hold her before she fell apart. With

226

her face pressed against his blue knitted sweater vest, she took a few deep breaths, inhaling his scent, and it calmed her.

'OK,' he said, lifting her chin to see her face. 'Then we hide it, but be prepared. I know that girl only too well, and if she sets her mind to being an artist, then nothing is going to stop her.'

'Then I will happily sit back and quietly live vicariously through her.' Evie smiled, and Jim leaned down to gently peck her on the lips.

Isla hadn't grown up to become an artist. She'd listened to her heart and gone to law school, becoming the first female head of Snow and Summer Ltd, and the first person to run the firm completely on her own. She was part Snow and part Summer, and what with August having no interest in law and Evie's brother having no children of his own, she happily succeeded Jim and ran the business better and more fairly than anyone before her. Edward Snow and James Summer Senior had no say in the matter, as they'd both passed away when August and Isla were children. Eleanor Snow followed shortly after her husband, but Jane Summer had lived into her nineties. After the death of her husband, she had become a completely different person, and had wholeheartedly agreed that Isla should take over the firm.

Although Isla had become a lawyer, her love of art had never gone away, and she drew and painted in her spare time, but she could never understand the look on her mother's face when she presented her with a new painting. She always looked so wistful, and perhaps even a little scared. Isla hated that look so much that she eventually stopped showing Evie her work, believing that her mother didn't think she was any good. That belief had stayed with her, and it made both of them sad.

Evie followed Isla down the hallway to the room she'd occupied as a child. When she opened the door, Evie slipped in behind her and stood looking around. She and Jim hadn't changed anything about the children's rooms when they'd moved out. Isla had always been headstrong and rather tomboyish, yet her colour of choice had been pale pink, and she'd insisted on as many objects as possible being sparkly or covered in jewels. Now Evie looked around at the pink-and-cream striped wallpaper and the glittery curtains. Little fake jewels shone out at her, gleaming from every nook and cranny, and her daughter's eyes shone back, full of sorrow. Isla ran to her bed and flung herself down on it as she'd done when she was a child, throwing a tantrum. She buried her face in the pillow and let her tears fall into the fabric. Evie looked on from the end of the bed, where she used to sit and watch her daughter sleep after she'd put her back to bed after a nightmare.

'I'm still here, Isla,' she whispered. 'I always will be.'

Isla fell asleep after mere minutes of sobbing, and Evie hoped it had something to do with her being so close. Now was her chance.

'Isla.'

Isla's eyebrows knitted as she recognised her name, even in sleep.

'Isla, my brilliant daughter. You are so clever. You always knew there was something wrong with me, something I was hiding from you, but you trusted me so much that you never questioned it. Thank you for letting me keep my secrets. I thought I was being brave hiding my past from you, but really I was just a coward. I didn't want to hurt any more. I wish you had asked me questions so I would have been forced to confront what I never had the courage to face in life, but in death . . . it turns out you have no choice but to stand up to your biggest demons, so my advice to you would be to get it over with while you're still alive and kicking.' Evie laughed at herself, and Isla relaxed into her laugh, just as she used to relax into Evie's warm hugs. 'But now, my darling girl, it's time you knew everything, so here we are. There's a box, Isla, a shoebox in my old flat. Jim . . . your father has the address. Under the rug in the living room there's a loose floorboard, and underneath that you'll find the box. In the box . . . well, you'll just have to have a look but I promise you things will become clear once you find it, but you need to promise me one thing. Look after them for me, OK? Look after them better than I did.'

Evie stood, brushed her skirt down and tiptoed closer to her sleeping child. Tentatively she stroked a few strands of Isla's hair away from her face, and when Isla didn't move, she leaned down and placed a kiss on her forehead. As soon as Evie's ghostly lips touched her daughter's skin, Isla sat bolt upright.

'Mum?' she yelped.

Evie gasped, but the gasp seemed to suck her backwards across the room, and her vision faded. She was being dragged out of the living world for a second time.

Evie found herself thudding across the basement floor. With a very inelegant roly-poly, she landed face down at Lieffe's feet.

'Well?' the little Dutchman asked impatiently.

Evie had had every breath beaten out of her on impact, so she merely pressed the tips of her thumb and index finger together to make a circle. That was all Lieffe needed to see. He picked up a cup of tea he'd made ready for her return, and placed it carefully on the floor next to her face.

9

magic

All the blood rushed to Isla's head. She was sure she hadn't been alone in the room just a moment ago. She'd felt another presence, gentle and calming, felt it so strongly that she'd been startled awake. However, when she'd awoken, she'd found the room empty. She rubbed her temples and laughed at how silly she was. Unlike her brother, she'd never believed in ghosts and ghouls, and while August often cowered in the dark or jumped at shadows, Isla slept soundly and never faltered. She looked across at the pink swirly clock on the wall and saw she'd only been asleep for a few minutes. She was still very tired, her eyelids heavy, so she took advantage of not having woken up fully and sank back down on to her pillows.

In her dreams, Isla found herself floating through a black sky, shards of glass suspended in the air around her. They glinted and sparkled in the moonlight, and some of them were so clean and clear that she could see her own reflection, but she wasn't her forty-seven-year-old self, her blonde hair turning grey and her skin starting to wrinkle. She was eleven again. She looked down and saw that her hands were covered in paint and coloured chalk, and her pink trousers and pale green top were smudged with colour too. Even the ends of her hair had been matted and meshed together with dried acrylic.

The glass started to vibrate with a warm tinkling noise and suddenly all the shards whizzed off, flying past her in one direction, careful to avoid piercing little Isla. All the slivers danced around each other in the sky like birds and Isla was mesmerised until one by one they started to take formation. It seemed that each piece slotted in with the next: a jigsaw puzzle made of glass. The final shard skipped about, teasing her, before it took its place with the rest, then the creases and cracks between each piece filled in until it was one clean sheet of glass – a window that shimmered. As Isla applauded, her reflection started fading, steadily at first, and then all at once she was gone. The glass was growing cloudy and the shining surface became rough. The edges curled, and Isla realised that the glass had turned to paper. *But why?* she thought and it was then that a black dot appeared on the centre of the blank page. A single black dot but then it became a curved line, like someone invisible was drawing it in front of her. She followed the line as it swirled and skated around the page until it took the familiar shape of her mother's drawing of Horace in his waistcoat and monocle.

'Horace!' she laughed in her high-pitched eleven-year-old voice.

The cat's ears pricked up.

'Horace?' Isla gasped.

The cat stretched out his paws in front of him, and then skidded to the bottom left-hand corner of the page and pointed to the empty space in the centre. The black dot appeared again, and this time it turned into a cartoon of a little boy dressed like a cowboy. Once he'd been fully drawn, he drew a toy pistol from his belt and the words *BANG! BANG!* appeared beside him as he pretended to fire his gun. He ran to the bottom right-hand corner, and the black dot appeared in the centre once more. One by one, more and more cartoons appeared. A stern mother. A happy couple. A mean-looking boss. A goose with an angry expression. The page became crowded with pencil sketches until only a tiny space in the middle was left bare. A few moments passed before the black dot returned, but this time it was not a drawing that followed. Instead, a signature appeared, a tiny, modest signature belonging, without a doubt, to the artist.

Evie Snow

All the drawings turned to look at the signature and silently they showed their appreciation to Isla's mother for bringing them to life. The people applauded, the goose flapped its beak open and shut, silently squawking, and Horace gave a low bow with one paw resting on his waistcoat over his heart. Eleven-year-old Isla's eyes widened, and suddenly she found herself staring up at her pink bedroom ceiling, no longer feeling small and nimble but heavy and tired.

She was awake. Back to reality. Back to being forty-seven.

But something was different. The dream had seemed so real. Isla even patted her clothes, searching for paint marks, but she was still in her clean clothes from the day before, and the pink swirly clock told her she'd slept for eight hours: it was almost nine in the morning. She groaned. She definitely didn't feel like she'd slept for that long.

Isla showered, changed and made herself feel more presentable, but all the time the sketches she'd seen in her dream chased each other round and round along the outside track of her brain. The boss chased the mother, trying to pinch her bum; the mother chased the couple, wagging her finger in disapproval; the couple chased after the boy as he tried to pull the goose's tail; the goose waddled after Horace, who enjoyed outsmarting them all; and poor Isla chased after them, trying to find the answers to her swarm of questions.

August was the first to realise there was something amiss.

'Dear sister. Your head is in the clouds today,' he mocked in a silly Shakespearean voice. He tiptoed around her as she washed up her breakfast dishes. 'Your head is never in the clouds,' he continued when Isla didn't respond, his voice now tinged with concern. He yanked the wet butter knife off her, splashing water over them both, and pointed it at her playfully. 'Who are you and what have you done with my smelly sister?'

Isla laughed and took the knife back and continued to wash the hardened egg yolk off its ridges. 'I didn't sleep well, that's all,' she said, staring at the shiny surfaces of the bubbles in the sink and thinking how they looked like the clear sheet of glass in her dream.

'Is Mum's ghost haunting you too?' August said, only half joking.

A plate slipped out of Isla's hand and clattered into the sink. Luckily, it hadn't broken, but water sloshed up and out in a great tidal wave and splashed over her cosy pink slippers.

'Argh!'

August stared at her soaking feet for a moment before bursting into laughter. 'What's got you spooked?' he said once he'd composed himself.

'You said *too*,' Isla said, spinning to face her brother. Her voice came out more harshly than she'd intended. 'What did you mean, is her ghost haunting me *too*?' The water was quickly sinking into her socks, so she sat down and slipped them off in a huff.

'It's silly really,' August said, now feeling sheepish. He'd not spoken about what had happened with the dream and the bird to anyone other than his Daphne, and he probably wouldn't have shared it with her had she not been there to witness the majority of it. But he was so very grateful that she *had* been there, because their marriage was now as good as the day they'd said their vows. 'I—' He paused, grabbed an apple from the fruit bowl and took a bite. As he chewed, he thought about how he was going to word this strange story.

'Go on,' Isla pushed.

'I had this . . . dream.'

Isla felt her heart clang against her ribs. 'A dream?'

'It's going to sound silly, but I could hear Mother's voice telling me about this . . . this bird. I could see it flapping its wings, and when I woke up, it didn't leave me alone.' He could feel the story spilling out of him like ink from a pen. 'It was like the bird was inside my head until he appeared. I mean, *really* appeared.'

'The bird?' Isla said, fearfully.

'Yes. This little blackbird, except he wasn't a blackbird at all! He was a white dove, but Mum and a man she was once in love with had covered him in love notes. The bird would fly back and forth between them when they were apart, carrying the notes they'd written on its wings.'

Isla just stared at him.

236

'I know it sounds crazy. But wait . . . '

August ran from the room and darted upstairs to where his suitcase lay. He dug around under clothes and underwear until he felt the familiar shape of the notebook. When he reappeared in the kitchen, Isla was still in exactly the same place, holding the exact same expression.

'We saved the love notes. Read it. You'll feel closer to her if you do.'

Isla took the book in silence, but couldn't bring herself to open it.

'Isla?' August was concerned at how pale she'd become.

'I'll be back later.' Isla slid out of the kitchen chair and started to pick up pace towards the stairs. 'Is Dad awake?' she called over her shoulder.

'I think I heard him moving around up there. Why? Isla, what's going on?'

But Isla was already up on the landing, heading towards their father's room. She knocked on the door, feverishly.

'Dad? Dad! Are you up?' She listened closely for an answer, but nothing came. 'Dad!' she called, her voice rising.

The bathroom door opened and her father stood there in his striped pyjamas with a toothbrush hanging out of his mouth.

'Whatever is the matter?' he gurgled through foaming toothpaste.

'I need Mum's address. Her *old* address,' she clarified when she saw his bushy eyebrows pull together.

Jim suddenly felt faint. He held on to the door frame with his spare hand.

'Dad?' Isla rushed to him just as he lost his balance and started to fall, the toothbrush landing on the floor and splattering paste across the wood. She caught him before he hit the ground and kept him upright using all of her strength. 'August!'

Jim came to almost immediately, and after a lot of fussing from August and Isla, he felt steady enough to get himself dressed. He met his children downstairs where they both sat whispering to each other in concerned tones but they fell silent when Jim reached the doorway and came into their sight.

'Don't stop on my account,' he said, feeling embarrassed that he'd shown his elderly fragility in front of them.

'Dad, I have a question. Well ... I have many questions,' Isla said. August's notebook rested open in her lap.

'About?' Jim walked carefully into the room, making certain every step was sure and steady.

'About Mum and ... her life before us,' August said, taking the book from his sister.

Jim's next step faltered and he had to try very hard not to lose his balance before his foot touched the floor again. He took a deep breath. 'I see.' He finally reached the

238

armchair opposite the sofa and cautiously inched himself into it.

'I ... found this,' August fibbed, not wanting to bother his father with his improbably odd tale. 'It's a notebook filled with notes. *Love* notes, to be specific. From Mum to—'

'Vincent?' Jim said with a slight smile.

'Yes,' Isla breathed. 'How did you ... ?'

'I met him once. Only briefly. Nice chap. Loved your mother dearly.'

'I can tell,' August said, passing the book to his father.

Jim flipped through the pages, enjoying seeing Evie's handwriting. When he spotted words only she used, like 'flollopy' and 'twerp', the gap in his heart that Evie used to fill ached.

'You didn't just ... *find* this, did you, August?' he said shrewdly.

August was stunned and silent.

'You met Little One,' Jim continued as though they were having a perfectly normal conversation. He looked up from the open pages, warmth radiating out of them. August looked more than a little confused, so Jim carried on. 'The blackbird that isn't a blackbird. Your mother always called him Little One. Again, I only ever met him once, but Evie told me all about him.'

That was all the invitation August needed. He launched into the tale of how awful things had been with Daphne, about the dream he'd had and how Little One had appeared and fixed everything.

'It felt like Mum was watching over me, and now ...' August's eyes shifted to Isla, who was looking at her father hopefully.

'And now I've had a similar dream. A dream that felt so real and so familiar, like ... It felt like Mum was trying to tell me something.'

Jim closed the book gently and rested his lightly shaking clasped hands on its cover. 'And what do you think she was saying?' The tone of his voice had shifted. He sounded sceptical, less willing to help, and Isla felt panic rise into her throat.

'She said she lived somewhere after she left her parents' house and before she got married. She left something there that she wants me to find. The dream I had was all about glass that turned into paper and ... and drawings that came to life, and—'

'I've heard enough.' Jim held up his hand and Isla held her breath. August leaned slightly to his left against Isla's shoulder to let her know he was on her side. 'You are meddling in things you shouldn't be meddling in. Your mother's life before us was her business. Not ours. Respect her decision not to tell you about it and stop digging up her past. I just ... can't bear it.' He put his head in his open hand, not wanting his children to see the tears in his eyes, and gently waved them away with the other. He didn't mean to be dismissive or cruel, but he felt too weak to haul himself out of the chair, and he needed a moment to himself.

August took his sister by the arm, but before they reached the stairs, Isla turned back to her father.

'Whatever she asked you to keep secret, Dad, she's now asking me to find. All I need is that address. That's all. You don't have to have anything further to do with it. Please just ... think about it. I want to know her like you knew her.'

Jim sat for a long while thinking and reading the notebook, wallowing in a past he'd not been allowed to talk about for a very long time, although he'd thought about it often. They'd never seen Vincent again, and whether Evie thought about him or not, she never mentioned it, but Jim wondered most days where Vincent was, and *how* he was, and whether he'd ever found someone else and lived a happy life. He had always hoped he had. But now Jim was lost. He'd kept Evie's past locked away at her request, and now it seemed her ghost was haunting his children and convincing them to find the key he still kept hidden.

'Oh Evie. What do I do?' he whispered just as he drifted off to sleep in the armchair by the fireplace.

'Something's not right,' Evie said. She'd been lying on her back on the basement floor for some while, only sitting

241

up for swigs of tea from her mug. 'I haven't felt anything yet.' She had been bracing herself for the tightening and vibrating in her chest that would ultimately leave her feeling lighter, but it had been a considerable amount of time since she'd arrived back in the building, and . . . nothing.

'Patience, Evie. Sometimes it takes a little while for the living to get the message,' Lieffe said.

'No . . . it's something more than that. It's . . .' Evie knew it wasn't her daughter holding things up. Isla might have a lawyer's head on her shoulders, but there was a bit of magic about that girl that would definitely latch on to what Evie had whispered to her. Isla would have wanted to see it through to the end, even if she found nothing. No, it wasn't Isla. But if not her, then who?

'It's Jim.' Evie sighed and took a large gulp of tea.

'What about him?' Lieffe asked, taking a smaller sip of his own.

'Jim's a Summer. He may have been different from his parents, he had an imagination but it was always *just* make believe. It could and would never be real. He's the only one who has my old address.'

'So . . . ?' Lieffe felt lost.

'I made him promise he would keep my past and everything in it a secret. He's not parting with my address because he thinks that is what I would have wanted. Oh Jim.' Evie felt touched that he was guarding her secrets so well, but she had to make him realise that she needed his help in a different way now.

Come on, Isla, she wished with all her heart. *Win him over.*

Isla found her father asleep in the armchair. She lit the fire to keep him warm as the afternoon turned to evening and the air in the spacious house became chillier. She sat herself down opposite and watched him sleep. Even unconscious, he found a way to look worried, and Isla wondered if her mother was haunting his dreams too. He must have sensed her there, as he started to stir, and eventually his eyes flickered open.

'Isla,' he said, his mouth sticking.

'Dad.' She smiled at him. 'Listen, about what I said earlier ...'

Jim hoisted himself up in the chair, his creaking joints protesting. 'Isla,' he said with a slight warning tone to his voice.

'I know Mum must have asked you to keep this a secret, otherwise you wouldn't be fighting it so hard. But if you give me the address, whatever I uncover will stay in the family. I won't even tell August if you don't want me to. I'll pretend I found nothing, if I do find anything at all. But I just have this ... this feeling. There's something I'm supposed to go looking for, I just know it.'

Jim could feel himself giving in. Everything he'd kept

locked away in his head was pushing against its cage, bending the bars a little further each time.

'There's something Mum left for me at that old address that she wants me to have.'

That was all she needed to say. The memory of the box of glass poured itself through the keyhole in Jim's mind, free at last.

'I don't know why I'm doing this,' he said.

'Doing what?' Isla asked, a slender eyebrow raised.

Jim closed his eyes and let the memory seep down into his chest, where his heart opened its mouth and called out. His silence unnerved Isla, but within a minute, there was a flutter of wings outside.

'Follow that blasted dove and discover what you will.' He smiled, defeated.

Isla turned to the window. Sitting on the sill was a pure white bird, who she could have sworn was smiling.

'Don't ask me how. I've never been able to figure it out, but your mother had a word for it.'

'And what was that?' Isla asked.

'Magic.'

10

apartment 72

The building had long been abandoned. Its exterior had been consumed by green weeds that had grown out so much that each balcony's foliage was entangling with the next. Windows had been shattered, and fresh, smooth paint had been replaced by dull, cracked flakes speckled with moss. But even though it was dilapidated and falling apart, Isla thought the building still had character. Like looking at a photograph of an elderly person from when they were younger. You could still now see that same youth in their eyes, even though their body had withered over the years. She wondered if she was putting her safety at risk by entering the building, or if she'd even be able to find a way in at all. One of the glass doors at the entrance had been shattered, and she considered the fact that there might be squatters living inside. She hoped this wasn't the worst idea she'd ever had, but she knew she had to try, at the very least.

As she stepped through the broken glass, she was glad she'd thought to switch her court shoes for trainers before she left. The foyer was dark, and she could smell the mouldering damp patches that were steadily climbing the walls. The only thing that seemed somewhat complete was the light fixture in the centre of the foyer. It was an exceedingly modest chandelier – if you could call it that at all – but even so, it shone through the dust and had yet to be vandalised like most of the furniture had been. There were marks in the dust where chairs had once stood, the wallpaper had graffiti all over it, and various rude words had been carved into the woodwork. Clearly the lift was out of service, and even if it had been in full working order, Isla wouldn't have chanced it. She looked at the stairs. The carpet had been eaten away by mice, but the steps themselves looked sturdy enough.

'Seventh floor, here I come.'

There was nothing unusual about the building and nothing that made Isla feel she should be scared, but it had an atmosphere she just couldn't explain. She felt like the place had died before its time, that its life and joy had been taken from it before it had had a chance to really make something of itself. She could almost hear music and laughter coming from behind the apartment doors, and picture people leaning over the banisters to

246

call down to each other, and the idea that this had been a community where everyone had been fond of each other and invited each other round for tea warmed her soul. She hoped it really had been like that in her mother's time. However, seeing the building now with its broken windows and its vandalised walls, sadness followed the idea that it had once been so loved.

By the time she reached the seventh floor, Isla had to sit on the top step to regain her breath. On second thoughts, if the lift had been working, she would have taken it. After a minute, though, she jumped up. Her breath was still short and her thighs were burning from a longer workout than she'd had in years, but she was so close now, and couldn't rest easy knowing she was only footsteps away from where her mother had once lived.

She walked quickly past the lift. Its rusty golden doors had *CB luvs PF* graffitied onto them in yellow, encircled with a lopsided heart. The corridor looked like many of the others she had passed, and yet something was so different. The closer she got to her mother's apartment, the louder she could hear that warm tinkling sound that she had heard in her dream. Soon she was standing outside the dirty wooden door with the number 72 glaring back at her through a glaze of dirt.

Her stomach flipped nervously when she realised the door was closed. *Of course it is*, she thought. *How stupid of me to think I would be able to waltz right in!* She took a chance and gave the doorknob a sharp twist, at the same time jolting the door with her left shoulder. Much to her surprise and delight, it creaked and cracked open in a cloud of dust. She stood back and let the dirt settle before she entered.

The apartment was entirely empty. No furniture, no curtains, no anything. Isla wasn't sure why she'd thought she'd find it filled with her mother's things. She'd imagined it would be bursting with character, splashed with green, burgundy and orange, cupboards full of tea bags and hard boiled sweets and the smell of treacle. Her mother had always smelled of treacle. Isla closed her eyes and tried to picture the young Evie she'd only seen in pictures buzzing around these rooms. She smiled, because it was so easy to imagine. She couldn't put her finger on it, but something in the walls and the atmosphere screamed Evie Snow. It was clear that this was where her mother had fitted in.

Standing in the middle of the empty apartment, Isla suddenly realised she had no idea what she was looking for, or if there was anything to look for at all. There was a familiar flutter as Little One flew on to the balcony and perched on the railings. Isla tugged at one of the windows and it put up a good fight, but eventually its hinges cracked and it opened. Before she had a chance to step outside, Little One hopped in.

'No!' Isla panicked that she would be there for hours trying to usher the bird out of the apartment. She wouldn't be able to lock him in and leave him for someone else to deal with, because she wasn't sure there was anyone left to care for this building. August had grown

248

so attached to the bird, she'd never be forgiven if she let something happen to him.

However, Little One wasn't panicked. He was calm and quiet as he paced the floor, waddling to and fro until he finally settled on a single floorboard, which he tapped with his beak three times. Isla tilted her head, confused. Little One pecked three times again, this time harder. Isla knelt down by the bird, who hopped off the board, and with her heart racing, eased the plank of wood up quite easily with her nails. Underneath was a dark hole, deeper than she'd imagined. She had uncharacteristic thoughts of reaching in and monsters grabbing her wrists and pulling her under, never to be seen again. She shook her head. Then an even worse thought struck her: *what if she reached in and found nothing at all?* It was more like Isla to be scared of reality than the unknown.

She looked at the bird, who was perched on the very edge, stretching out his neck to peer into the hole. 'Here we go,' she whispered, and lowered her right hand into the darkness.

She was almost shoulder-deep before her fingertips tapped against something solid. She jumped at the sudden feeling and retracted her arm instinctively. Then, laughing at herself and her silliness, she rolled up the sleeves of her jumper and plunged both arms in, grabbing whatever it was she had felt and bringing it into the light. What she found herself looking at was a very ordinary brown shoebox. It hadn't been sealed shut and it was covered with an inch of dust, but, amazingly, it hadn't been chewed to pieces by mice or termites. Isla blew on the lid like she was blowing out birthday candles, and Little One covered his head with his wings as dust billowed into the air around him.

'Oh, sorry!' she said, wafting the air around the dove with her hand. Little One cooed his acceptance of her apology and ruffled his feathers.

Isla shook the box lightly and was greeted with that tinkling sound again. Curiosity washed over her. She couldn't wait any longer. She flipped the lid open with her thumbs, and immediately her face was lit up by hundreds of slivers of glass catching the light from the windows and casting rainbows here, there and everywhere. She laughed, but it caught in her throat underneath a lump of emotion.

'It's like my dream,' she managed to say, although she still wasn't entirely sure what she was looking at. It was just a box of broken glass. There was no paper or drawings, and nothing that said this box had once belonged to her mother. For all she knew, this was simply a drinking glass that someone had once broken. But then why would it have been saved at all, let alone hidden away from the world under a loose floorboard? So many questions hummed in her head, and yet she still felt relieved that she'd found *something*, even though she wasn't entirely certain what that something was.

Isla closed the lid and all the light was sucked from the room once more, then with Little One close by, she left Apartment 72.

11

the greatest artist who ever lived

Isla refused to show August the box and its contents until she'd figured out the puzzle. She carefully tipped the glass on to a blanket on the floor of her bedroom and, with her gardening gloves on, tried to piece the glass together, but there were just too many shards. Some weren't pieces at all but more like ground-up glass dust that was no use at all. Some slivers fitted together perfectly and Isla would vocally triumph, causing August, Jim and Eddie to jump somewhere in the house and wonder what on earth she was up to. However, most pieces had cracked so badly and had edges so jagged that there was no guessing where they slotted in.

After hours of toiling and a few cuts despite the gloves,

Isla gave up trying to create that crystal-clear sheet of glass she still had glimmering in her mind. Carefully she poured the glass from blanket to box, then reluctantly closed it and pushed it under her bed out of sight. She pulled her legs towards her chest and hugged her knees tightly, fighting back tears of defeat.

No, she thought. *I'm not giving up. Mum wanted me to find that box for a reason, and if I can't create that impossible sheet of glass, I'll just have to make something else.*

With renewed determination she pulled the box out once more, then went to the desk. She quickly set aside all of her old, useless trinkets and rooted through cupboards and drawers, trying to find her old green box of tools and art and craft supplies. At last, two shoeboxes sat on the table: the fifty-five-year-old brown box from Apartment 72, and a thirty-six-year-old bright green box that had once contained a pair of school shoes Isla had worn when she was eleven. Isla opened her own box and in it were ribbons, string, glitter, sequins and buttons, and there at the bottom, neatly folded away, a drawing of Horace, his waistcoat neatly buttoned and his monocle in place. Isla waited for his ears to prick but they never did. She flattened out the piece of paper, smoothing its creases, then propped it against the wall so that Horace could watch her as she set to work.

She sorted out the pieces of glass that were useless and the pieces that were large enough to do something with.

She sanded the edges of each shard, taking away their ability to hurt or harm those who came into contact with them. She drilled a hole in the tip of each, being careful not to shatter them into further tiny pieces, then threaded a length of string through each hole and tied a secure knot. She fished out an old cross-stitch hoop from her box and tied the other end of each piece of string to it. All the while, Horace watched her, and Isla often glanced up, wondering if he'd been moving about the page when she hadn't been looking.

Finally, when the moon was almost saying its good-byes, she took out a piece of ribbon and tied both ends to either side of the wooden hoop so it could hang. She held it up to survey her hard work, the pieces of glass swaying happily, and Isla was happy too, so happy that she hung it from the handle of her bedroom window so that each piece would catch the light in the morning.

All of a sudden she felt exhausted, and she let tiredness take over. She hadn't realised how hard and for how long she'd pored over that glass. Her hands ached from hand-ling the sharp shards and sanding them down, and her neck was sore from craning over them, and for a second time that week, she fell asleep in her clothes.

The following morning, the sun had indeed flooded Isla's room through her window and caught the sun-catcher she had put together. But it wasn't patterns of light dancing around the walls that she could see. What she saw made her rub her eyes like a child.

'August!' she called. 'Come quickly!'

Like a gun from a bullet, August heard her cry from the kitchen and bolted up the stairs, taking them two at a time, believing his sister was in danger. However, when he rushed through her bedroom door, he was greeted not by trouble, but by a drawing of Horace, alive and running about the walls. A goose waddled across the ceiling, flapping its beak and its wings. A happy couple waltzed clumsily with each other. A little boy threw his hat into the air and then fired his pistols at it. After fifty-five years trapped in a shoebox, the drawings had found their way through the glass into the room and were celebrating their freedom at last.

Evie's children stood dumbfounded, tears spilling down their cheeks.

'Mum was an artist,' Isla sobbed.

'She was,' said a voice from the door. As Jim watched, the waltzing couple spotted him and waved, to which he doffed an imaginary cap and smiled.

'Why did she never tell me?' Isla asked, running her fingers up the wall for Horace to chase.

'There were lots of things she never told anyone, things that were all connected. If she told you one thing, she would have had to tell you them all, and she just . . . couldn't. That's why, when you showed not only an interest in art but a talent, she was terrified of sharing her own passion for it, just in case you asked questions. She hated keeping things from you, but now it seems she feels you need to know.' Jim looked upwards, as if gesturing to Evie, wherever she was.

Isla walked over to the drawing of Horace she'd found the night before in her own shoebox. She felt the eleven-year-old inside her rise to the surface as she asked, 'So she didn't think my drawings were awful?'

'Oh Isla. Is that what you thought?' August went to his sister and put his arm around her shoulders as she nodded tearfully.

'Isla,' Jim said, 'she saw herself in your drawings. You took after her so much in that respect.'

'That's good to know. Because to me,' Isla sniffed and smiled, looking up at the Horace that was watching her from across the room, 'she was the greatest artist who ever lived.'

Evie had been lying on the floor of the basement for what felt like years. The journeys through the wall had taken their toll. She wondered why she felt so exhausted when she wasn't even alive any more, but she was too drained to ask. She simply lay there, letting the hum of the wall comfort and warm her until, when she'd almost given up hope, she was aware of that feeling once more. It started in her nose, like she was about to sneeze, and spread down her throat and through her chest. She didn't move from where she lay, but Lieffe sensed the difference.

'Evie, is it happening?' he asked, and she nodded fever-ishly, her eyes shut tight. Something started to rattle and clang in her chest, ten times harder than before, and she had to use all her strength to keep herself clamped to the floor. She thought it might never stop and was about to cry out for help when all at once it disappeared, leaving her whole body tingling.

'Well . . . ?' asked Lieffe, wondering if she was still conscious.

Evie wiped the sweat from her brow. 'If these get pro-gressively worse with each journey through the wall,' she said, 'then I dread what's coming next.'

12

the final journey

Evie sat and told Lieffe all about her children. Lieffe had left the world before August and Isla were born, and she truly wished they had had the chance to meet.

'Isla is stubborn and very clever,' she said affectionately.

'A deadly combination,' Lieffe laughed.

'And doesn't her brother know it! August, bless him, was terrified of her growing up. August is creative. Unlike anything you've ever seen. The way his fingers move across a piano and the melodies he just plucks out of the air . . . he's astounding.' Evie's eyes had glazed over, but it wasn't her son she was thinking of now. Someone else had entered her mind. A brilliant musician she'd once known who would have been proud of the son she'd had and the man he'd grown up to be.

'Evie,' Lieffe said gently, breaking her out of her trance.

'Yes?'

'Is it time to get the sweets?' He smiled.

'Yes, Lieffe,' she said. 'It's time to get the sweets.'

Evie had been nervous about seeing her son and daughter, but there was nothing she could do to prepare for the next trip through the wall.

'Is Vincent still ... y'know?' Lieffe interrupted her thoughts.

'What?' Evie asked, confused.

'Alive?' Lieffe whispered.

Evie was pulling on her green coat. She dropped her hands by her sides, completely flabbergasted. 'I have absolutely no idea. I hadn't even thought of that. How had I not thought of that?'

'Maybe you've just been hoping for the best. If he's somewhere in *this* world, the wall won't do anything. I've seen it happen before. There are ways of seeking him out here, though, don't worry.'

To think that Vincent might have passed away before her without her knowing, and to think that he could be much closer than she'd initially imagined ... Evie experienced just about every feeling before she decided to settle on nausea.

'I hope that wherever he is, he's happy,' she said.

'Me too.' Lieffe smiled kindly. Although he hadn't really got to know Vincent like he knew Evie, he knew Vincent had been a nice man. He had seen how happy

Evie had become when Vincent had waltzed into her life. He'd hear her humming from two floors away, before she stepped out of the lift, and her hugs were warmer than they'd ever been.

Lieffe didn't have to know Vincent any better to know that he was a good man because he knew Evie.

Evie grabbed a handful of the sweets from the Lost Box and stuffed her pockets full.

'I think just the one will be enough,' Lieffe said, looking at the shiny wrappers spilling out of her coat.

'I think so too. The rest are for me,' she said, smiling. She plucked one out and laid it in her palm. 'It's so small. So simple.' She held it up to the dim lighting. 'A handful of these was what brought me closer to the only man I ever loved. They were the start of everything,' she said, marvelling at the huge significance of something so small.

'Some would say they were to blame!' Lieffe said. 'There are people who would never touch a hard boiled sweet again after going through what you went through.'

Lieffe moved the desk chair into the centre of the room so he could watch the entertainment unfold.

'Yes, it was horrible, and yes, I spent my whole life hiding it.' Evie unwrapped the sweet and popped it into her mouth. 'But that doesn't mean I'd change a moment of it. Not for the world.'

'Why not?' Lieffe asked, sitting himself down in the desk chair with a groan.

Evie smiled, remembering a similar conversation many

years ago. She pushed the sweet into her cheek and began to explain. 'Because if none of that had happened, I might have grown into a very different person. If I'd got everything I'd ever wanted in life, I might have become a spoiled brat. If I'd never bothered to pursue that dream of being an artist, if I'd never stood up to my mother, I might never have known what being in love with someone really felt like, because I never would have met Vincent. Yes, that dream ultimately failed, but I learned so much. Mostly tiny things, but it only takes a spark to light a fire. All those tiny things accumulated to make me who I am. If none of it had happened, I could have lived a far worse life than I did. That's why, despite all the heartbreak, the failure and the secrets, if I was given the chance to go back in time and change things, I wouldn't. Not even a second.'

Lieffe looked at her. When she was alive, she had been a singular person who'd had all this fire in her and nowhere for it to go. She'd pushed against boundaries and fought against people who told her no, but to no avail. For most people, that would have been the end; they would have given up and turned back the way they'd come. Some might even have become bitter, feeling like the universe owed them and begrudging those who did succeed, but not Evie. She'd lost the battle, but her war was won when she became the mother her children needed. When she allowed them to grow into the people they wanted to be. And most of all when she accepted the hand she was dealt

260

and made the absolute best of it. Part of Lieffe wished he could go back in time and change her past for her so she could have become everything she'd ever wanted to be, but he was also very glad that what had happened had resulted in the woman standing in front of him now, because he thought she was simply brilliant.

'Are you ready for this?' he asked, meshing his fingers together and sitting back in the chair.

'Ready as I'll ever be, which isn't very, but it'll do.'

Evie took the orange sweet out of her mouth. It was warm and sticky, so before it had a chance to dry out, she stuck it to the centre of the wall with a firm push. The humming stopped abruptly. She was expecting the sweet to disappear, or for the wall to turn into something that represented her long-lost love, but it remained the same plain yellowing surface with its jagged wallpaper around the edges. *Please be alive*, she chanted over and over in her head.

'Did I break it?' she asked, unwilling to take her eyes off it, just in case.

'I'm not sure.' Lieffe sat forward. 'Usually it only takes a couple of seconds before it—'

'Shh!' Evie hushed him suddenly. 'Can you hear that?' She pressed her ear to the wall, careful not to disturb the sweet. It was faint, but unmistakably there. 'He's playing. Wherever he is, he's playing.'

Evie felt relief wash over her. He was alive after all, and surely well if he was playing his violin. The sound gradually grew louder, and she wondered how she had lived so long without it. It made every bone in her body resonate and every nerve-ending fizz. It made her feel alive again.

'He's good.' Lieffe smiled.

'He's extraordinary.'

Evie laid a palm on the wall, but something behind it clunked, and she snatched her hand away as the orange sweet cracked down the middle. She crouched down to inspect the broken sweet closely, but as she did so, the wall followed suit and cracked down its centre too, so that half of the sweet was on either side, like tiny handles on a very large door.

'Step back, Evie,' Lieffe said, knowing the wall's temperamental nature. He'd seen it do a great deal of things, all of them unusual and unexpected.

Evie heeded his advice and moved to the back of the room, watching as each side of the wall slid apart, revealing a dark gap about the size of . . .

'An escalator. That's the sound of an escalator!' she exclaimed. 'Can you hear it?' The sound of the sliding metal stairs was one Evie had become accustomed to during her year of commuting, and she knew that was what they were hearing now.

Lieffe sniffed the breeze that was flowing into the room. 'Can you smell burgers?' he asked, and Evie laughed.

'Yes, I can!' She closed her eyes, remembering that night in the station and how perfect and uncomplicated

262

it had been. When she opened them again, she saw something pushing through the darkness, getting closer and
closer until the escalator she had heard came into sight.
The moving handrails lined up perfectly with the gap in
the wall, and there on the bottom steps, its pages getting
awfully creased, was a book. Evie rushed to pick it up.
It was the exact copy of the book she'd been reading the
night she'd first heard Vincent.

'I think he's waiting for you,' Lieffe said.

'I've been waiting for him,' Evie replied as she stepped
on to the stairs and they carried her upwards, towards the
sound of Vincent's playing.

the third
secret

the good
tree

7 · 2

24 December

The Wedding

Planning their wedding had been exceptionally easy, as Jim and Evie had left it up to their mothers. The wedding wasn't really for them, after all. The worst was over, and whatever their wedding day had in store for them, they would face it together, hand in hand.

Evie's heart had been weighing heavy in her chest since the day Vincent had left, and every day without him was another day her heart had to bear that burden. At first it had seemed bearable, but she'd not counted on her love growing and growing with nowhere to go, so that her heart just got heavier and heavier as the days went by. Now, sat at a dressing table in the Summers' house, fixing her make-up in the mirror, the idea of Vincent standing at the end of the aisle instead of Jim hit her and made her heart swell near to bursting point. She held on to the edge of the table to steady herself and knocked a pot of brushes to the floor. Eleanor tutted but didn't make a move to help. Instead, Evie composed herself, leaned down and retrieved the brushes, some of which had rolled under the hem of her wedding dress. Eleanor continued to tut.

'You're marrying one of the most handsome men this world has ever seen, your wedding dress has been designed by one of the greats, everything's been paid for by James's father and you're *still* miserable. What on earth do we have to do to make you happy?'

Evie tolerated Eleanor's attempts to make her feel ungrateful. It only reminded her of just how grateful she was that things could indeed have been far worse but Evie knew deep down that that didn't mean she had no reason to be sad.

'I'm grateful for everything I have, Mother, I truly am, but that's not to say everything I have is what I desire. You *know* I'd give everything up if it meant I could have just one more chance at being who I want to be.' She wasn't trying to convince her mother; she simply wished Eleanor understood, but when she glimpsed the disgusted look on the older woman's face, she wasn't sure why she bothered explaining at all.

'Then why did you agree to all of this? You could be out there now, living in your own filth with that hooligan, without any money, trying to fulfil those silly dreams of yours. Tell me, why ever did you give it up if it was all so glorious?'

'Firstly, you didn't give me much of a choice. Secondly ...' Evie glanced out of the window. Eddie was laughing with Jim over champagne on the lawn, while the other guests milled about in their fur coats and finery under the holly-clad marquee. Eddie looked excited. He was on the brink of a huge change in his life, and Evie couldn't have been happier that she was able to give him that chance. 'Actually, there is no secondly. You never gave me a choice.' She looked her mother in the eye.

'You had a year.' Eleanor brushed down her lilac dress, not impressed with where this conversation was headed. 'Be grateful for that.'

'Yes. I had a year. A whole wonderful year to see the life I'd been missing out on and the life I could have had.' Evie stood up. Eleanor had told her that if she wasn't so plump she might have looked beautiful, but looking sweet would have to do. The cut of the dress made her bust look phenomenal, and a jewelled band cinched in her waist so that the Cinderella-esque skirt appeared even fuller. She reached behind her head and pulled the veil over her face, but her stare didn't falter when she said, 'If only I'd had a mother and not a jailer.'

A few minutes before the wedding, just after Eleanor had stormed out of the Summers' living room, which Jane Summer had kindly dubbed 'the bridal suite' for the day, Eddie came to check on his sister.

'Oh Evie,' he gasped. 'You look ... incredible.' He rushed to take her hands, but dared not hug her in case he crumpled the fabric or stood on the hem.

'Eddie, just the person I need,' Evie said, wincing as her heart gained yet more weight and swayed in her chest.

'What is it?' he asked, sensing that all was not right.

'I need you to tell Jim just to wait another ...' she checked the clock on the wall, 'fifteen minutes before getting everyone seated.'

'Of course. But why?'

Evie was already gathering up her huge dress and attempting to run towards the door in her stupid white heels with her stupid heavy heart. 'Jim will understand.' And with an apologetic look, she was gone.

Evie ran out through the front door, astoundingly undetected. As the minutes had tick-tocked closer to the pivotal point of the day, the guests had filtered through the house to the garden, where white seats had been placed in neat rows, an archway of roses stood at the end of a perfectly straight aisle, and champagne and canapés were seemingly unlimited. It was far too cold for an outdoor wedding, but Eleanor, who wanted to ensure Evie didn't have enough time to change her mind, had insisted that it happen as soon as possible, and the short notice meant the venue had to be the Summers' house, since all the churches had been booked up months in advance.

She ran to her own house, which was only a short distance away through a small wood that separated the Snow acres from the Summer acres. She was a pure white cloud against the iced green and she moved with great speed and determination, despite her heels sinking into the ground every few steps and her heart thudding up and down with all its weight. When she reached the house, though, she realised with horror that she had no key. It was then, through the frosted window, that she saw a flash of red. Evie wondered if their house had been broken into but then remembered there had recently been a new addition to the Snows' staff.

'Clementine? Clementine!' She could see her breath in front of her, reaching out to the floating red ball that grew gradually larger as Clementine Frost rushed to the door.

'Whatever is the matter?' the girl asked underneath the safety chain stretched across the gap. Her voice was sing-song and sweet, her face round and unspeakably kind. Evie could see why Eddie had taken a shine to her.

'I'm Evie Snow, Eleanor and Edward's daughter. I'm getting married today and I'm afraid I've ... er ... left something here that I desperately need. Can I come in?'

Clementine was already closing the door to unlatch the chain and she welcomed Evie in immediately. 'How did you escape unseen?' she asked, leaning out of the door to check that no one had followed.

'Escape?' Evie laughed hysterically, her heart still racing from the run to the house. 'Whatever do you—'

'I've worked here long enough to know what your mother is like. If she knew you weren't in that house doing everything she said, she'd most likely have your head on a spike.'

'You're wrong,' Evie said. 'She'd *definitely* have my head on a spike!' They laughed, and their laughter partially warmed the icy air of the house.

'I'm Clementine.' She held out a dainty hand for Evie to shake, but instead Evie gently embraced her, careful not to suffocate her with reams of white fabric.

'I know. Eddie's told me all about you.'

Clementine grinned. 'Eddie's told me all about you too. Do you want a cup of tea? Some water? Anything to eat?' She was already in the kitchen, opening drawers and cupboards, searching for something to offer.

'No, no, honestly, I'm fine. I won't be more than five minutes. If I'm gone any longer, I won't be able to get married because my mother will have murdered me.' Evie squeezed her dress through the kitchen, not taking any care to make sure it didn't snag, and opened the back door. 'Oh, and Clementine.' She looked back over her shoulder, unable to turn around completely because of her full skirt. 'If I get caught, I'll tell Mother I snuck in through the back without you seeing. OK?'

Clementine sighed in relief. 'You've done this before.' It was a statement, not a question. She gave Evie an amused raise of her eyebrow and folded her arms, impressed.

'With a mother like Eleanor? Of course I have!'

Clementine unhooked a piece of fabric from a kitchen drawer and said, 'Thank you.'

'Oh don't be silly. Unfortunately, lying to my mother has become terribly necessary if I ever want to be some kind of happy,' Evie admitted.

'I'm sure! But actually,' Clementine found Evie's hand and squeezed it, 'I meant for not being like her.'

Evie hobbled through the back door, down the steps of the porch and to the end of the garden. Nothing ever grew there. Her mother thought flowers were frivolous, and trees blocked out the sunlight, so the large garden was simply surrounded by one long, plain, boring hedge. She knelt down halfway along the hedge at the very foot of the garden, careful to lift her dress so that only her white tights got dirty. No one would see them. She snapped off a twig from the hedge and started to dig through the soil, creating a hole about the size of a bowling ball. Her hands shook as she set the twig down, and she took a few deep, cold breaths to steady herself. Then carefully she pressed her hands to her ribcage and gave a sharp push. Something clicked within her, and as she pulled her hands away, her chest opened up like a cabinet. Her ribcage parted like two doors, revealing a large, glowing heart that radiated so much warmth that the frost started to melt on the leaves in front of her and Evie's nose and cheeks turned rosy.

Evie had never seen her heart before. It was red and

shimmering, flecked with dots of black from every time she'd lied, cheated or been knowingly bad. But there were flecks of gold, too, from each time she'd been there for someone in need, when she'd done something selfless or tried her hardest to be the best version of herself. The colours of her heart represented the deeds she'd done, both good and bad, but the faint smell of treacle told her that overall, she had a sweet heart.

Gently she reached into her chest with one hand and wrapped her fingers around her heart as best she could, but her palm was too small to encompass it. She sucked in a breath, watching her lungs expand, then gave a twist and a tug. It came out in one go, and she held it in her cupped hands. It glowed harder in protest, and its colours swirled worriedly.

'Shh,' she hushed. 'Everything's going to be OK.'

The heart thumped louder, and one of Evie's tears splashed on to its red surface. 'I can't give you to the man I love and yet I can't give you to the man I'm marrying either. I won't give you to someone just because I'm told to. You deserve more than that.' She stroked the almost-glassy surface with her thumbs in smooth circles. 'So I won't give you to anyone at all. You deserve to have the chance I will never have. The chance to be anything you want to be.'

As she placed her still-beating heart in the hole she'd dug, there on its surface another golden fleck swirled into existence. It was then that she knew she was doing the

274

right thing. Keeping her own heart when she'd already decided who it belonged to felt wrong, as if she was holding stolen possessions. No. Her heart was no longer hers, couldn't be Vincent's, and sadly, was never to be Jim's. So quickly, she pulled the mounds of soil she'd dug out back into the hole on top of her still-beating heart. When she ran a hand over the dirt to smooth it and make it look undisturbed, she could feel a warm patch where her heart lay. She hoped no one would notice that and go digging.

She closed the doors of her empty chest, and while she felt hollow, she also felt complete. Her heart had rattled around its cage for too long, yearning to be with the man it belonged to. Now it had a permanent home where it would be safe and well looked after, without any danger of falling into the wrong hands.

Evie walked down the aisle towards Jim, arm in arm with her father. Edward Snow had barely looked at her since she was a toddler, and he didn't make a special effort for her wedding day either, nor did Evie expect him to. She smiled, said her vows, they exchanged rings, and when the vicar gave the order, Evie kissed Jim for the first time, sealing their fate for good. Jim let her kiss him for as long as she felt necessary and made no sudden movements, unsure of how she was feeling. The last thing he wanted was to cause even more unnecessary hurt on her wedding day. As they walked back down the aisle, Jim squeezed her hand all the way, but it was only once they had their first dance as husband and wife that they had the chance to talk.

'You didn't kiss me back,' Evie said, a little wounded.

'No. I wasn't sure how you were feeling. I . . . I'm worried about you.' He held her closer to him as they slowly twirled around the floor of the warmly lit marquee with their family and friends watching.

'Does it seem like you need to be?' Evie looked up at him, the weight in her chest, now buried, leaving her feeling lighter.

Jim moved her away from him, taking her by the hand and spinning her under his arm, just the once. 'You do seem surprisingly OK.' He held her close again, careful not to push the boundaries.

'We still have a life to lead. Either I lust after the life I want, knowing full well I can't have it, or I get on with the one I have and make the most of it.' Evie shrugged and rested her head on Jim's shoulder. 'It doesn't mean it will always be easy. There will be times when it gets hard for both of us because of what's happened, but we're very lucky we've got each other.'

'I feel lucky,' he squeezed her, 'but I also feel bad.'

Evie lifted her head to look at him. 'None of what has happened is your fault, Jim. Just because you married the girl you love and got your way in some shape or form does not make you the bad guy. It just means you got away with fewer cuts and bruises than the rest of us, but you still got your fair share of hurt.' She stroked his cheek, wishing she could take that worry out of his eyes and bury it along with her heart for good.

'I feel bad for all of us. Especially . . . ' Jim dared not say his name, but Evie knew who he meant.

'He understood why this had to happen. He'll manage. We all will.'

Jim let Evie's eyes calm his thoughts, then he nodded.

'Now, how about that kiss?' Evie asked. 'We are husband and wife after all. Our friends might start getting suspicious.' She smiled, and Jim's stomach flipped as he wondered how many times he'd imagined her asking him to kiss her. Gently he moved a fluffy caramel curl of hair that had caught in her eyelashes, then he tilted her chin upwards with his finger and kissed her with all the love he had.

Evie and Jim didn't have a honeymoon. They didn't feel it was necessary or appropriate. Instead, they found a house near the sea, as far away from their parents as possible, and packed their bags, ready to move in on New Year's Day. The house had four bedrooms. One for them, one for guests, one for any potential children and one for a certain someone who they had promised not to leave behind.

'Do you want me to come in with you?' Evie and her brother stood outside the door to the living room in their parents' house. As Evie squeezed Eddie's hand, she could feel his heartbeat in the ends of his fingertips. 'Eddie, you're shaking. Don't do this alone.'

'No. No, I can't tell you how ready I am for this. I'm not scared. I know things will be OK no matter what they say. Thanks to you.' Eddie hugged his big sister for the millionth time since the wedding. Evie didn't think he knew the extent of what she had given up for him, but he wasn't stupid, and even just the inkling he had that Evie agreeing to marry Jim had something to do with him made him thank her every moment he could. Suddenly the boy who had once shied away from affection now embraced his beloved sister numerous times each day.

'And now I can start the new year as who *I* want to be. Here goes!' Eddie grinned.

'I'll be waiting right here.' Evie pointed at her feet and stood very still, assuring him that she wouldn't move from that spot until she saw him again.

Eddie pushed the door open. 'Mother, Father. May I have a word?' he said and stepped inside.

Evie felt like every second was a year and she'd be old and grey by the time she saw her brother once more. *He's been in there far too long*, she thought. All her worries were about to come to a head when the door opened and Eddie reappeared, completely unharmed.

'What happened? What did they say?'

Eddie grabbed her by the arm and started to push her towards the front door, rather forcefully.

'What's going on, Eddie? Didn't you tell them?'

'Of course . . . well . . . sort of. They don't know yet.' He spoke quickly, his cheeks red and hot.

'You couldn't do it?' Evie felt disappointed, but she knew she couldn't push him to do it if he wasn't ready.

'No, no, I could! I just—' Before Eddie could continue, their mother let out a scream from the living room that shook the very foundations of the house.

'I gave us a head start,' he said.

The door burst open and there stood their father, his face puce, the veins on his neck close to bursting. In his sweaty hand was a crumpled piece of paper, which he balled up and threw at Eddie. He missed, and Evie caught it in the crook of her arm. She quickly unfolded it and read:

Mother and Father,

I like men so I'll be moving out. Maybe one day you'll be decent human beings and accept me as I am, but until then, fuck you.

Eddie

Evie was sure that Eleanor's sobbing and wailing could be heard for miles, but the noise was rivalled by Edward Snow's pounding footsteps as he charged towards them.

'*Go!*' Eddie pushed Evie out of the front door, following

close behind. They ran straight into Jim, who had come to collect them to drive them to the new house. '*Car!*' they both screeched at him. 'Get in the car!'

Jim panicked, and slipped down the front steps, but the Snow siblings picked him up and thrust him towards the vehicle piled high with their belongings. Evie clambered into the back of the car with the boxes, and Jim started the engine before Eddie had even closed his door. For most of the way down the drive, Eddie was hanging out of the passenger seat, dangerously close to slipping out onto the road.

Evie thought it couldn't have gone any worse, but when at last Eddie got a grip on the handle and slammed the door shut, he yelled for joy, hit the dashboard with his fists in celebration and laughed all the way home.

Ten Years Later

A Surprise Awaits

James Summer Senior passed away just after Isla was born. Jim was sad that his father never got to meet her, but he was also glad that Isla wouldn't have to grow up in the shadow of such a cold and unloving man. Evie's father passed away three years later, and only a few months after that, Eleanor joined him, wherever he was. Jim and Evie attended the funerals, but few tears were shed by anyone. Evie would miss her parents, as any daughter would, but her world became far less complicated now that they were gone.

When August was ten years old and Isla five, Evie and Jim felt it was time to sell their house by the sea and move back to look after Jim's mother, Jane. The Snows' house had been left to Evie in her parents' will, but she refused to go back to a place that had been more of a cage to her than a home. She handed the keys over to Eddie, who was overwhelmed by the thought of having his own place to share with the love of his life.

Oliver Hart was a humble boy who had grown up in the seaside town they'd moved to and worked in a café on the promenade. Eddie had gone in there mainly because he kept being given free coffee, but when Evie accompanied him one day and pointed out who was responsible for the generous gesture, Eddie couldn't catch his breath. Oliver was full-faced, partial to chunky knitwear, and cut his own hair as well as his father's, making them look oddly alike. Eddie had enjoyed meeting new people who shared his interests, not just in men but in every aspect of his life that he'd never been allowed to explore before now. He'd dated various guys whom Evie had loved, thinking her brother's taste in men wasn't unlike her own. Evie had wondered aloud what was wrong with each guy every time Eddie announced they'd parted ways and he'd just reply 'when you know, you just know'. This time, Eddie knew. Oliver was the man for him and Oliver seemed to feel the same about Eddie. Their relationship developed without any complications which couldn't have pleased Evie more. Even Oliver's dad was accepting of their relationship.

Although Evie refused to live in the Snows' old house, there was still something she was curious to see, so she agreed to go with Eddie to look at the place before he and Oliver moved in. As they drove up the driveway, her questions were answered.

'What is *that*?' Eddie asked.

They all bent their heads to look through the windscreen. Behind the house they could see a huge tree with dozens of long and twisted branches.

'Beats me,' Evie said with a knowing smile that caught Jim's attention as he pulled on the handbrake. 'Right, kids! Wanna see where Mummy and Uncle Eddie grew up?'

Isla cheered; August, humming and tapping out melodies with his fingers on his knee, missed the second half of the sentence but followed his Uncle Eddie anyway. Eddie ran up the steps, excited to open the door with the keys for the first time since the house had become his. He fist-pumped the air with both hands and fake-cheered at Jim and Evie, who were watching from the car. Then he picked up Isla and took August by the hand, and started telling them ridiculous made-up stories about his childhood.

'All right, what's going on, you?' Jim asked, once Eddie and the children had disappeared into the house.

'I don't know what you're talking about.' Evie couldn't look him in the eye, but she also couldn't keep the smile off her face.

'I know that smile. It's the "Evie knows something no one else does" smile, and it drives me mad!' He laughed, only half joking.

'I'll tell you later. You're going to need to look for yourself first.' She got out of the car, but not before she'd poked her tongue out at him.

Evie couldn't contain herself. She ran straight through the house, unlatched the back door and dashed out into the garden. At the end of the lawn, pushing through the centre of the plain, boring hedge that bordered the garden, was a tree that stood a good ten feet taller than the house. It was dark brown, with a strange orange sheen to its bark. There were a few leaves on its branches, yet none on the ground beneath it. Evie wondered if it would ever bloom. She couldn't wait to see how it would look, or what would grow on it, if anything.

'Can it really be?' she asked out loud. When she touched the tree's trunk, she could feel the warmth radiating from every crack in its bark, and the unmistakable beat of her own heart pulsed faintly underneath her palm. The tree's branches shuddered, knowing that its owner had finally returned.

'What kind of tree is that?' August called from the centre of the lawn, his fingers still playing mindless melodies by his sides. Jim stood behind their son, watching Evie being welcomed home.

'A special one, no doubt,' he said, and he smiled at his wife, still trying to figure her out.

'It's average, at best,' she shrugged, 'but it's good. It's a good tree.'

August tilted his head at the strange interaction between

his parents. 'It's just a tree,' he said, furrowing his brow and squinting up at the highest branches.

'It's not *just* anything! Some might say you're *just* a child, but *are* you?' Evie ran to him, picked him up and tickled him.

'No!' he laughed.

'What are you, then?' she asked, setting him down on his feet and kneeling in front of him, not caring that the grassy dew was soaking into her tights. She looked him square in the eyes, pretending to be menacing.

'Anything I want to be,' he said, reciting back with a nod what Evie had told him a million times.

'Exactly. Well, I once told this tree it could be anything it wanted to be, and it decided to be good.' Evie pressed his nose once with her finger.

'OK,' August said, understanding. 'It's a good tree.'

'I think it's *the* Good Tree,' Jim said. 'Probably one of a kind.' He, like his son, was beginning to understand. Thunder rumbled in the distance. 'Let's get inside before that reaches us.' He pointed to the angry clouds looming closer in the sky.

'Awww, but I like rain!' August moaned as Jim ushered him towards the back door.

'You're so much like your mother.' Jim rolled his eyes affectionately towards Evie, who glanced back at the tree one last time before joining her family indoors.

Oliver joined Eddie at the house later that day, and Evie and Jim left them to their first night officially living together and drove the almost pointlessly short distance to Jim's mother's house, which was to be their new home.

As soon as Jim stepped inside, he stopped short in the hallway and gazed around in disbelief. 'Why are the walls . . . blue?' Jim was so used to the house being dull and grey, full of stuffed and mounted animal heads from his father's hunting trips. Now the walls were wallpapered in a pleasant blue dotted with violets, and Jane Summer rushed towards them in a bright pink silk trouser suit and startled them all.

'I needed a change. I also needed a life, so I went out and got one. No more being held back. Oh, I can't believe how good it is to see you!' She flung her arms around her son and then the rest of the family in turn. Isla and August loved the attention, but Evie and Jim were stunned.

'Mother . . . what on earth has happened?'

Jane stood between the children, covered their outside ears with her hands and pressed their other ears against her body so they couldn't hear her say, 'Your father died. That's what happened. I loved him, I truly did, but I spent the best part of my life doing everything for him and putting my own life on hold. No more!' she said with a flourish and let the children go, not realising they had, in fact, heard every word. They ran off into the house, giggling at mad Grandma Jane.

'Mother, I . . . I . . . '

286

Jane braced herself for her son's opinion.

'I couldn't be happier for you!'

'Me too!' Evie said, embracing her for a second time, loving the idea that Jane might now be more of a mother figure to her, and a proper grandmother to the children.

Jane wiped away a tear. 'Well, what are you waiting for? Come in and see what I've done to the rest of the house!'

They emptied the car and the van, chose whose room was whose and fell asleep quite quickly due to the long drive, the exertion of lifting all the heavy boxes and trying to explain to a tired, sulking Isla why August should have the bigger room. Thunder rumbled through the night and rain pounded the roof and Isla dreamed of lots of tiny people knocking on the roof to come in and make friends.

The following morning, Evie came downstairs to find Eddie and Oliver in the kitchen chatting away to Jane, who was laughing hysterically at Oliver's jokes.

'Morning, all. Everything OK here?' Evie asked, mainly directing the question at Eddie, wondering how Jane was taking to the couple standing in her kitchen – or if, indeed, she even realised they were gay.

'Everything's fine, dear. It was Jim's father who had the old-fashioned take on life, not me!' Jane grinned and touched Oliver's arm in a way that seemed more flirty than accepting, but as long as she wasn't screaming the house down like her own mother had, Evie was happy.

'I baked a pie this morning.' Eddie pushed a dish towards her, and the smell that wafted up from it had Evie's stomach growling. 'Oooh! Best brother ever!'

Jane handed her a knife. Evie cut herself a large slice, and as soon as the first forkful touched her lips, she knew something was odd. She kept chewing, not sure what flavour she was tasting or what fruit was in the filling.

'What kind of pie is this?' she said with her mouth full.

'We have absolutely no idea,' Oliver said, backing imperceptibly away from Jane, who wouldn't take her eyes off him.

'What?' Evie said, setting the plate down, no longer trusting what she was swallowing. 'I thought you baked it?'

'We did,' Evie said. 'But we got the fruit from that weird tree at the end of our garden. We looked it up and couldn't find anything like it. We thought maybe cooking it might be better than just trying it on its own, so we baked it into a pie. What's it like?'

'OK, firstly, are you trying to kill me? What if it's poisonous?'

Oliver glanced at Eddie. 'Whoops,' Eddie said apologetically. 'We didn't think of that. Are you feeling OK?'

'I think I'm fine. I *think*. If I collapse, you'll know why. Secondly, haven't you tried it yourselves?'

Eddie shook his head. 'I thought we could all try it together.'

288

'Convenient that you made me go first.' Evie pushed the pie dish towards them and took another, smaller forkful of her own slice. She dissected and inspected it, not really seeing much wrong with the fruit inside. It was a nice ripe orange colour and didn't appear to be bad or mouldy. It just tasted unlike anything she'd ever eaten before but she knew she'd finish the slice without an issue. Evie watched as Eddie took his own big mouthful, but the moment his taste buds got a load of its flavour, he spat it into the sink behind him with an exclamation of disgust.

'Holy smokes! Evie! I'm so sorry! Don't eat any more. That's the foulest thing I've ever had.' He was already carrying the pie dish over to the bin when Oliver stopped him.

'I gotta try this!' Oliver took a piece of the fruit out of the open side of the pie with his fingers and popped it into his mouth. Evie hoped he'd like it, but he pulled the same faces and made the same noises as Eddie. He persevered through the taste and swallowed but could barely ask for a glass of water afterwards. Jane tried it too, and daintily spat her piece out into a tissue, trying not to offend Eddie and Oliver. One by one the whole family tasted the pie, and it seemed the only one who didn't find its flavour completely repulsive was Evie.

'Hang on,' Jim said. 'That tree was entirely bare yesterday. Are you sure this fruit came from that tree in particular?'

'There's only one tree in the garden, but come and see for yourselves!' Eddie said.

Together, one Hart, one Snow and five Summers headed to Eddie's garden, and through its few green leaves, they could see it was indeed completely covered in the strange fruit.

'See?' Eddie said, pointing up to the highest branches.

'How odd,' Evie said. 'It must have liked the thunderstorm.' She smiled, picking up an oval orange fruit from the ground.

It fitted perfectly within the palm of her hand. It was where it belonged.

Over the next few months, they all kept a watchful eye on the tree. They soon realised that it only ever bore fruit when thunder and lightning were ruling the skies. It had no seasonal order. It just loved the rain.

One day, Jim asked, 'I wonder, how would it taste in jam?' He was partial to strawberry jam on his toast in the mornings, but when Eddie tested the theory, it put Jim off toast for weeks. They tried pies and jellies, cakes and cookies, until eventually they gave up and the tree at the end of the garden simply remained the tree at the end of the garden. A tree that was pretty but useless, a tree that produced fruit that made everyone except Evie feel sick.

'Isn't it odd how the tree only grows fruit after a storm,' August said one evening, tapping his fingers on the windowsill as he looked out through the rain. Jim stood beside him, and together they watched tiny orange spots appear on the highest dark brown branches that they could see all the way from their house. One by one the spots would soak up the rain and pop into the form of fruit. August giggled each time a new one burst to life, the popping sound audible from where they stood. Jim, though, knew that the tree was more than it seemed, although what it seemed was really quite extraordinary.

He knew there was something more behind its story.

'The tree likes to make the best out of a bad situation,' Jim answered, looking at his wife who was sat by the fire in the armchair, pretending to read, but she couldn't hide her smirk.

'What do you think, Evie?' Jim asked pointedly.

'Seems that way.' She shrugged without looking up from her book, still smirking.

'August, I think it's time for bed.' The boy was about to run for the stairs, but Jim caught him by the scruff of his pyjama top and pulled him backwards into a hug. 'Good-night, rascal.'

'Love you, Dad,' August whispered.

'Love you too.'

Once his son had scampered up to his room, Jim sat in the armchair opposite his wife. 'That tree,' he said.

'Mmm?' Evie turned a page.

'It seems to be rather . . . familiar.' Jim leaned his elbows on his knees to closely inspect her expression.

'Mmm.' Evie smiled.

'Evie?' he said with concern, and she looked up at him. 'How did you grow it?'

Evie lost her playfulness a little when she thought about explaining her literal lack of a heart, and why she'd buried it in the garden. But she had to tell him. They didn't keep secrets from one another. When she eventually found the words, Jim simply listened and nodded.

'So the tree is so much like you because . . . well, it *is* you,' he said, laughing. He held up a finger. 'But why does the fruit taste so bad?' He stuck out his tongue in disgust. Even the memory caused his taste buds to shudder.

'Now that I can't answer.' Evie frowned.

'You don't know?'

'I don't know,' she confirmed.

'Just one more question.'

Evie nodded, enjoying sharing what she knew.

'Are there any more secrets you're hiding away, in your old house . . . or this one?' Jim's eyes darted about the room, looking for odd artefacts he'd not noticed before that might conceal untold truths, truths that would come teeming out like termites should they be removed from their rightful place.

'None,' Evie said firmly.

'None?' Jim pressed once more, just to be sure.

'None. Now you know them all.'

13

the single greatest adventure

The escalator rattled upwards into an all-consuming darkness that made Evie wonder if she was still conscious or whether she'd slipped into sleep without realising. She stepped forward when it flattened out, but caught her heel and stumbled. A train in the distance sounded its horn in one short burst, then again but this time it seemed much closer to Evie, lost in the dark, until the driver blew the horn so loudly and for so long that Evie was sure she was going to be squashed flat. She balled her fists over her eyes, bracing herself for the excruciating pain that she thought would be inevitable but the sound flew past her. A gust of wind from the train rushing by made her lose her balance, and when she threw her arms out to steady herself, she uncovered her eyes and saw that she was at the station she used to change platforms in when heading home from *The Teller* offices. Not only that, but she was stood opposite Vincent's old busking spot. An old man was playing there now. His violin was black like Vincent's had been, but this man was very obviously in his eighties. He played sitting in a little green canvas fold-out chair, presumably because his legs wouldn't hold him up for as long as he'd want to busk which, judging by the amount of coins in his case, was a long while.

Evie wandered towards the entrance to the platform, but something about the violinist caught her eye. Something that was out of place and yet completely familiar. His eyes were closed as he played a beautiful soft tune, and at his feet was a little silver bowl filled with individually wrapped, hard boiled sweets. Orange ones, to be precise. Propped up next to it was a small handwritten cardboard sign. It read:

> Great adventures can start small.
> Even as small as a sweet.
> Help yourself to an adventure.

Evie read those words over and over until the violinist stopped playing. Then she looked up at him, his violin resting on his lap, and although he seemed an entirely different person, his hair short and grey, his skin leathery

294

and sallow and his weathered hands trembling, those green eyes hadn't changed at all.

'Vincent.'

Vincent Winters packed up his violin and his sweets, folded away his chair and slowly trundled out of the station to make the walk home. The weather wasn't cold, but the pavements were wet from earlier rain, so it took him a long time to get to his house, making sure every step was placed correctly so he wouldn't slip. Evie walked with him, and even though he didn't have a clue she was there, she was glad he wasn't alone.

Together they walked across a bridge to a quaint part of town where the houses were joined together in neat little rows, the fronts painted in various pastel colours. Vincent hobbled up the steps, holding on to the railings with one hand, his violin in the other and his chair under his arm, and Evie wished she could lend a hand with her restored and capable twenty-seven-year-old body. Instead she just watched, helplessly, praying that he didn't fall.

The house was small but clearly worth more than the Vincent she once knew could have afforded. Evie felt proud. He must have done well for himself in the end. She slipped in through the black front door before he closed it, and watched as he took off his coat and hung it on the stand in the hallway. The black coat swung open, revealing its purple silk lining, and Evie smiled.

Vincent steadily trudged into the sitting room so Evie took a moment to look at her surroundings.

The hallway walls were covered in framed photos, mostly of Vincent when he was younger with a woman Evie didn't recognise. She looked small and happy, and she fitted perfectly next to him, like they were jigsaw pieces that slotted satisfyingly together. A pang of jealousy shot through Evie's stomach, but she was glad Vincent hadn't wallowed in their failed relationship, as she so easily could have done herself. He'd moved on and found someone who clearly brought him happiness. The photographs showed adventure after adventure, the pair of them doing extraordinary things against foreign backdrops. In one, they stood either side of a lion, their arms around his thick mane and the lion licking its lips. In another, they were balancing on the wings of an aeroplane, thousands of feet in the air. They stood atop mountains, knee-deep in snow. They held hands on a tightrope above an audience of hundreds. They sat in the lotus position on beds of needles with calm faces.

Each picture was another pang in Evie's gut. It was the life she'd wished she'd led. The life she'd given up for her own security and that of her brother. The life she'd never known.

She turned away from the pictures, unsure of what else this happy house had in store for her, but all the same, she followed Vincent into the sitting room, where he sat down in a large armchair. The room had many shelves, all covered in books, mainly fiction, but next to Vincent's chair, they held sheet music and biographies of great musicians he admired. There was a silver music stand by the front window that looked out onto the street. The stand was set to around the height Vincent was when sitting in his armchair. Evie remembered how her own back used to ache in her seventies when standing for more than a few minutes at a time, and how she'd wished there was something she could do to ease that for him.

She spent the evening sat on the sitting room floor watching Vincent read, yawn, play his violin, yawn, drink a small glass of port, yawn and then finally concede to the idea of going to bed. He seemed so alone, so quiet, and she wondered whether he felt that himself as much as she did from observation. Even when Evie was older, she got agitated if she sat still for too long, and had to find things to keep her busy. She'd learned to knit and crochet, and made scarf after scarf to keep her family warm during the winter, while during the summer she'd crochet cushion covers and tea cosies. She'd write letters and cards to her friends back in the little village they'd lived in after she and Jim had married or she'd bake for hours in the kitchen. She was always busy and bustling, even when her old body resisted. Vincent, however, seemed calm and quite content to sit and do nothing, but then, she thought, he'd always been that way. While she frantically drew or cooked dinner or made tea, he would sit on the sofa with a book in his hand. She'd leave him in one place knowing he'd still be there when she got back.

He took the stairs carefully, bringing both feet together on each step before moving on to the next, but Evie loitered in the hallway. She wondered if the girl from the photos was still alive, and if they were still together. The stillness of the house suggested that Vincent lived here alone, but the presence of the photographs told her that it hadn't always been that way, that they'd once lived in this house together. A thought struck her. Looking at the pictures again, she realised they were only ever of the two of them. Vincent had never had children.

Her eyes fell on the single picture that wasn't of Vincent and his girl. It was a face she recognised, and she laughed when she saw the image of Sonny Shine kissing Vincent's cheek so hard that Sonny's face was squashed and distorted. It was Vincent how she'd known him, looking fed up with Sonny but smiling nonetheless. His hair had fallen in front of his left eye, but the brilliant green had caught the flash of the camera and shone through the dark strands. He didn't look like a model, a Greek God or a fictional character dreamed up by a woman to make women lust after him. His nose was round and crooked, his teeth were slightly stained from smoking through his teenage years and from drinking too much tea, and his facial hair had always been scruffy and untamed . . . but he was Vincent. Evie had loved him for everything he was, not only the parts of him that were universally accepted as beautiful. The parts that weren't conventional were the bits that set him apart from everyone else. She remembered how he used to sleep with his hand resting on her fleshy stomach, how he told her she was beautiful even when she wasn't wearing any makeup, how he'd kiss the bridge of her nose between her eyes, even though she always said it was slightly too wide and made her eyes look funny. Individually, the two of them had been flawed, as all people are, but together they had been perfect, because they'd embraced the parts of each other that weren't quite as they wanted them to be. She touched Vincent's nose in the picture with a single finger, missing him more than ever. The Vincent upstairs wasn't a man she knew. She hadn't been there through the years that had created him.

She tiptoed up the stairs and carefully pushed herself through two closed doors before she found Vincent's room at the end of the corridor. The door was propped open by a doorstop that looked like a black cat. Vincent was already tucked up in bed and lightly snoring. The room was dark, but in the moonlight Evie could make out the floral duvet cover, which looked too well matched to the room's decor to have been Vincent's doing. There was a desk in the corner where he had left his wallet and pocket watch, and a wardrobe stood against the wall, but aside from the bare essentials, the room seemed cold and empty. None of the character that Evie knew Vincent once had shone from any corner of the house, and Evie wondered how long the woman from the pictures had been gone. A long while, she assumed.

She walked around the bed to get a better look at Vincent's face, and found that in sleep, he looked more like the man she had known. He carried his burdens on his face but when he slept, his face relaxed into the face Evie knew. He had been relatively carefree and untroubled when she had first met him, but when she'd seen him in the station, now an old man, his careworn face had been like a mask she couldn't see past. Now, in sleep, she had found the Vincent she'd fallen in love with, just a little more wrinkly.

'Vincent?' she whispered, the name feeling strange on her tongue. His eyebrows rose a little, like a dog's ears pricking at the familiar sound of its name. 'Vincent. It's ... it's Evie.' She couldn't put her finger on it, but something changed in his face, and he looked inconsolably sad. Her voice must be affecting his dreams, and she wondered what he was seeing in his mind to make him so upset. She wanted nothing more than to touch his face and smooth out the valleys of worry that had formed in his brow. 'Vincent. There's so much I could say. So much I have wanted to say for so many years. Firstly, you should know that Eddie became the man I always hoped he would. He found a loving partner and is living a happy life. Our ending wasn't for nothing, but not a day has gone by when I haven't wondered what would have happened if we'd gone against everyone and everything. I wonder what our alternative ending would have been. I wonder if Eddie would have found happiness without having the security we gave him, and I wonder whether our lives would have been any better or worse than they actually turned out to be.

'I did find happiness, eventually. I found it in my two children. They became my world and I would never wish to change anything that would mean they didn't exist, because a world without August and Isla would be a far less brilliant place to live. But I did still go through each day wishing you were by my side and wondering where you were and if you were missing me too. It's hard living with "what ifs", but living with one so big was unbearable. The weight on my heart became so heavy that I . . . well, I took it out and buried it in the garden on my wedding day.'

Vincent's face crumpled, and a single tear rolled down the bridge of his nose and soaked into his pillow.

'Out of my heart grew a tree. A giant tree, taller than all the houses for miles, and it bears this strange fruit that no one can stand the taste of except me . . . and possibly you, I don't know.' That thought hadn't occurred to Evie before now. 'Will you visit it? I think if you saw it, you'd understand. You'd know how much I missed you each and every day, and you'd see that I never stopped loving you. Not once.'

Vincent suddenly whimpered and rolled on to his back, tears streaming down the sides of his face and into his grey hair. He mumbled something, and Evie thought he'd said her name, but she couldn't be sure. Then he sniffed in his sleep and seemed to compose himself and Evie wondered if he was dreaming of her.

'Evie . . . '

This time it was clearer. She was sure he knew she was there, and oh, how she wished he would wake up and see her, so that they could talk and reminisce and be together again, even if only for a short while. But Evie could feel that pull on the back of her neck. The world of lost souls was calling her once more. She didn't feel like she'd said all she needed to say, but then there was so much she wanted to tell him that if she carried on, she'd never leave.

She closed her eyes, and was just giving in to hands that were dragging her back to Dr Lieffe when she heard Vincent whisper, 'Evie,' and she opened her eyes to watch him say, 'You were my single greatest adventure.'

The noise of a train whizzed through Evie's brain and rattled her ribcage like the tracks it rode on. She pushed through the wall all at once in a great *whoosh!* but then halted abruptly, suspended in the air, and was gradually lowered to the floor, as if she was standing on an invisible escalator.

'Well that was a lot more pleasant than it has been before!' she told the wall, which rippled its surface in reply.

'How was it?' Lieffe helped Evie off with her coat and wheeled the chair behind her so she could flop backwards into it.

'It was ... Well, it just was. I'm not entirely sure how I feel, but I know I'm feeling.'

Lieffe nodded and left the room for what seemed only like seconds before returning with two freshly brewed cups of tea.

'You don't have to talk about it if you don't want to, but you know I'm here if you do.' He handed her the tea and stood awkwardly with his own steaming mug. 'Do you want some time on your own?' he asked.

'No.' She shook her head immediately. 'I'd be glad of company. All we do now, after all, is wait.'

14

impossible ideas before breakfast

Vincent woke the next morning in a pool of tears. His pillow was sodden and his hair was damp. He'd dreamed of Evie, as he did many nights, but this time she had been so vivid, her voice so clear. He swivelled carefully out of bed and put his feet directly into his slippers. On his way downstairs to make some breakfast, he slid open a drawer in a chest in the hallway, pulled out an envelope and took it into the kitchen with him. Over porridge, he read the invitation to Evie's funeral, or a 'celebration of her life', as it was described.

The news that Evie had passed away had affected Vincent in a way he hadn't imagined. After they'd parted all those years ago, he'd spent four years alone, mourning the loss of a woman he didn't want to live his life without.

He'd poured himself into his studies and his music, graduated with the highest grade, and was invited to play in an orchestra for a ballet that was set to travel around the world on a three-year tour. It was on that tour that one of the ballerinas, Cynthia Petal, fell in love with the handsome violinist. Truth be told, every ballerina fell in love with Vincent, but it was Cynthia he'd taken a shine to, because she was so unlike Evie.

Cynthia was kind, of course, and well deserving of Vincent's affections, but she was small and angular, and her laugh could shatter glass. Every time a girl had shown interest in Vincent, he'd found something in her to associate with Evie Snow. When she smiled with all her teeth, he saw Evie. When she had curves in all the 'wrong' places, he felt Evie, and when her laugh warmed the atmosphere ten feet around her, he heard Evie. He saw her everywhere except in Cynthia Petal. He could stand to be around Cynthia without feeling his heart break every ten seconds, and so he stuck close to her and she let him.

Every stop they made on tour, in every foreign land, Vincent and Cynthia found an adventure. They had so much fun that when the tour ended, they saw no reason for their adventures to end too, so they carried on travelling, using the money they'd made from dancing and playing in the ballet. It was only when they stopped in Las Vegas and passed a drive-in wedding chapel that marriage was mentioned. By this point, Vincent hadn't heard from Evie in nine years and knew he never would, and the four years he'd spent with Cynthia had been truly blissful. He saw no reason why they shouldn't be together for the rest of their lives. He loved Cynthia in a very different way to how he'd once loved Evie, but he did love her all the same, and her feelings for him were never in question, for they were ever present in her eyes. So Vincent pulled hard on the wheel and swerved the car into the 'Say I Do Wedding Drive-Thru' to start a very new kind of adventure.

Vincent and Cynthia spent their years together dancing and playing to make money and then splashing out on plane tickets and hotel rooms. It was only when they came home for a while that they realised they hadn't been travelling, they'd been running. Running from the very real truth that they couldn't have children. They'd been trying for so long, and not once had there been even a glimmer of hope. So to distract themselves, they would flit from place to place, pretending they were still young and had all the time in the world, denying their reality until it was too late. Now they accepted that there were to be no little ones, and finally settled down in their old home town, where they had first met.

They were both offered jobs at a school for performing arts just outside town. Vincent taught violin and Cynthia taught ballet, and although they never had children, they had each other, and that was enough. At least Vincent thought so, until, at the age of forty-six, Cynthia started showing signs of pregnancy. Vincent would wake in the early hours to the sound of her vomiting and would rush to the bathroom, hoping she'd give him good news, but she'd maintain it was just something she'd eaten. After six weeks of holding back her hair most mornings, he insisted she go to the doctor to find out what was wrong. That was when she broke down and admitted that she was pregnant. Vincent was over the moon and tried to kiss her, but she turned away from him, tears spilling down her cheeks, and told him the truth.

When Cynthia had finally realised that she and Vincent weren't ever to have children, she had turned elsewhere for comfort, indulging in the affections of a male dancer whose lustful advances she'd fought off for years. In a moment of weakness, however, she'd given in to the dancer – but it turned out that Cynthia was prone to moments of weakness and an affair had flourished. She had convinced herself that she was barren, so she was sure Vincent would never find out about the affair, but the truth was that Cynthia wasn't the one who was unable to have children. Only weeks into her affair with Antoine Blanc, she realised something was amiss, and after weeks of vomiting, tender breasts and no sign of Aunt Flo, she could no longer deny that she was with child, and that that child didn't belong to her husband.

Vincent was devastated. Cynthia, in a cruel act of self-preservation, had lashed out and blamed him for preventing her from having children earlier in her life, and Vincent could only agree and apologise. She went to live with her mother for a while, leaving Vincent alone with several bottles of cheap whisky to drink himself into oblivion. Until an old friend showed up on his doorstep.

Sonny Shine, inebriated as always, had obtained Vincent's new address from Violet Winters, and when Vincent opened the door to find his ex-flatmate lying on his front steps because he'd thrown himself at the door by way of knocking, it was enough to sober him up. Subsequent conversation showed him that Sonny's life hadn't changed at all over the years they hadn't seen each other and when Sonny offered him a swig from his hip flask, Vincent declined. He didn't want people looking at him and seeing what he saw in Sonny.

The very next day he called Cynthia and told her he would look after the child and raise it as if it were his own if only she would come home. Life would continue as normal, he told her. Her answer came in sobs down the crackling line. Cynthia had lost the baby. According to the doctors, it was a miracle she'd fallen pregnant in the first place, but sustaining the pregnancy would never have been possible.

Cynthia came home full of remorse and promises that it was over with Antoine, and Vincent found it in his big heart to forgive her. She was the only woman who had ever made him any kind of happy after Evie, and he just couldn't lose her. Their lives resumed, except they now had a fragility about them that everyone who knew them could sense. As individuals they were stone, but together they were glass, and their friends and families danced a ballet around them, careful not to ripple the peace they had found. They lived happily but quietly and their adventures became few and far between, until they stopped altogether. Cynthia passed away when she was seventy-six, leaving Vincent with only pictures of their adventures to keep him company.

Vincent Winters read the cursive writing on the invitation over and over. He desperately wished he'd gone to Evie's funeral to pay his respects properly, but he hadn't had the courage and had convinced himself it was what Evie would have wanted. Jim had sent the invitation, so it wasn't concern about Jim's reaction that had stopped him; more the fact that he was sure Evie wouldn't have wanted her children to start asking questions about the strange old man from their mother's past who they'd never seen or heard of before. He didn't think his heart would be able to handle it either. Not a day went by that he didn't think of Evie, but he'd had good practice at pushing thoughts of her away and hiding them in the tiniest corners of his mind. Meeting her children, though, who he already believed would look like her, talk like her and hold pieces of her in everything they did, would be like losing her all over again.

He'd made up his mind not to go as soon as he'd seen the invitation, and the funeral had taken place weeks ago anyway, but now he was rethinking his decision and he didn't know why. The dream he'd had about Evie had filled every pore with this strange, inconceivable hope.

The same hope and energy he'd had when he'd asked her to run away with him all those years ago. It had been an impossible and downright foolish idea, but he'd believed with all his heart that they could make it work. That was exactly the same kind of belief he had now.

Vincent flipped the invitation over to read the address of the Summers' house. He'd never thought it before, but now, although impossible and downright foolish, he somehow believed, over his breakfast porridge, that one day he'd see Evie Snow once more.

15

hello, goodbye

Vincent stood on the bottom step of a grand house, looking up at a blue door. He tapped his walking stick nervously on the gravel, enjoying the sound it made, then turned and watched the taxi drive further and further away, wishing he'd asked it to wait in case he changed his mind. *This is good*, he thought. *Can't back out now*, and with a brave push forward, he climbed the steps and knocked on the door with his knuckles, quite hard. The moments that followed turned his stomach. He dreaded one of Evie's children answering the door and turning the crazy old man away, but the face that greeted him, though one he didn't know well, was at the very least one he knew.

'James Summer?' Vincent croaked, then coughed to clear his dry throat.

'Yes, that's me.' Jim took a step forward, pulling the door mostly closed behind him. He knew that he knew this man from somewhere. Quickly he rattled through his mental Filofax, trying to fit a name to the face.

'Jim . . .' Vincent said to break the silence as he watched the other man trying desperately to place this blast from the past. The dawning realisation on his face was picture-worthy.

'Vincent Winters,' he breathed, and before Vincent could back down the steps and forget all about this silly idea of his, Jim had hobbled down towards him and embraced him. 'I can't tell you how good it is to see you,' he said, the words muffled as they caught in his throat.

Vincent's back stiffened. The last time he'd been hugged like this was by his own mother, the night she had passed away twenty years before. 'It's good to see you too,' he said, returning the hug, relaxing into it and enjoying the interaction with another human. Something he'd had little of in recent years.

'Are you well? You look well.' Jim couldn't contain his excitement. He'd spent so many years wondering how Vincent was, whether he was coping and what he'd done with his life. Out of respect for his wife's wishes, he'd never dared find out, but now the man himself was on his doorstep, and he felt he owed it to Vincent to ask all the questions he wished he'd asked and to offer him the friendship he'd always wanted to offer.

'Yes, I am. I think I am. I've had a strange few weeks ...' Vincent said. Both men had shrunk in height now that they were elderly, but Vincent still had half a foot over Jim and looked down on him even when hunched over his walking stick.

'Since Evie died?' Jim asked, and Vincent nodded sheepishly. 'We all have. Would you like to come in? Meet the family?'

The front door had swung open a little in the wind, and Vincent could hear voices talking over each other, laughing, tutting, making a din somewhere in the house. His heart strained forward in his chest, trying to urge him towards the sound, but he dug his heels in.

'Won't they ask questions?' he asked.

Jim nodded. 'Probably. There's a lot they've already learned about you in the last few weeks, but even so, I think it's about time they knew everything ... don't you?' He put his arm around Vincent's shoulders and together they walked inside. 'They've all been staying here for the last few weeks to sort through Evie's things. Now, though, it feels like they're staying to look after me.'

'How've you been? Since ...' Vincent asked, feeling as though he'd forgotten how to make conversation with people.

Jim sighed and leaned gently on a chest of drawers in the hallway. 'You know what it's like losing Evie.'

A familiar sting prickled through Vincent like electricity.

'But I'm doing ... better. Thank you.' Jim smiled with

his lips but not his eyes, and Vincent understood only too well.

'Dad?' a woman's voice called.

'You arrived just at the right time, Vincent,' Jim said quickly as the sound of footsteps got louder. 'Isla's making lunch and usually she recruits me, only to tell me I'm not doing things fast enough.' He rolled his eyes with warm affection.

'Am I getting you out of kitchen duties?' Vincent smiled, amused.

'No, you'll be taking my place!' Jim laughed as a middle-aged woman appeared at the end of the hall in baggy tracksuit bottoms, a bright pink T-shirt and a frilly red apron covered in flour.

'There you are! You're supposed to be helping, and ... Oh. Who's this?'

Vincent couldn't take his eyes off her round face. It was like not wanting to look away from a car crash. In truth, she looked more like Jim, but her lips moved in the same way as Evie's, and, although greying slightly, her hair was the same shade of blonde.

'This is Isla, my daughter.'

Isla walked towards them, her floury hand outstretched to take Vincent's. He shook it, hoping she didn't notice how sweaty his palm was. He hated how awkward and out of place he felt.

'Isla, this is Vincent.'

Isla abruptly stopped shaking his hand and simply held

it there, her mouth now slightly agape. 'You ... you're Vincent? Vincent Winters?'

Vincent took a deep breath. 'I am.'

Neither Vincent nor Jim knew what was rushing through Isla's head, as the expression on her face didn't change, but neither of them expected her to ...

'AAAUUUUGGGGGUUUUSSSSTTT!!!!' Both men jumped at her yell. 'Oh goodness! I'm so sorry, but ... you're here! It's you! You're you and you're actually here!' After reading and rereading the notebook August, Daphne and Little One had put together, Isla felt as if one of her favourite fictional characters had come to life and was standing in the hallway.

August rushed in from the kitchen brandishing a wooden spatula, his clothes just as floury as Isla's apron. 'What's going on!' he yelled as he slipped on the rug in his socks, crashing into the wall at high speed but keeping hold of the spatula at all times.

It was clear to Vincent that August had got most of Evie's genes. His eyes were as big and brown as hers had been, and his face was round, his cheeks pinchable. The bridge of his nose was slightly too wide, but it didn't make his eyes look funny, in the same way it had never made Evie's look funny. Just big, bright and full of happiness and mischief.

'It's OK, it's OK! There's someone here you need to meet!' Isla said excitedly. 'Dad ...' She gestured to Jim to do the introductions.

'You're impossible,' Jim said, laughing at his daughter but very aware that all this might be too much for Vincent, until he saw that a smile was creeping on to the other man's lips.

'Daaaad,' Isla moaned like she was a teenager again. 'August.' She turned to her brother, who was holding the spatula higher in the air than was necessary, still unsure if he was supposed to hit the intruder or cook him lunch. 'This is Vincent Winters!' she said with a squeak.

'What?' August dropped his arms to his sides in one great swoop, and sauce slopped off the end of the spatula and on to the rug. 'You're Vincent? *The* Vincent?'

'I ... I think so.' Vincent, now feeling a little more confident, held out his hand, which August shook with pleasure.

'Well I'll be damned. I can't believe it! Come in, come in!' August and Isla bustled towards the kitchen, tripping over each other. Vincent shot a glance at Jim as they started to follow.

'I don't know what's got into them,' Jim confessed.

'It's what's always been in them, I'm sure,' Vincent said. 'Their mother.'

August and Isla cooked lunch while Jim and Vincent set the table and sat down to talk.

'How do they know who I am?' Vincent leaned across the table to Jim, nodding towards the siblings, who wouldn't stop looking at him and whispering to each other like kids in a school cafeteria.

'How long do you have?' Jim asked rhetorically, but Vincent checked his watch and replied, 'Probably only a couple of years left in me, but tell me anyway. It's been a long time since I heard a good story.'

August appeared with a notebook and surreptitiously placed it on the table in front of Vincent, trying to pretend he'd not been listening to their conversation. Vincent flipped it open to find his own handwriting, far steadier and neater than it had been for years, but his all the same.

'Where did you get this?' He closed the book and turned it over in his hands, sure that he'd never seen it before.

'Little One,' Jim said.

'Little One,' Vincent repeated, and laughed, remembering the blackbird that wasn't a blackbird.

'August had a dream about that bird, and that very night Little One turned up in his garden,' Jim explained. 'In the dream, he'd heard Evie's voice telling him to wash the bird's wings and relieve him of his duties, and when they cleaned him, all your notes to each other were revealed. August's wife Daphne had the bright idea to save them all in a notebook.'

Vincent flipped the pages of a past he never thought he'd see again in such detail. He closed the book and placed it on the table before his tears could splash on to the pages.

'May I borrow this?' he asked.

'Oh Vincent, they're your memories. The book belongs to you.' Jim pushed it towards him, and forgetting himself, Vincent picked it up again and hugged it to his chest.

'Then Isla had a dream too. Long story short, she found a shoebox that Evie and I hid under the floor of her old flat in which she'd hidden all her drawings.'

'Can I see them?' Vincent asked.

'You can, absolutely, but maybe not quite in the way you remember.' Jim stood halfway out of his chair to go upstairs to retrieve the sun catcher before seeing Isla stood in the doorway holding it delicately in her hands, with a sheepish smile.

'I thought Vincent might want to see this at some point,' she said placing it on the table. Before she returned to the kitchen, she turned back and said, 'I've not been listening . . .' Jim gave her a disapproving look but shooed her away playfully.

'In Isla's dream, she heard her mother's voice telling her to find the shoebox, and when she did, she made this.' Jim took the suncatcher and hung it from the light fitting above the table where the sun from the windows could hit it when it came out from behind the clouds. 'Brace yourself. Just one moment . . . there!'

The sun shone through the window, hit the glass: the drawings came to life. Startled, Vincent clutched the

320

book tighter, but as soon as he recognised the goose that had caused him to fall in the pond, he howled with laughter. He even recognised the drawing of himself and Evie huddled under an umbrella. The Vincent drawing waved at the real one, but the sketched-out Evie was miming, like she was trying to tell him something. She was pointing at Vincent with a jabbing finger, then gesturing to her own lips and moving her hands to suggest sound coming out of her mouth. Then she pushed both palms flat together, put them under her head and pretended to sleep.

'What's she doing?' Jim asked.

Vincent shook his head, knowing full well that the drawing was miming *Tell him about your dream*. He wasn't sure he could handle anything extraordinary happening to him at his age. Just being around this family had his old heart fighting to keep him upright. Telling Jim about his own dream of Evie might invite strange goings-on, and Vincent was too tired to be played with. Evie was still dead, and that was all that mattered. No matter how many extraordinary things happened that made it feel like she was still here, none of them would bring her back.

'I should really be going,' he said, avoiding eye contact with the drawing, who was still waving her hands about. He turned to leave, but the cartoon Evie jumped on to a sunbeam and appeared on the wall beside the door, hands on hips and nose scrunched up in frustration.

'Vincent . . .' Jim was concerned, but he had a feeling he knew what had got Vincent so skittish. 'You've had a dream of your own, haven't you?'

Vincent was staring at the version of Evie on the wall. It was Evie as she saw herself. Big cheeks, funny eyes and far bigger around the middle than she'd ever been, but even so, he couldn't ignore it. He turned to Jim and nodded.

Over a roast lunch, Vincent recounted his dream. How real Evie had seemed, what she'd said, and his speculations about why he'd had the dream at all.

'Why does she want you to see the tree?' Isla laughed. 'It's nothing special.' Vincent felt a little disappointed that he wasn't here to see something marvellous, but he caught Jim looking quickly away from both his children and into his gravy.

'Well, it's very clear that he needs to see it all the same,' Jim said, not looking up from cutting his meat far more precisely than necessary.

'All these dreams,' August said. 'It makes you wonder what really happens after you die.'

'You really think it's Mum doing this?' Isla asked in a challenging tone. 'From beyond the grave!' She wiggled her fingers at her brother, teasing him.

'You're more than willing to believe it when all those

322

drawings are dancing about the place!' August said, trying to keep his cool.

'That's just a trick of the light,' Isla said feebly.

'It's not!' August put his fork down with force.

'It is!' Isla did the same. Gravy splattered across the tablecloth and on to Vincent's sleeve.

'Right, you two. That's enough,' Jim said sternly, handing Vincent a napkin. 'It doesn't matter why you've been having these dreams. What matters is what they've led you to. You've learned so much about your mother. Things that have made you feel closer to her now that she's gone. That's what's important, and don't forget it.'

'Sorry, Vincent,' Isla said, touching his arm apologetically.

'Yes, sorry,' August said sheepishly. 'Don't know what came over us. It does seem odd, though. The three of us all having dreams about Mum that have led us to things she hid for most of her life.'

'If Evie remained anything like she was when I knew her,' Vincent said quietly, not wanting to make Jim feel uncomfortable, 'I wouldn't put it past her to find a way to talk to us from another realm.' He laughed.

'Yes,' Jim chimed in. 'Much like you, Isla, she was always fighting against the odds and usually winning.'

Jim and Vincent shared a knowing look. Although they both knew it was completely impossible, neither man was willing to rule out the supernatural where Evie was involved, but Jim thought it best not to scare his imaginative son or argue with his realistic daughter.

'So,' Jim wiped his mouth, placed the napkin on the table next to his plate and looked at Vincent. 'I think it's time you saw this tree.'

As the sky darkened, three Summers and a Winters walked slowly through the woods with lanterns. Isla had called ahead, so Eddie and Oliver were on the porch waiting for them when they arrived. Vincent had never met Eddie, but for a while, he'd blamed him for the end of his relationship with Evie. Over time, he'd come to his senses and realised that Eddie had no idea how much his sister had really done for him, or how much she'd given up. Even so, he wasn't sure how he was going to feel when he met him.

Although Vincent was well aware of how much time had passed since he'd packed his things and left Evie sleeping on the balcony, he had expected to be meeting the Eddie she had always talked about: a boy with bright eyes, barely old enough to drink. Instead he was greeted with the reality of a man in his seventies standing arm in arm with another elderly man, both of whom Vincent would have guessed were his own age had he seen them casually in the street. The gap between ages grows closer and closer as you get older, until decades seem like mere cracks in the pavement. Vincent, Jim, Eddie and Oliver were all old men. A fact they'd all deny until death, if death wasn't so close.

'Vincent.' Eddie greeted him with a smile, but he held on tight to Oliver anxiously. 'It really is a pleasure to meet you.'

'And you, Eddie. I was once told so much about you, but that was more than fifty years ago now,' Vincent said.

'I doubt much has changed,' Isla said, prodding Eddie with a finger.

The Summers' house had been very much a family home where children had once played, and the rooms were still filled with nostalgia. However, although the Snows' house had been occupied by Eddie and Oliver for so many years, and now by August and Daphne too, Vincent could feel an inexplicable chill in the air. *Left behind by Evie's mother, no doubt*, he thought.

'Lead the way, Eddie.' Jim gestured for Vincent to follow Eddie through to the back door and into the garden.

Against the dark grey sky, the impressive tree loomed almost black. Vincent couldn't quite believe the height of it, and his poor aching neck wasn't able to crane up to see it in its entirety.

'Wow ...' He laughed. 'What have you been feeding that thing?'

As the wind whipped its branches and blew all around them, Vincent was sure he heard something out of the ordinary, but his hearing wasn't what it used to be and he'd probably been mistaken. Still, he felt hot under the collar all of a sudden and leaned on his walking stick a little harder.

'Are you OK?' Isla asked, touching his arm, ready to catch him should he fall.

'Yes, yes. Just a little warm, that's all.' Thunder

rumbled overhead and the dark clouds shifted directly above them.

'The rain should clear the humidity,' Oliver said, feeling a couple of drops hit his forehead.

'Vincent, do you have a little more time? I think you might want to stay for the storm.' Jim smiled, an odd, knowing sort of smile that, despite feeling tired and overwhelmed, Vincent couldn't resist.

'Of course. Does the tree put on a show? Sing a song? Do a dance?' he joked.

'Better,' Eddie said, before leading them all back into the house.

Jim had gestured to everyone, letting them know that they should leave him alone with Vincent for a little while. The two men sat in the armchairs by the fire, both of them taking their time lowering themselves into them, and laughing when they were finally seated with an *oomph!*

'I think it's best we both speak quite frankly ... don't you?' Jim said, trying to hold his nerve. Outside, rain drizzled down the windows and thunder rumbled above the house. Vincent was sweating despite having taken off his black jacket. 'Absolutely,' he replied, undoing the top button on his shirt.

Jim took a deep breath before beginning. 'Evie was an ... extraordinary woman. She was a pain in the arse at times,' Vincent nodded in agreement, 'but she was extraordinary nonetheless and she did some inexplicable things in her lifetime – mostly good, some bad and some that no one will ever know the answers to but one of the most extraordinary things she ever did was plant that tree.' Jim shifted in his seat to see if the others were eavesdropping, but it seemed they'd formed their own gathering in the kitchen to discuss Vincent's unexpected arrival.

'It's a very impressive tree.' Vincent shrugged, unsure of what else he could say. To tell the truth, he had been a little disappointed that he hadn't found something that made the trip more worthwhile.

'It's more impressive than you think. Can I tell you a story?' Jim was enjoying his chance to retell Evie's tale. Vincent nodded, blinking slowly. 'On the day Evie and I got married, before she walked down the aisle and before we said our vows, she ran to this house in her white dress and knelt in the mud at the bottom of the garden. She'd realised she could never give her heart to you, and she didn't want to give it to me, so she decided she would never give it to anyone. There and then, she took her own heart out of her chest and buried it in the ground.'

Vincent suddenly felt more awake, and he sat up in his chair, looking at Jim with interest and a hint of amusement at what would have sounded like a tall tale if he hadn't once known Evie.

Jim continued. 'When we returned to this house ten years later, that tree had appeared, right on the spot where Evie had buried her heart.' He was pleased to hear a muffled yet very familiar popping sound resonating through the house. 'It was a tree that seemed familiar to us all, and yet none of us really knew why. A tree that was warm to the touch, a tree that whispered words of comfort when the wind caught its branches just right, a tree that only bore fruit after a thunderstorm because it liked to make the best ...'

'... out of a bad situation,' they said in unison, and smiled.

'You hear that?' Jim asked.

Vincent strained his poor ears and could just about make out what sounded like corn kernels popping in a frying pan. 'What *is* that?' he asked.

'I think you might want to take another look at the tree.'

Together they heaved themselves out of their chairs and walked to the back door. Vincent laughed heartily when he saw the orange fruit appearing on the branches, some popping to life so hard they immediately fell to the ground with a thud.

'The only tree to guarantee a fruit basket every time it rains,' he said, satisfied now that it was worth all the anxiety the trip had caused him.

'If only it was edible,' Jim said.

'Is it poisonous?' Vincent asked.

'Not as such. It just tastes disgusting. You're welcome to try it, should you wish.'

'I'll take your word for it ...' Vincent said, just as he heard Evie's voice in his mind. *A giant tree, taller than all the houses for miles, and it bears this strange fruit that no one can stand the taste of except me . . . and possibly you, I don't know.* 'On second thoughts . . .'

Vincent strode out into the rain, his breath spilling out in smoky plumes and his walking stick thumping into the mud with every step. Something in him told him this was how he could be closer to Evie. This was his chance to see her again, he was sure.

'At least take an umbrella!' Jim called after him, but Vincent's only thought was of getting to that tree. As he neared it, he could feel its heat. It warmed the raindrops as they fell, and he could no longer see his breath in front of him. He kicked one of the fruit lightly with the tip of his shoe. Its surface seemed soft enough to bite into, but he wondered how ripe it would be if it had only just fallen. The wind rustled through the branches, and Vincent was sure he could hear his name being called by a voice he'd not heard in over fifty years.

Vincent, Evie called. *Vincent.*

'Evie?' he whispered. He turned back to the house, where Jim had been joined by August and Isla. His cheeks turned red with embarrassment.

Vincent.

No, he was certain that was Evie's voice.

'Evie!' he called over the noise of the rain and the thunder.

'Vincent! Come back inside! You'll catch your death out there!' Eddie was now on the back porch too, and

329

Oliver was watching from a window. Isla noticed Little One appear in the sky and land on one of the tree's tallest branches.

Lightning struck close by, so close that Vincent heard the crackle of electricity, and it lit up the concerned faces of Evie's family. He looked up to the sky just as another fruit burst from a branch and fell right into his open hand. Without thinking, just trusting his own instincts, he bit into it. His taste buds reeled as they lapped up the familiar taste of toffee apples, treacle and cream. He closed his eyes as its juices, warm in his mouth, slid sweetly down his chin. As he swallowed, his lips tingled as though he'd just been kissed by someone who'd recently sipped a mug of tea.

'Evie . . .' he breathed.

The storm was dying out, the rain merely a pitter-patter now and the thunder sounding distant. Vincent waited for the warmth on his skin to subside, but it didn't. Instead it spread through his body, reaching the very tips of his fingers. He felt like he was sitting just that bit too close to a roaring fire. He dropped his walking stick in the mud, but he didn't fall. He felt sturdier than he had in the longest time.

'Vincent! Can you hear me?' Isla stepped off the porch to go to him, but Jim put a hand on her shoulder and shook his head.

'If he needs us, he'll tell us. I'm sure of it,' he said, and Isla nodded, but even so, no one went back inside.

They all sensed this wasn't just an elderly man grieving an old flame. This was something different, something *special*.

The heat in Vincent's body danced and swirled in his blood and finally found its way to his heart, caressing it, teasing around its edges. The wind dropped completely, the rain stopped and everything went deathly quiet. Vincent opened his eyes for a moment and saw Eddie, Oliver, Isla, August and Jim huddled together against the cold, watching him with bated breath and fearful eyes. He knew something wonderful was about to happen and he closed his eyes for what he was sure would be the last time.

'Goodbye,' he whispered as the flames in his body consumed his heart completely and all at once he was alight with Evie's love.

Lightning struck the tree with one huge, crackling bolt, the rain poured once more and the thunder laughed. Every ache Evie had felt over the last fifty-five years, every moment she'd longed for Vincent and every day she'd still been in love with the memory of him, Vincent felt all of it, all at once, and it was too much for his eighty-three-year-old body to take. All he could do was give in to the force of the love Evie's heart had held. His knees buckled, slamming into the mud, and as he collapsed, the tree collapsed with him, with Little One's lifeless body tangled in its twigs.

The family gasped and called out, and Jim ran to him,

as best as the old man could, but it was already much too late. Vincent's life was gone, pouring out of him like smoke, drifting up through the air to a place he'd been dreaming of for far too long.

16

at long last

Evie and Lieffe sat in comfortable silence. She sipped her tea and Lieffe had his eyes lightly closed, happily thinking the time away. Evie truly didn't know how she felt after seeing Vincent. She'd spent her whole life pushing thoughts of him away, but those thoughts had been of the Vincent she'd known. The Vincent she'd visited on the other side of the wall was a very different man. Not just because he was older, but because he'd lived a life that Evie had not been a part of, and it had shaped and moulded him into a lonely man with no family left to love. The Vincent she had met was a man she didn't recognise, and that made her incredibly sad. Should she have run away with him? Would that have made them both happier? Helping her brother and staying with Jim had made her happy eventually, but it had meant that Vincent had lived a life of heartache … yet how could she have known he wouldn't find someone else he'd love as much as if not more than her? Evie shook her head, not enjoying the game of what-if she'd been playing since she'd arrived back.

'Lieffe.' Her voice croaked and Lieffe opened his eyes a little, but she didn't look at him. She couldn't. 'Did I do the right thing? Keeping my secrets?' she asked.

'Did it feel like the right thing?' Lieffe asked, closing his eyes again, for which she was glad. She felt less judged when he wasn't watching her.

She found herself nodding. 'Yes. It did. At the time. It was right for me, anyway.'

'Did you hurt your children by not telling them about your past?' Lieffe hummed, his eyes still closed.

'They didn't know me as well as they could have,' she said.

'But did you hurt them? Was anyone hurt by your actions?'

'No.' She shook her head.

'Well then,' he concluded.

'But we could have had much stronger relationships,' she said feebly, not knowing if that was true.

Lieffe opened his eyes fully. 'Maybe,' he said, shocking Evie with his sudden blunt reply.

'They might have talked to me more as they were growing up if they'd known me better,' Evie said, running through it in her mind.

'Yes,' Lieffe agreed.

'Trusted me more.'

'They may have loved you better had they known the *real* you,' Lieffe said.

'Well I don't think—' she started, but Lieffe cut her off.

'Technically you didn't hurt them or lie to them, but you never told them the whole truth, and that probably did affect your relationship with them more than you'll ever realise,' he said, and then leaned back in his chair and closed his eyes once more.

Evie took a moment to process what she'd just heard. 'No,' she said, and Lieffe opened one eye. 'No. That's not true.' She put her tea down on the floor by her feet. 'My kids knew the version of me that was created by my life before I married their father, and that's all that matters. Bad stories can create good people, and I wanted to protect them from those bad stories so they could live with the good person they'd created without ever worrying about what I had to go through to become that person. I kept those secrets because I needed to, and . . . and sometimes it's OK to make those kinds of decisions for the sake of your own happiness.'

Evie stood and paced across the room. 'All that matters is that I was the mother they deserved, and I was able to become that mother because of my life before they even existed. My mother showed me how *not* to be a parent, and so I made sure my children had everything I never did. Jim showed me how to love someone unconditionally, no matter what, and Vincent showed me just how much love I had inside me to give. So no, I didn't hurt my children. They're happy because of me and Jim and because of the life we gave them.' She stopped, suddenly out of breath.

Lieffe leaned forward, his elbows on his knees. 'Then I think you have your answer.' He smiled fiendishly.

'I did the right thing?' Evie said.

'You did the right thing,' he said, nodding.

All of a sudden the wall began to hum, and Evie felt that strange pull towards it, the hairs on her arms and neck standing on end. She let it bring her closer, until she was standing in the centre of the room. Its yellowing surface started to spin like a whirlpool, a hole appearing in its centre; only a pinprick at first, but as the swirling gradually became faster, it opened up to the size of a bowling ball. A breeze filled the room, blowing Evie's hair in every direction, making it hard for her to see properly. She heard a clunking sound come from inside her, and before she knew what was happening, the doors of her chest started to open. Panicked, she put her hands on them, trying to close them, but they were out of her control and they pushed back.

'Don't fight it, Evie. Nothing can hurt you here. Whatever's happening is for the best,' Lieffe called to her over the wind, trying his best to comfort her. 'You're safe here.'

Evie took as many deep breaths as she could, trying to calm herself. The black hole was still spinning, and now she could hear a noise coming from the darkness, a noise that put her entirely at ease and even placed a smile of relief on her lips.

Thump-thump. Thump-thump. Thump-thump.

Through the hole in the wall floated her black-and-gold flecked heart, twirling and shining, putting on a show for the owner it hadn't seen in half a century. Evie stopped resisting and let her hands fall to her sides. Her heart floated on the wind towards her and, without any hesitation, positioned itself back in the hollow of her chest, where it belonged. The doors swung shut with one last solid clunk, and Evie touched her chest, finally able to feel her heart beating beneath the skin and bone. She frowned.

'Is something the matter?' Lieffe asked, rushing to her with the chair.

'No, nothing's wrong. It's just . . . I have my heart back, but it hasn't made me feel heavier. In fact I feel lighter. Much lighter than before.' She looked at Lieffe hopefully.

'That can only mean one thing.'

They were eight floors away, but Evie heard the click of the lock on the door of Apartment 72. It was finally open.

She couldn't help herself. She let out a laugh so big and full of joy that she almost knocked Lieffe off his feet. She laughed so hard and so heartily that she began to float upwards, almost hitting her head on the ceiling.

'Come on!' she said to Lieffe between her happy laughs.

She used her hands to move herself along the ceiling and out of the room. Her happiness and her new-found lightness meant her feet didn't touch the ground, literally. She floated up the stairs, Lieffe hot on her heels. Before she could float all the way to the top of the building, Lieffe grabbed her ankle and guided her to the seventh floor, where he pulled her downwards until her feet finally did touch the ground. She gave one huge happy sigh and wiped the tears from her cheeks.

'Are you all right?' Lieffe chuckled.

'Yes,' she said happily. 'I'm OK. More than.'

'Good. I'm glad. Well, Evie,' he gave the tops of her arms a squeeze, 'this is where I leave you.'

'I will see you again, won't I?' Evie asked, suddenly panicked.

'Whenever you want! Through that door is your heaven. If you ever want to invite me in for tea, I'll be there, but this time, it's your turn to make it.'

'Of course. I promise. You're welcome any time.' She hugged him, hard. 'Thank you for everything, Lieffe. I never would have got this far without you.'

'Oh Evie. I know you. Of course you would have.'

'Maybe, but it would have taken me twice as long.'

'Well,' Lieffe said, 'it's been a true pleasure.' He hugged her back, even harder.

After a long moment, Evie finally pulled away. 'Time to go,' she said.

Lieffe gave her a final smile of encouragement before she turned away and walked purposefully down the corridor.

When she reached Apartment 72, the excitement she'd

been feeling a second ago gave way to the fear that her keys would refuse to turn again. She moved closer to her door and leaned her forehead against it, praying that there wasn't something she'd forgotten, something else that she'd need to go back and fix. Just then, she heard a noise coming from inside. She pressed her ear against the wood. She was certain it was the sound of clinking porcelain and boiling water. Her curiosity eclipsed her last-minute worries and she scrambled to get her keys out of her pocket. Her hands shook, flustered, and she missed the lock several times, scratching the wood of the door, before she finally slid the key perfectly into the keyhole. For the first time in a long time, she could feel her heart thumping in her chest.

One, she counted in her head, *two ... three ...* She pushed the key with her thumb to the right.

It turned.

Her breath caught in her throat. She turned the doorknob and it swivelled easily. Carefully she pushed on the door and it opened. Just a crack at first – it was all she could manage – then with one deep breath she shoved it all the way open.

The room was warmly lit, just as it had always been when she'd lived there. The green armchair sat by the door, looking comfortable and slightly worn. The rug was where it always had been, the sofas were in their rightful places, everything was as it should be. Evie was turning around to close the door, putting the keys in her pocket, so happy to be home, when she heard a noise behind her: the unmistakable flutter of wings.

Slowly she turned, her back against the door, and looked out through the doors to the balcony. Against the setting sun, she could see the silhouette of Little One perched on the railings.

He wasn't alone.

Evie couldn't breathe. The scruffiness ... the shaggy hair ... the green eyes ... The one thing the apartment had been missing. The one *person* her life had been missing for far too long.

'Vincent?'

The man on the balcony stepped into the room. His face was stubbly and flushed, the smile under his rounded nose was kind and crooked, but it was his eyes, his green eyes, shining through his raven hair, that made Evie's heart burst into a thousand speckled pieces.

'Evie?' he said, his voice breaking.

Evie ran into his open arms, and the feel of him against her body was so *real*. He took her face in his rough hands and brushed his nose against hers, convincing himself that this wasn't a dream, she was real too and she was there with him. Evie rested her hands on his chest, feeling his heart beating beneath his skin, and she ran her fingers up through his hair, convincing herself of the same thing.

Vincent moved his lips to hers, and just before he kissed her Evie whispered, 'At long last.'

Acknowledgements

Firstly I'd like to thank all the people who helped this book to physically exist in the world. My agent Hannah Ferguson, without you and the faith you've put in me, my ideas and stories would still be pages in notebooks that no one's ever seen. Thank you for your continued support! My editor, Manpreet Grewal. You've been spectacularly patient with me and so wonderful at accepting my truly mad ideas. Thanks for not screaming wildly down the corridor when you read that Horace the cat would swallow the heroine and that Evie and Vincent would be using a bird as a notebook! To Stephanie Melrose who has arranged many an event, flapped many a book and taken many a photo with those who have come to said events. You work so hard and I can't tell you how much I appreciate it. To Rhiannon for always putting up with me being scatty and late for deadlines. To the designer, Bekki Guyatt, and artist, Helen Crawford-White, of this book's cover, it's truly beautiful and I couldn't have dreamed it better. To Hannah Boursnell, for being just as excited about this book as you were the last! Also to Sara Talbot, Rachel Wilkie and Marie Hrynczak for making sure everything runs smoothly and for being so behind this book and for always providing tea and treats whenever I visit!

Secondly, to all the people who helped this story exist. Evie is a woman I aspire to be like myself and without my incredibly strong, brilliant and slightly crazy friends, I wouldn't have had half the inspiration to make her who she is. Celinde Schoenmaker, my Dutch mermaid! We may not share a dressing room any longer but you're always there and I will love you, always. *Ik hou van jou.* Louise Jones, you are the slug to my lettuce and boy have we been through it all! But here we are, stronger than ever, ready to take on the world with our words and our sass ...TOGETHER. Katy Secombe, never have I ever had the pleasure to meet and work with someone as truly bonkers as you! Thank you for all your stories and your magic. Calling you my friend is an honour. Zoe Doano, your kindness, patience, peace and love towards this fast-paced and frightening world is a rare gem and I am lucky to have spent so much time surrounded by your aura. Here's to a long and lovely friendship! Emma Kingston, what can I say? You're just brilliant! You deserve so much success and I can't wait for the day I'm pointing at your name in the programme of your own hit Broadway show and I'm disrupting the audience by yelling about how we used to work together. (I won't take any photos during the show though, promise! :P) There are so many people I can't go without mentioning! Hazel Hayes, Dodie Clark, Emma Blackery,

Rachelle Ann Go; you've all inspired me in ways I can't begin to express. Thank you!!!

Thirdly, I have a lot of love for the friends who inspired the men in *On the Other Side* too. Alex Banks, your friendship is one of a kind. You're hilariously wonderful in every way and you never fail to make me laugh. Gary C, you are a star. Always there and always shining. I have so much love for you. Jack Howard . . .I am so proud of you, Jackaroo. Simply for the man you are. Everything else you do knocks me flat. You hugely inspired this book and I hope you always know how highly I think of you. Rock 'n' Roll. Always. Pete Bucknall. My Big Tree. You understand me better than anyone ever has and you're always there to lean on. Even when we both know I'm being utterly crazy. I love you so much.

Fourthly, to my family! My mum and dad, you're the most loving, supportive, crazy people and I can't thank you enough for all you've done for me and for all you continue to do. Nan and Grandad, I couldn't have coped without your support over the years. So much of this book is about marriage and relationships and if you hadn't set such a shining example of what a marriage should be, I wouldn't have been able to write this book. Thank you! Tom and Gi, you're always there with words of wisdom and silliness and watching you both work so hard AND juggle your own lives is a huge inspiration. I don't know how you do it. You're superheroes! Buzz and Buddy, you're both too young to read this book or to know that I'm thanking you but your gorgeous little faces make me want to be a better person and create a better world for you to live in when you're older. I'll always be here if EVER you need me.

Fifthly, I want to say a massive thank you to everyone who has supported me, helped me and believed in me over the years. Marc Samuelson, thank you for putting your faith in me. Without you, I never would have got here as quickly and I won't ever be able to thank you enough. Ray Lamb, my singing teacher when I was a young'un. You taught me the true meaning of confidence and that knowledge has been invaluable. I owe you more Rolos than you could ever know! Mr David Brown, my English teacher in secondary school. Thank you for putting up with all of my overenthusiastic attempts at writing a novel when I was in my teens. I reckon this one's a bit better than whatever I used to dump on your desk and ask you to mark. Sorry for that but thank you for always being so encouraging. That's something I'll never forget. Dr Ian Roche, my secondary school music teacher. You weren't just a teacher but a friend and you always pushed me to be my best. Thank you for getting me out of physics and maths lessons to focus on the things that mattered to me most. And to everyone at Northwood College who taught me and supported me in my time there. I will always make sure that the knowledge, confidence and encouragement you gave me will always be put to good use. And to Helen, Simon, Nick, Jono and Ang for accepting me into your group with so much warmth and love. You all mean the world to me. <3

Sixthly, to all at Curtis Brown. I can't begin to thank you enough for being so supportive, being there every step of the way and believing in me, even when I don't believe in myself. You've encouraged me to try new things which in turn has helped me develop, not just as an actress and a singer, but as a person too. So thank you, Fran, Jess, Emma, Flo, Alastair and Helen. I am SO lucky to have you all by my side.

Finally, thank you to those who have supported me over the years from afar. Anyone who's ever watched a video, read my books, come to see me perform in shows or simply sent me a tweet of kindness. It's all so appreciated and although I can't reach out to everyone individually, I do see it all and I am often overcome with your love and support. THANK YOU! <3

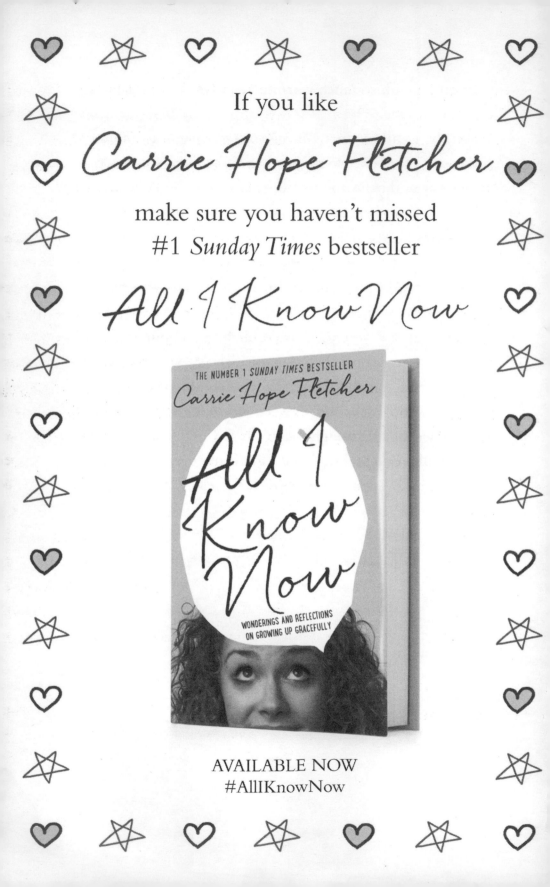